# ROCK MY SOCKS OFF

# ROCK MY SOCKS OFF

## JEREMY EDWARDS

Published by Accent Press Ltd – 2010

ISBN 9781907016011

Printed and bound in the UK


Cover Design by Red Dot Design

For Helia Brookes, with all my love

# Acknowledgements

The author's rocking horse runneth over with gratitude for the support, guidance, opportunities, inspiration, and friendship that pulse through the erotic literature galaxy. Professor Edwards would like to point his telescope of appreciation at such luminous loci as A Slip of a Girl, Tara Alton, Neil Anthony, Janine Ashbless, Bearded Confidant, H.L. Berry, Sarah Berry, Neve Black, Kathleen Bradean, Alessia Brio, Rachel Kramer Bussel, Elizabeth Cage, Heidi Champa, M. Christian, Elizabeth Coldwell, Cathryn Cooper, Danielle de Santiago, Desdmona Dodd, Carly Drew, Jolie du Pré, Emily Dubberley, Amanda Earl, Robin Elizabeth, EllaRegina, Justine Elyot, Emerald, Samantha Capps Emerson, Cassie Exline, Nicky Falkof, Alyson Fixter, Shanna Germain, Laura Godman, Allison Goldstein, Sunny Goodman, P.S. Haven, Aimee Herman, Jolene Hui, Maxim Jakubowski, Kay Jaybee, Stacie Joy, Stan Kent, Isabel Kerr, D. L. King, Olivia Knight, Jordan LaRousse, Ashley Lister, Kristina Lloyd, Nikki Magennis, Gina Marie, Sommer Marsden, Gwen Masters, Susana Mayer, Madeline Moore, Jenny Mount, Bill Noble, Gracie Passette, Roxanne Rhoads, Justus Roux, Samantha Sade, Craig J. Sorensen, Marina St. Clare, Angela St. Lawrence, Charlotte Stein, Donna George Storey, Lisa T, Ellen Tevault, Alison Tyler, Alana Noël Voth, Richard Wagner, Saskia Walker, and Kristina Wright.

A special round of rockin' applause goes out to Hazel, Bob, Miranda, Karen, Alison, and everyone else at Xcite Books.

Finally, I send a loving thank-you to my family and

other cherished friends. Your enthusiasm for my adventures is astronomically precious to me.

# Chapter One

NORMANDIE STEPHENS HAD JACOB smiling within moments of shaking his hand.

'Normandie.' Jacob echoed the introduction. 'That's a charming name.'

'It's a silly name,' she retorted with a laugh, 'and you know it.' Normandie had no reason to know anything about Jacob or his opinions, but she seemed unshakably certain of this last assertion. 'My parents called me Brittany, and when I turned sixteen in a sea of other young Brittanys, I said, "Fuck this" and swapped it for the next French province over.'

He liked the way the word *fuck* had tripped off her tongue.

'It's interesting,' he said. 'As I understand it, those French provinces don't have an official meaning any more. They're culturally and historically significant, of course – but they haven't been recognised by the French government in centuries.'

She stared at him for a moment, sizing him up. 'I bet you say that to all the girls,' she finally replied.

Her hair was a lazy shade of sand blonde. But her eyes, which Jacob later described to her as 'green-traffic-light green', harboured the sort of energetic intensity that could get you out of bed in the morning – and then straight back into bed, if you could catch up with her.

Just minutes before, Jacob had been silently resenting Brandon for inviting him to this party.

'OK, dude, if you have everything you need, I'm going to lock up,' the San Francisco satellite office contact for *Hip Hip*

1

*Horizon* magazine had said. 'I'm supposed to drop by this party at my brother's. Come along if you want. Open shindig in a big-ass Victorian. Lots of, y'know, grad student types – *you* might like it.'

Jacob had tried not to take the last comment as an insult, coming from this twenty-one-year-old clubber. Brandon was essentially a glorified intern who spent all day in an iPod-and-MySpace trance; but he kept the phones from going unanswered at the token West Coast outpost maintained by *HHH*, and he'd fulfilled his obligations to Jacob by meeting him at the office after his flight got in.

And, since he'd had nothing better to do with his first night in SF, Jacob had tagged along to the party, stopping only to purchase a bottle of wine – of a quality that he knew perfectly well might be wasted on a bunch of twenty-something revellers.

But when he'd jumped into the vicinity of Brandon's elbow to prompt an introduction to the alluring woman who had arrived fashionably late, he was logging Brandon as a friend for life.

The first thing he'd noticed when she arrived was her look of radiant intelligence. The second thing he'd noticed was that everyone seemed to know her. And yet she had an air of self-protective aloofness. She smiled warmly at people but looked past them, laughed politely at their jokes but projected a certain reserve. And though she could not have been taller than five foot four, she gave the appearance of floating above the party.

Jacob had felt at once that she was somehow better than everyone else and more vulnerable. He had wanted to admire her and nurture her. Oh, and undress her.

He had decided that maybe he should talk to her first.

And when he did, he didn't see her eye avoiding his or hear her laughter ringing with overtones of remoteness. He didn't know how or why, but somehow he'd managed to cut through all that.

But after the introduction, she was swept away in a sea,

not of sixteen-year-old Brittanys this time, but of convivial grad students. It was a good forty-five minutes before Jacob spotted her standing by the trolley of wine bottles, apparently deciding what to have next.

'I recommend the old-vine Zinfandel,' he said, tapping the label of a bottle that he had taken the liberty of opening half an hour earlier. 'It's excellent.'

'Thank you. I brought it.'

'Ah. I brought a Cabernet Franc, but I don't know what the host did with it.'

'If it's really good, he's probably saving it for a more important party,' said Normandie. 'He's very calculating, you know.'

'No. To be honest, I don't know him at all – though I think he was pointed out to me somewhere along the line. I'm just a tag-along, you see. He's calculating?'

'Oh, yes. Of course, I'm the same way. That's why I can recognise it.'

'Interesting,' said Jacob.

'Mind you, I'm not *manipulative*. That would be bad. You see the difference, don't you?'

'I think so. Now that you've highlighted it.'

'I'm not interested in making anybody do something he shouldn't do or doesn't want to do. But I want to see where things are headed, to plan and plot a course, to act with forethought and foresight and maybe a bit of cunning.'

'Got it,' he said agreeably. 'So you're not manipulative, but you *are* calculating. And have you made any good calculations lately?'

Normandie smiled with what looked like a mixture of pride and sexual appetite. 'As a matter of fact, yes.' She hesitated a titillating moment, as if she had a secret. 'You see, I'm an astronomer.'

'That's funny. I always think of astronomers as being tall. Stupid, isn't it?'

'Oh, I don't know. If you're tall, I suppose you're that much closer to all those ridiculous objects that are billions of

3

miles away. Yet somehow, I manage. Poor little me, the stars just out of reach.' She let out a comical, exaggerated sigh. Then they chuckled together. Her hand brushed his elbow as she swayed slightly with mirth.

'Shall we sit down?' he said.

'Sure, Mr Tag-Along,' she answered. 'I'll tag along with you.'

They had settled onto a cushioned window seat. Almost reluctantly, he explained to her that he was a writer from New York.

'Hmm ... Jacob Hastings. Should I have heard of you?'

'Whether or not you *should* have heard of me is between me and my ego – or possibly a problem for my publicist,' he answered with a hint of bitterness. 'The point is that you obviously *haven't* heard of me. Which is fine. In fact, there are days when I wish *I* hadn't heard of me.'

'Aw,' she said, patting his cheek. Her manner was at once sympathetic and gently mocking, and Jacob loved it. And, of course, she had touched him.

'I think you need another drink,' she prescribed, gesturing at his glassless hands. 'Or maybe a good screw.'

'Do I have to choose?'

Her gaze became intent. 'And here I was just half an hour ago, telling myself I'd have to go home alone and dial my own number for kicks.' She stood up. 'But first things first – another glass of Zin for the mysterious, underexposed author.'

Jacob admired her ass as she crossed the room. He decided it was an ass of confidence.

Soon she had parked it back on the window seat.

'You know,' said Jacob. 'I'm usually a one-drink man. The second drink is not unheard of for me, but it's a delicious exception.'

'I like that,' said Normandie. '*Delicious exception*.' She appeared to relish the phrase, much as she was relishing the wine on her tongue.

'It's true,' he continued. 'Like many one-drink people,

4

I've discovered that when I have that second glass, I imagine that I'm enjoying myself more, even if I'm not.'

She looked like she was about to protest, but he caught her eyebrow in mid-ascent. 'In this case, however, I promise you that I am actually enjoying myself as much as the wine makes me think I am.' He patted her knee, in a gesture that both of them knew meant more than simple reassurance.

'It's a good thing I have a PhD, Jacob Hastings. Not everyone would be able to follow your double-talk.'

He laughed. 'At the moment, you're the only one who needs to follow it. Everyone else can go to the movies, as far as I'm concerned.'

She took another sip. 'So what's your claim to fame, as a writer?'

'My claim to fame is that I'm one of the world's foremost authorities on the history of typography. Unfortunately, that's also my claim to obscurity.'

'I never tolerate obscurity in my life,' said Normandie helpfully. 'It just won't do.' She took a decisive gulp.

'Normandie Stephens, are you the sort of woman who always has spare light bulbs on hand? Answer carefully, because a yes may plunge me into love.'

'With me, or the light bulbs?'

'Why are you here?'

'It's where the free food and drinks are,' Jacob explained. 'Besides, all the other houses in the Haight were locked.'

'Smartass.' She said it like a term of endearment, a testimony to how comfortable they'd become in the course of an hour on the window seat. 'I'll try again. Why are you here in *San Francisco*?'

'To get laid.'

'Long way to go for it. Are you intent on doing it on the Golden Gate Bridge, or something?'

'No, the paint job would clash with my polka-dotted pyjamas.'

'Polka-dotted pyjamas? No deal. Unless we actually get to

poke the dots.'

If there was one kind of woman Jacob could fall for, it was a woman who could trump him at repartee. 'If it's all right with the dots, it's all right with me. I'm serious, though.'

'About the pyjamas?'

'About all of it. Look, I could have told you I came out here to write a magazine article – and I did – but I turn down offers like that all the time. I took this particular one because it was in SF, and SF seemed like a good place to get laid after a rather discouraging spring in New York.'

'That's logical, I guess. For a non-scientist. Did you have anyone particular in mind?'

'*Did* I have someone in mind? You mean, as in before I boarded the plane?'

'Yes.'

'Not *do* I, as in at the present moment?'

'No – that one I know the answer to, I hope. Otherwise we've been wasting a perfectly good window seat.'

He could feel the sexual electricity charging the air around their wine-buoyant heads. 'Good point. I just wanted to make sure I was answering the correct question. Isn't that something you scientists are always talking about? To get the right answers, you have to make sure you choose the right questions?'

'That's "Who Am I?" you're thinking of, not science. But never mind. I've decided I like the other question better.'

'The one you already know the answer to.'

'Yes.'

'Typical scientist.'

They laughed long enough that other people looked their way, wondering what could be so funny on a window seat for two.

'So,' said Jacob when they'd quieted down, 'why are *you* here?'

'It's where the guys in polka-dotted pyjamas are.'

'That's all right,' he said. 'I don't care why you're here so much as I care *that* you're here.'

'I should tell you, though. It may not be interesting, but it is only fair.'

With an old-fashioned wave of his hand, he encouraged her to proceed.

'What's this?' She imitated his gesture, making a quizzical face.

'I was simply indicating that I hoped you'd continue talking. It was supposed to be courteous.'

She chortled into another sip of wine. 'I guess it is, in an old-school, no-longer-recognised-by-the-French-government sort of way.'

'Are you making fun of me?'

'Of course.' She patted his thigh, and Jacob became even more comfortable with being made fun of.

'Actually, Jacob, would you do it again?'

'What – this?' He imitated her imitation of his quaint gesture.

'Yeah.' Her voice sounded slightly husky now. 'Yeah. Maybe it's sexy after all.'

'Let me know when you've made a final decision about that.'

She stood up. 'Let's get out of here.'


'So you're writing a typography-related magazine article.' Normandie's voice had a crisp, refreshing lilt to it as they walked. The extra bit of projection she gave to make her voice carry over the traffic added an attractive, theatrical quality to her remarks.

'I wish!' was his reply. 'When was the last time you read a typography-related magazine article?'

'I – uh – I'm afraid I don't get much time to read, aside from professional journals.'

He smiled appreciatively, taking his gaze off the stretch of sidewalk ahead of them to meet her eyes. 'Oh, you *are* smooth. No,' he sighed, 'the assignment I've taken cannot, by any stretch of even an astronomer's imagination, be described as "typography-related". It's about rocking horses.'

'How cute!'

'Rocking horses may, in fact, be cute. Personally, I find them repellent, but I won't argue that point with a woman I'm hoping to go to bed with shortly. In any event, you have every right to find them cute, and I hope you have a nice day for it. However – and on this I must insist – being required to write 5,000 words about rocking horses is not cute. It's not even polite.'

'This may be a silly question … but they *are* paying you, right? And you *did* voluntarily accept the assignment, yes?'

'That's two silly questions.' He took her hand and pulled her into the doorway.

# Chapter Two

'NICE,' SAID NORMANDIE, BOUNCING her ass on the edge of a love seat as if it were her personal 'fuck-me' bed. 'Did this place come with the rocking horse assignment?'

'It came with my old college roommate, Harlan. Who is in Europe for the entire length of my stay in San Francisco, unfortunately.' He handed her a glass of Harlan's Pinot Noir and sat down next to her. 'Or fortunately.'

'Great kitchen ... great view ... what else does your roommate come with?'

He looked her over. 'I'm more interested in what you come with.'

'Me? I usually come with an assortment of screams and giggles.'

'Excellent. Of course, anyone can *say* that.'

'Are you challenging me, Jacob?' She sipped her wine but appeared to have little interest in it.

'I'm not sure, but I think what I'm doing is propositioning you.'

'Too late. I propositioned you way back at 3475 Haight Street.' She stuck her tongue out. 'Or weren't you paying attention?'

'I do seem to recall something along those lines, now that you mention it,' he said with affected vagueness. 'This is indeed a quandary, our having both propositioned each other. How do we sort it out?'

'Dunno.' She put her arms around his neck and kissed him. 'We may have to fuck twice, just to keep it fair.'

'How about eating your pussy?'

'Yeah, how about it?'

'I mean ... does that count as one of the fucks?'

'Good question. Does your old roommate have a copy of *Robert's Rules of Order*?'

Jacob eyed the bookcase. 'All I see is *Joy of Cooking*.'

'Well then,' said Normandie, 'let's get cooking.'

Judging from the dampness of her panties, things were already cooking in there. And when Jacob pulled her toward him, one hand on her ass and the other stroking her gusset, he felt her pelvis gyrate and her thighs clench. The hot breath in his ear articulated an almost inaudible 'Eat me, Jacob'. He stroked her clinging fabric again, more forcefully this time, and the breath in his ear gained volume while losing definition. 'Oourghmm,' it said sexily, the amorphous syllables dripping with feminine lust. His cock tingled.

Her fingers were soon on the snaps of his trousers. Avoiding the fly slit in his briefs, she pulled his cock up and out of them. She tugged the elastic down just enough for his balls to rest on top, his package displayed for her over the border. She left him like that, preciously exposed, when she slithered backward onto the love seat to receive his tongue between her creamy legs.

She tasted like an exotic liqueur, and her essence dribbled daintily around his face as he teased and tickled her intimate receptors. When she pushed his head into her cavity with a gentle determination, he was engulfed by the heartbeat of her thighs and the fragrant, liquid gift of her ecstasy. His ears, cuddled by her flesh, might have been insensible to her vocal passion, had she not been shrieking so loudly with pleasure.

Shortly after it finished singing its wild screams, her mouth became the warmest, wettest thing he could remember ever touching him down there. He came almost instantly, a melting Popsicle.

'I never told you why I'm in San Francisco.'

'Tell me why you're in San Francisco,' Jacob suggested.

'I'm doing research at Hauser University. Actually, you probably could have guessed this, from the fact that I, for example, am an astronomer, and Hauser University, for example, has a big observatory. Got me an associate professorship there, though it won't last. Loves me some seminars. Rock on.' Normandie, after plenty of wine, plenty of oral sex, and only five hours of sleep, was trying out Harlan's treadmill on a setting so high it fatigued Jacob just to know it existed.

'Are you sure you're old enough to have a job?' he teased.

'Thirty-one next April, gramps.'

He adored her for being funny first thing in the morning. How could she be his contemporary, thirty-four-year-old Jacob wondered, and yet be so full of an almost juvenile vitality? Already he knew that if he saw more of Normandie, he would be hopelessly taken with her. And he intended to prove that.

He sipped coffee and admired the focussed, dynamic energy of her perspiration-radiant body. She was working out in a minimalist get-up of bra and panties – panties that Jacob knew were fragrant from last night – and he watched the special sweat mark develop on her crotch.

When she relaxed and stepped off the treadmill, he was ready for her, and it was the work of a moment to slip her panties down and begin the job of kissing from the small of her back on to and all over her glistening ass. Finding a vigour he didn't know he had, he actually carried her to the bedroom, with her panties halfway down her legs. She was kissing his ear as they travelled.

He was now glad that they hadn't, per se, fucked before falling asleep last night, sated with cunnilingus and fellatio. It felt more meaningful to be depositing her on the bed for a sweaty morning shag, with coffee rather than wine in their veins, with sunlight rolling in through the generous windows in Harlan's condo, saying *this is the morning after, this is daylight, this is reality*.

The wetness in her crotch was more than just perspiration. Jacob slid into her easily, and they fucked with all the passion and hunger that they'd saved from last night. Normandie, setting the rhythm and the pace, rocked and writhed as if she couldn't get enough fast enough, and Jacob almost had trouble keeping up with her. She jammed her own fingers between them to make sure her hot spot was in the loop, and the slippery, ticklish sensations soon overwhelmed them both. They exploded together in a reckless, sweaty lushness that left them incapable of anything but a shower.

A shower and a piss. Normandie spread her legs naturally and unabashedly on the seat, avoiding both a posture of modesty and one of display. She chattered casually about her plans for the day, and her eyes met Jacob's with post-coital warmth. Though limpness for the moment prevailed, his cock hardened just a little as he watched the water hiss out of her.

'You know, I didn't come to San Francisco to fall in love,' Jacob confessed between mouthfuls of multigrain sandwich.

'I remember, Prince Charming. You came here to get laid. And, unless it was all a vivid and wonderful dream, I believe that goal has been attained.'

He winced. 'Yeah, well, I think I got a bonus. A big bonus.'

Normandie toyed with the crumbled blue cheese on her salad.

'What do you think of that?' Jacob was asking.

'Needs more dressing,' said Normandie.

He laughed indulgently. 'OK, we don't have to talk about this. It's only my heart, after all.'

'No,' she said seriously. 'It's not only *your* heart.'

He watched her eat. He noticed how sensuous her lips looked as she flirted with each lettuce leaf before finally committing to it.

'Am I nuts to want to fuck you while you eat salad?' he asked.

'Don't ask me. Ask the proprietor. People might be waiting for the booth.'

Jacob got up, snatched the bill off the table, and headed for the cash register. He turned to look at Normandie, hoping to catch sight of her expression without her knowing. She was smiling, and her right hand nestled prettily, napkin in hand, at the centre of her denim crotch.

During the walk home, she spoke only once.

'There's something different about the way you arouse me. It's like different hormones are engaged, compared to what I'm used to. It's interesting.'

It was *interesting,* Jacob repeated in his mind.

He was tracing soft circles along her flank when she confessed herself preoccupied.

'At least now I know there's something better than tenure,' she sighed.

'No offence, Dee, but from where I stand – er, *lie* – that's quite a non sequitur.'

'I'm sure that's true. But it's only because you can't read my mind.'

'I'll try to do something about that. Meanwhile … what's all this about tenure?'

She sighed again. 'I'm probably not going to get tenure, that's all. The budget is tight and the university wants the department to downsize, and even though Kate adores me, she can't …'

'Who's Kate? You don't need to explain why she adores you – who wouldn't adore you? – but just tell me who she is, so I can follow on my scorecard.'

'My good friend Professor Katherine G. Passky is the brilliant, sexy, silver-haired chair of our department. I sort of idolise her.'

'She sounds like you in twenty or thirty years.'

Normandie kissed him. It was about eighty per cent sexual and twenty per cent tender, and it made Jacob feel as if he'd taken a slug of scotch.

'Twenty-two years. I think she's fifty-three. Anyway, she's written astrophysics books that would make your head swim.'

'Trust me,' said Jacob, holding up a cautionary hand. 'Even the *title* of an astrophysics book would make my head swim.'

She smiled. 'I keep forgetting you're a layman.'

'So soon?' He began caressing the smooth globes of her behind, by way of refreshing her memory.

'Mmm. This is why I said there was something better than tenure. Where was I?'

'Kate.'

'Yes. Kate thinks I'm a genius. Granted, I am … but it's so hard to find people who properly acknowledge that.'

Jacob got into a rhythm, kneading her flesh. 'Is there anything that can be done to put you over the top?'

'Just keep doing what you're doing for a while, darling.'

'I mean, to get the university to give you a permanent position.'

'At this point, I think they'd have to be convinced that I was doing not only important work but spectacular work.'

'But I don't understand. If your Kate thinks you're such hot stuff, why can't she help?'

'She can't pay me a salary with nonexistent money. Even a really good knowledge of quantum physics doesn't enable *that*.' Normandie suddenly inhaled sharply with surprise and pleasure. 'Ooh, do that again.'

# Chapter Three

ALMOST EVERYONE JACOB HAD ever known fell into one of two categories: people who knew exactly what they wanted and were too busy pursuing it to stop and chat; and people who didn't know what they wanted and were happy to talk all night. From the latter population, Jacob had consistently drawn his friends and his lovers.

But Normandie was a strange, wonderful hybrid of the two types. She knew what she wanted – and she wanted a lot. She wanted vast galaxies of knowledge. She wanted acclaim. She wanted the respect of her peers. She wanted a bigger telescope, and a building to put it in.

And she seemed, judging from the past week and a half, to want Jacob. But she didn't seem to want him in the calculating way she wanted these other things. She seemed to want Jacob because something delicate inside her responded to him. Her manner seemed to say that although she couldn't have predicted his existence, he made her smile. And that even though she was very, very busy and very, very focussed, she could always make time to laugh, and play, and perhaps love.

He had never met anyone like her. That had been obvious at once. But the amazing thing, to him, was that she claimed she'd never met anyone like him, either.

'You're not a little boy who's trying to compete with me, and you're not a big boy who's trying to own me, and you're not a selfish boy who wants me just to shut up and fuck.'

'Thank you,' said Jacob.

'You – you just *are*. Do you realise how special that makes you? How easy to be with? How nice to wake up next to?'

He didn't really know if he was special, but it certainly made him feel special to hear her say it.

She was hugging him tightly in her strength-training-strengthened grip. She was almost tearful. 'You make me feel that no matter what happens to all my distant stars, there's something solid and organic in my life.'

Jacob stroked her along the length of her back, laughing. 'I'm like a bag of granola.'

'Thanks for showin' up, dude,' said Brandon. 'Gary totally wanted me to get your input on the photographer.' He produced a crisp white envelope of sample photos.

Jacob quickly wiped away the excess beer on their table, trying not to take offence at the vulgar implication that he, a professional writer, might have considered not 'showin' up' for an appointed meeting with a representative of his publisher. Why Gary, his editor back in New York, had chosen this particular individual to represent him in San Francisco remained a mystery.

'These are the three people Gary likes,' Brandon explained. 'They're all here in SF and available.'

Jacob squinted at the photos in the dim pub lighting, pretending that he gave a damn who was going to take pictures of rocking horses for *Hip Hip Horizon*.

He could tell at a glance that all the photographers were competent, more than capable of doing justice to the appalling subject.

'Excellent,' he said noncommittally. 'Which candidate does Gary favour?'

'He's sort of jonesin' for this one,' said Brandon, touching the part of the picture you're not supposed to touch with his beer-moistened forefinger. 'Susan Weedon.'

'Oh, good,' said Jacob, handing back the materials. 'She's my first choice, too.'

The lights went down a notch further – though Jacob wouldn't have thought it possible – and a throb of house music replaced the pop that had been playing. A fluorescent light revealed a DJ rising from his cocoon in a booth in the far corner, and a few figures began to float out onto what passed for a small dance floor.

Their business was concluded, but Jacob hadn't finished his beer. He was comfortable where he was, and he knew that Normandie might not be done in the lab until almost midnight.

'So, Brandon,' he said with forced affability, 'what are you studying?'

'Y'know, like, communications,' Brandon replied absently. The young man's attention was clearly wandering as the dance floor began to heat up. Now Jacob understood why Brandon had suggested they meet at this particular pub at the hour of 10 p.m. This was evidently where he had planned on spending the next chunk of his evening.

'Very nice,' Jacob said drily. 'Look, I'm going to nurse this beer a while, but you don't have to babysit me. If you're eager to get out there and –'

He didn't even have time to finish the thought before Brandon had hopped up and joined a group of lithe young women.

Jacob could see Brandon through their eyes – an easy-mannered, nimble young guy in hip clothes, as strikingly handsome as he was, to Jacob, strikingly vacant. But Jacob was much more interested in seeing the women – through Brandon's eyes, his own eyes, or any eyes that happened to be available. They were lovely, indeed, and the knowledge that he probably had little in common with them and that mutual boredom would ensue from any direct interaction did not prevent him from enjoying the sight of ice-cream-scoop bottoms, tickle-me midriffs, and fluffy mops of hair, all bringing sparkles of feminine life to the otherwise drab environment.

He sat there contentedly for forty-five minutes, allowing the beer to mellow him and the women to arouse him. Then he headed for his borrowed apartment, fairly confident that Normandie would eventually invite herself over and finish what the dancers had started.

Sure enough, an hour and a half later, he was sprawled naked on the bed.

'Relax,' said Normandie, from the level of his crotch. She kissed the underside of his balls. 'I want to kiss and lick every bit of you … show you how much I appreciate who you are, and what you are.'

'That tickles beautifully.'

'*Tickles* is only the beginning, my friend. On the scale of pleasure I'm planning on giving you, *tickles* is, like, a one.'

He reclined his head again and closed his eyes.

He heard the lewd *pop* of the massage oil being opened. He heard its drunken, reverse guzzling as it globbed into Normandie's hand, and he smelled an appetising, oily cocktail of raspberry and banana.

'Oh!' The first cool stroke of her moistened fingers around his groin surprised him.

It dawned on him that she was the first woman with whom he felt comfortable being really passive in bed. A dynamo like Normandie was just what it took to make him want to be deliciously inactive sometimes, to glide into a zone where she could spoon dollops of pleasure onto his body and he had no responsibility but to wallow in it.

It used to be that he didn't like having his ass touched beyond a basic functional grip during fucking. But now she was reaching under and caressing his cheeks, pinching them, titillating between them. It felt good, and he told her so. He could never remember feeling so relaxed and aroused at the same time.

He hadn't ever trusted a woman in this way. Not that he'd been afraid they would hurt him; but he had always felt compelled to keep his sexual steering wheel in his own hands. With Normandie, he was happy to be taken, to be driven, to let her try things on him, to raise his erection to monumental proportions in whatever way she chose.

'You can play with my ass anytime you want,' he said.

'Thank you. We'll make a note of that.'

18

With his mind and body at rest, he continued to let her cover him in slickness, caressing him at every turn, stimulating invisible muscles and awakening latent erogenous zones. Never before had he felt so many sensory points being discovered and nurtured – along his ribcage, under his arms, along the inner lengths of his thighs … He felt that he could lie here and absorb pleasure forever – except for the little matter of his flouncing cock, which she had lubed early on and returned to stroke every so often. It was now craving her full attention, and she took notice of this.

She kissed it. 'Be with you in a moment, baby,' she said sweetly – to Jacob's prick, not Jacob senior.

She reared up on her knees and, quickly but erotically, began to cover her own body in lube, as if it were indoor suntan lotion.

'Would you like me to do that for you?' he asked.

'Not this time. You just lie there.'

Her face rang the changes on tactile delight and sexual excitement as she sensuously finger-painted herself. Her body was sinuous and tense beneath the pressure of her own hands.

She saved her inner thighs for last, and as she moved her hands closer and closer to her pouting pussy, Jacob could not only see but smell how aroused she was.

Then she let herself fall forward, clambering back on top of him and manoeuvring her ass until she had her cunt satisfactorily skewered. She ran her slippery hands all over his slippery body, while her slippery rump bounced against his slippery legs and her slippery love channel clutched at and pumped around his slippery dick. The entire experience was almost frictionless, save for the tight interplay of cock and pussy, and the effect was like that of fucking weightless in space. When Normandie bounced herself into climax and milked Jacob's own orgasm into her screaming body, he felt as if he would never return to earth.

'Now that was my idea of a good time,' she told him calmly afterward.

# Chapter Four

THE LIVING MUSEUM OF the American Rocking Horse was, by contrast, not Jacob's idea of a good time. His tastes ran to fanciful fonts – not prancing, rococo animals with wild, Victorian-era eyes. But the success of a book on fonts had proved to be a fanciful notion itself; and with Jacob's handsome jacket-flap photo flapping impotently over stacks of unsold books that were now headed back to the publisher's warehouse, well-paid magazine features were something he knew he had to get used to again.

So he was forcing himself to spend this Tuesday morning at the museum, which was housed in a huge warehouse along the city's Pacific frontage.

He was surprised to find that an attendant had to unlock the main display area for him.

'When is the museum open to the public?' asked Jacob.

'Oh, it's not open to the *public*,' said the attendant, a fussy little trout-eyed man whose picture, Jacob decided, probably appeared next to the word 'officious' in any good illustrated dictionary.

'That's an interesting interpretation of the phrase *living museum*, isn't it?' Jacob couldn't help saying. 'But I'm sure it's not your fault. It's just a comment for the curator, really.'

'*I* am the curator,' the man responded. 'No matter what Sylvia Hodgeport says.'

Jacob had no idea who Sylvia Hodgeport was, or why her opinion regarding who was or was not the curator of an obscure, perpetually closed museum should be a controversial one. Fortunately, as Jacob was a feature writer and not an investigative journalist, he felt no obligation to pursue the topic. So he merely nodded.

The airplane-hangar-sized building was immaculately clean. The floor had been polished, the walls had been painted a delicate shade of cream ... in short, a beautiful space had been designed to house and display these grotesque creations.

God, they were hideous. They really *might* have been cute, Jacob admitted, had they been the size of mantelpiece ornaments. But, large as life, they made his mind run to firewood rather than feather dusters.

They resembled real horses the way a cupcake decorated by a committee of kindergartners might resemble a slice of bread. The wood of their flesh had been carved here into unwieldy braids, there into an impossible gown or an ostentatious waistcoat, and everywhere into mismatched garlands that hurdled the boundaries of good taste and kept galloping on. Their facial expressions all managed to blend some degree of equine arrogance with a healthy dose of human idiocy.

And so many of them! At floor level ... on risers ... some even hanging from skyhooks like absurd, repulsive Pegasuses. For the purposes of the assignment, the setup was ideal – down to the fact that everything was extremely well labelled, with a surfeit of historical documentation. There was good lighting, and, thanks to the never-open-to-the-public policy, there were no distractions. It was enough to make Jacob want to either throw up or take a nap.

He sat down on a bench and closed his eyes to reflect. Would he always have been so devoid of interest in an assignment like this, he asked himself, or was it simply that it could not successfully compete for his attention with Normandie's magnetism? Maybe he was getting too old to divide his enthusiasm efficiently between demanding work and incipient love. And there was no denying that love was what it was – he was certainly old enough to recognise *that*.

He opened his eyes. He shuddered. No, this was not a side effect of love. The rocking horses were simply horrible, and that was that.

By noon, he felt he needed a gallon of coffee and a world

full of sunshine to shake him out of the unpleasant combination of nausea and stupor. It was, unfortunately, raining; but he grabbed a latte from the nearest barista and walked briskly in the direction of food. He slipped into a burrito joint he'd noticed in the neighbourhood and sat with his back to the door, testing his reading knowledge of simple Spanish by means of the imported movie posters on the wall.

'Is this seat taken?' Normandie had materialised from behind and glided swiftly into the chair across from him.

'No,' said Jacob. 'Is your ass taken?'

'You took it last night,' she said. 'Don't you remember?'

'Hmm. Yeah, I thought it looked familiar. Hey, how in the world did you know I was eating lunch here?'

'I was about to ask you the same question.'

'Pure serendipity!' he marvelled.

'Or maybe I was subconsciously drawn here by your irresistible, masculine pheromones, luring me across Golden Gate Park.'

'How did your subconscious know the irresistible animal scent was me, and not those Golden Gate Park bison?'

'I think you've showered more recently.' She leaned across the small Formica table to nuzzle under his arm. 'Mmm,' she said approvingly.

He couldn't pretend that he fully understood her aversion to planned hook-ups. She had warned him at the outset that he shouldn't rely on her to commit to premeditated dinners, theatre outings, concerts … And yet, she had already established a pattern of casually but consistently showing up in his space and in his life – and she welcomed it when he did the same. And, whenever and practically wherever they coincided, they meshed, coupled, and merged. They had begun to speak openly in the language of partnership, but they lived as if the thread of their relationship were quasi-accidental. Normandie seemed to thrive on a predictable pattern of spontaneity, and Jacob was wise enough not to disrupt or even question that.

'It seems that we're always walking down streets,' he said as they headed toward the LMARH.

'What else would we walk down – the sides of buildings?'

'I just mean that so much of our interaction occurs while we're en route from one place to another. Sometimes it seems we spend almost as much time coming from places and going to places as being places.'

'I see.' She thought about this for a minute, while their solid, waterproof shoes went *clomp clomp clomp* along slick cobblestones and skimmed the occasional puddles.

'I have to admit,' she finally said, 'I often find it even more fun to be on my way someplace than to actually be someplace.'

'You're kinetic.'

She stopped, took his hand, and pressed her body against his. 'That's one of the sweetest things anyone's ever said to me.'

The light rain poured daintily around them while they kissed.

'They're enough to make you puke, aren't they.' Though he was very glad of her company for his afternoon session with the rocking horses – he would have been glad of just about anyone's company, with the possible exception of the troutly curator – he took pains to distance himself from the cloyingly precious subjects of his 5,000-word article-in-progress.

'Remember, Jacob,' Normandie said valiantly, 'they were originally made for children.'

'Quite true,' he said. 'I don't blame the children. Kids just hop on and ride. They can't be expected to have good aesthetic sensibilities. The important thing,' he added grudgingly, 'is that they have fun.'

'The important thing is that we have fun, too,' said Normandie, stroking Jacob's arm. Then she whispered, 'I forgot to wear panties today.'

He pressed his fingers against the lightweight fabric of her summer skirt, and verified what she'd just told him.

She smirked. 'And what was that you just said – *hop on and ride*?' In another moment, she had straddled the largest – and possibly the most hideous – rocking horse in sight, one that had evidently been built to accommodate an entire small family of aesthetically undiscriminating children.

'Dee!' Jacob knew that the officious management could walk in at any time.

She looked back at him, with a challenge in her eyes. 'Hop on and ride,' was all she said.

It was an offer he could not refuse.

'Don't you get turned on by the thrill of possibly getting caught?' she asked as he snuggled up behind her and the contraption began to jiggle equivocally beneath them.

'No. Personally, I'm more into the thrill of *not* getting caught. However, I'm turned on enough by your bare cunt on a rocking horse that the getting or not getting caught is incidental.'

While clinging to her waist with one hand, he reached underneath her with the other and nestled his fingers into her wet spot. They would just have to hope that this additional layer of varnish wouldn't damage the antique finish.

Sensuously, they began to rock, their combined weight easily directing the horse back and forth. Jacob kept two fingers firmly implanted in Normandie's pussy, and as their bodies travelled to and fro the fingers did the same: a delectable microcosm.

His free arm was wrapped tightly around her, and he could feel her heartbeat reverberating through her entire torso. She was rocking within the rocking – she was evidently using the sculpted saddle horn to generate the friction she needed against her clit. Soon she was coming, her cunt clenching and her firm bottom pressing frantically against his stiff crotch. He wondered how he was going to dismount from the ridiculous vehicle under the burden of such a huge hard-on.

With the grace of a lewd ballerina, Normandie scooted herself 180 degrees, using her slippery, gaping snatch as a fulcrum. Once she was facing him, she unzipped his jeans while Jacob rested his hands on her shoulders. They rocked more slowly now, her ass doing the work. With a glint in her eye, she reached underneath herself to moisten her hand, then stroked him, rocking all the while. She brought him off quietly, directing his spurts of release right onto the summer fabric of her lap. Then she kissed him, as if the mess had been his gift to her.

'I may have to reconsider my opinions about rocking horses,' said Jacob.

# Chapter Five

AFTER ANOTHER DAY OF observing and note-taking at the LMARH – including two delicate hours guiding the efficient but monosyllabic photographer Susan Weedon – Jacob was ready to write the damn article.

*On the shores of the galloping Pacific, in the shadow of San Francisco's most cavalier skyscrapers, lives a curious herd of once-tame horses. Now semi-wild, they have been led to water but show no signs of drinking ...*

And so on, for 5,000 nauseating words that made Jacob himself feel like drinking. Thank goodness it was the editor back in New York who would have to sift through the dozens of pictures that Susan was likely to turn in. Jacob had conscientiously directed the photographer to the specimens he was planning on writing about, but she had taken each one from six or seven angles, and he really didn't want to have to look at the results.

He had not had the courage to inspect the big horse that Normandie had tamed with her delicious wetness for any residual stains. And if Susan had noticed any unusual glimmerings through her lens, she hadn't said anything. But, then again, she would hardly be likely to break her near-total silence to exclaim, 'Look, Jacob! I think that's a *sex stain*!'

The door to the lab admitted him silently. Normandie was, as usual, alone here – the department hadn't been able to grant her an assistant – and Jacob admired her back before announcing his presence. Though she was faced away from him while working at her computer, it excited him to note that her legs were spread apart, that under her desk she flashed the wall from inside her miniskirt. Even if she chanced to be wearing panties – which Jacob was lucky enough to know was a big *if* – he could get into the image of her soft, cotton-clad pussy beaming from between her legs.

Jacob was a man whom many friends and acquaintances admired for his ability to put ideas into words. And yet sometimes he felt that he hid behind the words – or, more accurately, that he used words as a substitute for the vivid emotions he sometimes seemed to lack. But around Normandie, there were times when he felt that it was the words that were lacking and the emotions that were having their day in the sun.

'I thought you might like lunch.' Those words would do, for the moment.

She swivelled to greet him, flashing him in the process. Ah, so we're in lime green panties today, Jacob observed to himself with a twitch in his groin.

'You look lovely in lime,' he said.

She looked confused. Her eyes scanned her aqua top and black denim mini. Then the light went on, and a mischievous, hungry smile shone out.

She glided forward on her task chair until she nearly collided with him. 'Did you really come here for lunch?' she asked, using a forefinger to tease a line above his belt. 'Or did you come here, for example, to get your hands on some lime green panties?'

'Mm,' said Jacob, nibbling from the base of her throat toward her shoulder. He loved these low-on-the-shoulder summer jerseys.

'Or perhaps,' she said, 'you came here to tweak some nipples. *They're itching for it today*,' she confided conspiratorially, directing his hand onto her chest and positioning his fingers.

Their mouths ate each other while he tweaked.

'Then again,' Normandie panted, 'maybe you came here to touch some soft ass.' She pushed her chair back, hopped out, and grabbed hold of a nearby filing cabinet, jutting her tight-skirted rump his way.

Jacob had hardly ever seen her quite this randy in the middle of the day, and he congratulated himself on having chosen this particular point in the week for dropping by the lab. He immediately gave her the firm but painless swats she craved. He could see her lime panties again, from behind this time, see them moistening before his eyes. He dropped to his knees.

Cotton had never tasted so good. He was eating her pussy right through the panties – sucking, licking, nibbling. She was saturating them with nectar, and the filing cabinet was rattling ridiculously as she shimmied in place, clutching the damn thing.

He wrapped a hand around her waist to seek her clit. The clit finger did her from above, descending from the waistband of the panties, while his mouth continued to dance against her panty-encased cunt. When she pressed her ass against his forehead and brazenly squeegeed a damp, trembling orgasm across his face, Jacob came in his pants like a happy, helpless virgin. She collapsed on top of him, and he felt the oily pleasure of her hot, dripping cunt pulsing onto his sticky trousers.

It was a hot day, and they didn't mind taking their lunchtime walk without reference to a change of underwear. Normandie whispered that the warm breeze was tickling her moist panties back to dryness, and Jacob could feel his recent splash of come baking onto his boxers. Her hair was a lewd blonde in the afternoon sunlight, and Jacob felt ecstatically dirty to be on post-fuck parade with her, reeking of sex, knowing her neat little lime panties were stained and sagging as her creamy thighs advanced along the sidewalk.

Back at the lab, he gave those panties extra attention before inching them downward, savouring their aroma and their fatigued limpness as he caressed her through, around, and within them. When, at last, she wiggled them impatiently down and off, he claimed them and held them briefly to his face, before placing them lovingly on her desk.

'Enough with the panties,' she exclaimed, leaping for his fly and hustling him out of his pants. She sank into the couch, oblivious to the heavy reference books scattered to each side of her, and moved him into position, guiding his cock to where it belonged. Jacob took her cues – and her knees – and, within moments, he was pounding her into the cool vinyl, moving like a corkscrew … until he ultimately popped. In his throes, he wedged the heel of his hand against her mound and pressed, until he felt her inner volcano erupting in response.

'I want your hands all over my body. Isn't that crazy?'

They were talking in the lab bathroom, where Jacob had just unzipped. 'Crazy?' he said. 'Why? I mean, it works for me.'

'It's crazy because we just fucked thirty minutes ago. I can't spend all day, every day, naked beneath you, soaking up pleasure with every cell of my body.'

'Of course not. Sometimes I should be beneath *you*.'

Normandie studied his steady stream of piss. It seemed to soothe, almost hypnotise her. 'Do you think I'll lose my grant if I turn in a pair of sex-stained panties instead of a report next month?'

'I think you should compromise, and turn in a sex-stained report.'

'Has anyone ever told you that you're a very attractive pisser?' she asked.

'No. Put it in the report.'

But Normandie did resume working, and Jacob sat quietly in her office, making fussy hand-written revisions to the manuscript of his magazine article.

'What would you do if I discovered a new galaxy?' she asked, just when he was getting ready to leave.

'Congratulate you.'

'Would you feel threatened?'

'By a galaxy billions of miles away?'

'By all the attention I'd get.'

'No. You *should* get attention.'

'The media might be on my ass 24/7.'

'For that, the line forms here.'

He stepped forward to kiss her goodbye, then stopped. 'And what would *you* do if I won a Pulitzer Prize?'

'Fuck your brains out – same as always. Oh, and maybe we could do some champagne or something.'

# Chapter Six

ON FRIDAY, NORMANDIE 'HAPPENED' to show up at Jacob's (technically, Harlan's) when supper time was approaching. Another non-date restaurant dinner was enjoyed, and the couple drifted to Normandie's place afterward. It became obvious to Jacob, though, that this was a working evening. He grazed at a novel while Normandie attacked her work, biding his time before trying to seduce her.

After about an hour, he put the book down and stood behind her at her desk, just giving her shoulders a hint of erotic massage. 'So, tell me again why you have to finish going over this research tonight, instead of letting me nibble your ass cheeks like you ought to.'

'Because, Mr Asscheek Nibbler, tomorrow is the deadline for submitting results to the journal. If I want them to commission my article for the winter issue, they need to see the research results now. And if I want to impress the pants off the tenure committee, I need to be in that issue.'

'Oh. I don't suppose you'd settle for impressing the pants off of *me*.'

'Tomorrow.'

'I'm expected to stand here in my underwear until tomorrow?'

'Of course not. You can sit down.'

Jacob had always loved intellectual women, had always loved the way their passion flowed as freely for ideas and discoveries as it did for his brown eyes and his soft caresses to their sensuous zones. Sometimes more freely, he had learned in one or two less-than-satisfactory relationships.

He kept quiet, honouring her work time and the privilege of sharing it, appreciating this opportunity to watch her sink

31

into an orgy of intellectual stimulation ... and quietly counting the minutes till he could screw her intellectual ass off. He was patient, fully aware that if they could fuck in her lab on a weekday afternoon, it was only fair that she could work at home on a Friday night. She had to go to bed eventually, and that was all he needed to know.

He asked if there were some way he could help her, and she thanked him and said she'd let him know.

When her energy flagged, he made her a pot of tea. When her attention wandered, he read her the funniest bit from the novel. It made for a nice, relaxing evening.

'Jacob.'

He realised he'd dozed off.

'Would you do me a favour and proofread this table?'

She passed him a sheaf of documents, fresh from the ink-jet printer.

'Proofread *what*? This is just a bunch of numbers.'

'They'd better be numbers – because if they're colours or ice cream flavours, I'm a lousy scientist. Just check 'em for alignment, decimal places, etc. Please, that is.' The smile she bestowed was worth a thousand *pleases*.

They were just columns of figures – meaningless to him, or by all rights, they should have been – but they became a sacred text, or an inscrutable poem. They were her art, wrung from absurdly distant galaxies by means of impossibly complicated mathematics.

'Looks good to me,' he said when he'd finished. 'Though the 4.793 in the third column could use a little salt.'

'So, what's the next step?' he said on Monday morning, after he'd given himself breakfast in bed between her thighs.

'The next step is that I do you, I guess.' She dipped beneath the covers and grabbed his cock, like a swimming-pool diver grabbing a rubber-coated brick.

'Actually,' he said after she'd sucked him dry, 'when I said "What's the next step?" I meant what's the next step in your grand scheme to acquire tenure? While you wait for the journal to give you the green light, I mean.'

'Oh,' said Normandie. 'I hope you don't regret the blow-job.'

'Not a concern,' said Jacob. 'Technically, though, I owe you one instalment of oral sex. Do you want it now?' He was already lifting the hem of her negligee.

'Silly boy. I just had one.'

'And that's a problem because ...?' He enunciated the words between kisses as his mouth played around her upper thighs.

'Oh!' she conceded. 'You're right, it's not a problem. Mmm, not a problem.'

Thus encouraged, Jacob proceeded. He officially extended his visit from thighs to tender feminine lips, kissing up blushes and tonguing his way into favourite places, where he was welcomed with libations.

'No, this isn't problematic at all,' she was saying in quick breaths. 'Wow, goodness, Jacob, I'm having quite a remarkable absence of problems with this. I'm having – ee!' She ended on a squeal.

It was the wittiest little orgasm she'd ever had for him, to date. He clutched her ass and buried his face in her warmth, wetness, and wit.


Normandie had submitted her research, as planned. But she had explained to Jacob that, as with just about anything these days, it wasn't enough to do solid work. One had to market. Promote. Schmooze.

In addition to making arrangements to appear at some upcoming conferences, this week's schmoozing entailed a visit to Kate Passky's office. Jacob had turned in the final revisions on his article, and his only career-related obligation was mulling over an unappealing but lucrative editorial job he'd been offered back in New York. He was intrigued by the very concept of someone so impressive that even Normandie was in awe of her, and he was pleased when Normandie invited him to tag along. She even made a quick call to Kate to let her know, explaining to Jacob that in the backbiting, super-bureaucratic world of academia, even a phone call was really just a shortcut, a memo being the more usual procedure for announcing events as trivial as putting cream in one's coffee. 'You never know when some rival will make a stink because *his* friend didn't get to sit in on a casual meeting with the chair, and why wasn't the entire department notified, and how come there's no paper trail, etc.' From the exasperation in her voice, it sounded like she might have a particular rival in mind.

It seemed incongruous that one of the most important decisions of Normandie's life would emanate from such an inconspicuous, insignificant-looking office. Jacob couldn't have said what, exactly, he'd been expecting, but it was something more along the lines of vaulted ceilings, dancing spotlights, and probably lots of neon that would ask, WILL NORMANDIE STEPHENS GET TENURE? Times Square style.

But the only neon was in Jacob's mind. And, perhaps, Normandie's – though she looked cool to the point of seeming blasé. In this dim, bookshelf-crammed room with one window and barely enough floor space to accommodate visitors, Kate sat behind a desk of modest proportions, looking like the most important question on her mind was whether or not it was time to order more paperclips. The cosy array of open reference books, semi-shuffled manuscripts, and rampant sticky notes did not, collectively, give the impression of holding anyone's career in the balance.

When she looked up, Kate's personal magnetism was as good as any neon. Though his knowledge of astronomy stopped at the fourth-grade level, Jacob could see why this handsome woman with intelligence and humanity shining out of her museum-quality grey eyes would be an inspiring leader in whatever field she might have chosen. Add to that the exceptional professional genius that Normandie vouched for, and it was easy to see why she had used the word *idolise*.

The two of them were of necessity squeezed right up

against Kate's desk, and Jacob could smell both the mints on Kate's breath and the sweet, fresh smell of Normandie. The chair nodded graciously at him, but her first words took him aback.

'So this is the writer you've been fucking,' she said to Normandie.

Normandie rolled her eyes.

'Oh, all right. I'm sorry.' Kate smiled indulgently. '*Seeing*. The writer you've been *seeing*. There, is that better?' She patted Normandie's hand, condescendingly. 'Young academics have become so uptight since my day.' She looked at Jacob. 'Don't you think so –'

'Jacob,' he gulped.

'Don't you think so, Jacob?' She winked at him, enjoying the tease around the obvious fact that Jacob had not been old enough to make the scene in her 'day'. Normandie, whose composure never eluded her for more than a moment, was now chuckling into her hand, and her cheeks were rosy and cheerful.

'Maybe I'd better wait outside,' said Jacob, between dry-throated ahems.

'Oh, he *is* cute,' said Professor Passky to Professor Stephens, as though Jacob were already out of earshot.

'Please stay, Jacob,' said Normandie lightly. 'It would be stupid for you to leave after coming all this way, just because Kate used a particular verb.'

Now Kate was chuckling too, and Jacob couldn't help smiling. 'Professor Passky, I'm very pleased to meet your verb, and I hope you'll use it again sometime.'

'That's the spirit,' said the chair of the Astronomy Department, giving Jacob a punch on the arm – an interaction, like the patting of Normandie's hand, that was made possible only by the small size of the office.

Then she became businesslike. 'Normandie, I have to tell you that I still can't swing assigning you a research assistant. There just aren't enough to go around.'

'OK,' said Normandie, with a shrug.

'You don't mean *OK*,' Kate argued. 'You mean *oh, shit*. Because it's not OK. But there's nothing I can do about it. And, speaking of things that are not OK but about which I can do nothing: I've been given next year's preliminary budget, and unfortunately it's looking like I can't create any new tenured positions. Don't think I didn't try. And, hell, I'll *keep* trying. But unless something changes …'

# Chapter Seven

HE'D NEVER KNOWN ANYONE whose personality was quite so revved up. Normandie wasn't overbearing, she wasn't tiresome, she wasn't ridiculous … she was just, it seemed, one hundred and ten per cent herself. Every word and action had a signature upon it – from the crisp way she chewed, to the elongated posture in which she habitually fell asleep, to her trademark laughter, bright on top with undertones of secret wisdom. Her laughter connoted sex, to Jacob. Not surprisingly, he liked to tickle her all over, and her laughter always tickled him back.

He hadn't noted the precise day on which his centre of gravity had shifted from speculating about the depth of his attractiveness to her to deliberately presenting himself in the way he hoped would please her; or the precise week when striving explicitly to please her had shifted to automatically, unconsciously being the person he wanted to be for her. By now, his every thought and decision reverberated against an image of her, when the real thing wasn't close at hand. His idea or ideal of her had become his touchstone.

'You're my touchstone,' he told her one morning.

'No wonder you touch me so much,' she said with approval. 'But just move your thumb down a few millimetres … Oh! Yeah.'

'Now I understand why you scientists are always pushing the metric system.'

'Mmm-hmm,' she purred, with an unscientific wiggle. 'Push my metric system.'

It felt strange when he had the epiphany that she was, in some ways, like the sister he'd never had. A buddy. A playmate. An ally through life's uncertainties. He'd never before been romantically involved with a woman who felt so much like 'home'.

'Am I the type of woman you imagined you'd end up with?'

'First of all, let's dispense with that expression "end up with", if you please. It sounds so depressing.'

'Good point. What should we say instead? "Start out with" doesn't convey the full extent of my meaning.'

'How about "go around with"?'

'Deal.'

'And, to answer your question: No. Do you really think I could have imagined anything remotely like you?'

'Ha! I'll try to take that as a compliment.'

'Please do. And, while you're at it, you can take *this* as a compliment as well.' *This* was a combination lip lock and nipple pinch. 'So what about you … Am I the type of man you imagined you'd go around with?'

'No. I thought I'd end up with a woman.'

'You thought you were a lesbian?' She'd told him she enjoyed boy-girl-girl threesomes – as did he – but his understanding was that her primary interest had always been in men.

'No, I knew I wasn't a lesbian. But I was a dating-fatigued girl who thought she'd eventually just pack it in and find a congenial housemate – whom I always visualised as a woman.'

'What did she look like?'

'Sort of like me.'

'Why, you vain creature!' Jacob beaned her with a throw cushion.

'Hey, I said I wasn't a lesbian; I never said I wasn't a narcissist. Anyway, my gorgeous imaginary roommate was quieter than I am. A quieter version of myself. Wouldn't that make an ideal housemate?'

'Depends. Do I get to go to bed with both of you at once?'

'No, we take turns with you. It's a small bed.'

'Fair enough.'

'So, you can see that it's a big adjustment for me … giving up on giving up, reorienting myself to "going around" with someone to whom I'm sexually attracted.'

'Even more than you are to yourself, you mean.'

This time, she beaned him with the cushion. 'Oh, and I suppose you've never indulged in the delicate art of self-love?'

'Maybe once or twice,' he conceded. 'Per day.'

'Be careful you don't use it all up, with none left for me.'

'There's plenty for you. And your non-existent housemate.'

'Let's see.' She grabbed at his jeans and, with practised fingers, unzipped them in an instant. The zipper made a noise that sounded like '*Yep.*'

'Told you,' he said. 'You see, I – ahhh.' There was that mouth again.

That evening, the sky was scheduled to clear, and Normandie seized the day – or rather the night – to take a trip out to the observatory. She invited Jacob to accompany her, and, for the first time, they held hands on a commuter train.

Her opportunity for serious work would come later in the evening, but they went early enough to 'play with the big telescope', as she so scientifically put it. Jupiter was awaiting them in the sky upon arrival, and Normandie made haste to set things up just the way she wanted.

Then she dropped her pants.

'This is one of the reasons I became an astronomer.' Her eyes were gleaming like stars.

She had positioned the eyepiece of the monstrous telescope so that she'd be able to gaze on the warm, sensuous shape of Jupiter while Jacob fucked her from behind. She steadied herself with the telescope's handles and pointed her bottom his way, her feet playing restlessly within the nest of jeans. She was already breathless. 'You think I'm kidding.'

'No,' he said. 'I think you're wonderful. Delicious. Irresistible.' He punctuated the last adjective with a playful slap to her rump. 'But kidding? No way.' He peeled the panties down and slapped her again, even more softly this time – sensually.

Then he couldn't wait any longer. She was so wet, so enticing. Soon his own trousers were at his feet and he was pushing sweetly into her, holding her by the elbows while she continued to clutch the telescope handles.

Even Jacob knew what Jupiter looked like – he loved the famous red spot that resembled a hungry cunt, and the liquid stripes that enveloped the planet in what looked like layers of feminine desire. Though he couldn't see what she was seeing, he visualised the planet throbbing around him as her moist warmth responded to his thrusts.

'My clit,' breathed Normandie. 'Can't let go.'

He got her drift: she needed to keep a symmetrical grasp on the handles, and so it was his responsibility to trigger her climax. He'd certainly had far less appealing jobs in his time.

And it was not only an appealing job – it was also an easy one. A tender push of her button made her tremble. Her chasm oozed for him, and the substance of her body seemed to coalesce into an orgasmic homogeneity. She maintained her grip on the telescope, but, apart from that, she seemed to lose contact with the world around her.

The pulsating, striped planet exploded in Jacob's mind, and his corporeal explosion followed suit.

Afterward, he found a blanket in the utility closet and spread it on the floor by the window, so that they could camp there peacefully and look – with the naked eye and the naked everything – at the deepening starscape.

'It's even more beautiful when you understand it,' Normandie said.

'I don't think it would be for me,' said Jacob. 'I think it might lose something if I could analyse its mysteries.'

'I guess I'm just turned on by knowledge.'

'Thank goodness,' he replied, drawing a finger along her slit.

She kissed him. 'Are you sure you don't want me to start

rattling off facts about the constellations we're looking at?' she offered.

'No, please don't. I love the stars for their inarticulate beauty. And I love you for your *articulate* beauty. But it's two different kinds of beauty.'

'I understand. How about if I just point and say, "Ooh! I know something about that star!"'

'That will work.'

She immediately tried it out. 'Ooh! I know something about that star!' She specified a particular point of light with an eager forefinger.

'You're brilliant,' said Jacob.

She pointed in a slightly different direction. 'And I know something about *that* star, too.'

'You're gifted.'

'And that one!'

'You are exceptionally well qualified for your job as an astronomy scholar. And you have the cutest fingers.' He took hold of the one she'd been pointing with and brought it to his lips.

She sighed. 'I wish you had something to be as passionate about as I am about all that.' She gestured at the heavens.

'I do. You.'

'That doesn't count,' she said, wagging the famously cute, recently kissed finger. 'Though I'm glad you said it.'

After last night – the telescope had been just the first act – Jacob was not quite sexually depleted, but he was physically exhausted. So, he lay there lazily and watched Normandie, who was reading an astronomy journal and sliding a finger idly in and out of her snatch. He focussed on listening for the telltale squelchy sound.

'Is it soup yet?' he eventually inquired.

In response to this obvious clue that he was awake, she put down the expensive, quarterly periodical and climbed on top of him.

'Good morning and I love you,' he said. 'But I'm tired.'

'Too tired even for this?' she said seductively.

'Maybe.'

'I feel like a ripe fruit this morning. Grab me and plunge in.'

She was so horny he could smell it. 'I think I need breakfast.'

'Fruit is perfect for breakfast.'

Jacob closed his eyes.

'How about this, lazy boy?' She crouched over him, a squatter staking her claim and claiming her stake. 'I'll do it to you, until you're doing it to me without even trying.'

'Well ... if you really don't mind doing all the work.'

'Do I look like I mind? Come on, hungry man. A nice, warm cup of cunt for breakfast.' And she slid herself slowly down his pole.

The feeling was luscious – each up stroke felt, impossibly, more delicious than the preceding down stroke, only to be superseded itself by the down stroke that followed. Jacob could not believe that, minutes before, he had been inclined to turn this down in favour of Cheerios.

'I've decided to stay here for a while,' he said later, at the lab.

'I'm afraid you can't,' Normandie replied. 'I need to spread some charts out there in a minute.'

'I don't mean here on the couch. I mean here in *San Francisco.*'

Though she was smiling at what had become a favourite running joke, she looked a little concerned beneath her sparkle. He knew she was afraid that he would do his career damage. It was touching.

'Relax.' He abandoned the couch to the forthcoming charts and came forward to take her hand. 'The editorial job in New York would have been too much of a bore, and not what I should be doing with my energy.'

'As long as you're sure ...' She trusted his judgment enough to look relieved, and this, too, made him feel good.

'*But,*' he clarified, 'I wouldn't have taken a better offer in

New York, either. Not under these circumstances.' He gestured grandly toward Normandie, his 'circumstances'.

'So what *will* you be doing with your energy?' she asked. 'Such as it is.' She poked him in the chest, the memory of her recent anxiety already submerged beneath the latest wave of puckishness.

'Eventually, I'll find something here. Something, hopefully, that doesn't involve rocking horses. Till then, I thought I could keep myself occupied by helping you.'

'Helping me?'

'Exactly. In a just world, you would have been given a research assistant, and I can think of nothing better to do with my time right now than pitch in around your lab.'

'But you're a writer, Jacob!'

'The glorious and non-existent Freelance Writers' Union has nothing in its rules against members assisting beautiful astronomers. And the non-fiction literary world won't miss me if I wash bottles for you for a month or two.'

'We don't wash bottles in astronomy.'

'Fine. Scrub planets. Whatever. Let's get started.' And he actually rolled up his sleeves.

# Chapter Eight

'DUDE, ARE YOU REALLY going out with Normandie Stephens?' said Brandon, as though the idea surprised him.

This was, Jacob hoped, his final meeting with the *HHH* liaison – a lunch meeting to submit local expense records and make sure the magazine had a complete package for Jacob's contracted feature story. The Normandie angle represented the only time Brandon had shown any interest in Jacob's affairs, and this expression of interest did not fill any deep voids in Jacob's life.

'What is this – high school? I'm "going out" with her?' He was sincerely amused, if also irritated. 'Yes, we're in a relationship, if that's what you mean.' Overall, he preferred the way Kate had put it.

He reflected that, for Brandon, high school was the relatively recent past.

'It's cool,' said Brandon, irrelevantly. Then, in a display of unjustified camaraderie, he helped himself to a handful of Jacob's french fries.

Jacob absorbed the fact that by having a beer with Brandon the other night, he had evidently cooperated in degrading their relationship from a professional one to a french-fry-snatching one. He sort of wished he'd insisted that the meeting at the pub occur at the office instead, despite the conspicuous absence there of agreeable, house-dancing nymphs.

'Not that I care … but what, pray tell, makes you raise an eyebrow – and a fistful of my personal french fries – at my relationship with Normandie?'

'Y'know, I just never thought of her as your type.'

He knew that Brandon couldn't help being annoying; but

he wondered why the guy couldn't at least be annoying in a slightly less annoying way. 'You barely know me, Brandon. Since when do you spend your time thinking about what my "type" is?'

'Hey, don't forget, dude, you met her at *my* brother's party.'

Jacob was blinded by the flash of illogic, and he literally blinked. 'OK ... Does that mean you're in on the ground floor? Am I supposed to invite you into bed with us or something?'

'No can do. Busy week.'

'Have some more french fries,' Jacob said.

'This may be a stupid question ... but if you insist that there are no bottles for me to wash, then why are you wearing a white laboratory coat?' He had arrived for a working evening to find her absorbed in her latest research, but dressed with uncharacteristic scientific formality. He now looked briefly around the room, pretending that he was still not one hundred per cent convinced that the lab held no dirty bottles.

She turned to face him. 'Sometimes I just want to feel like a glamorous scientist. It helps when the research becomes tedious.' She advanced on him. 'But, on this occasion, I had you in mind.'

And before he could articulate another question, she unbuttoned and shed the garment, revealing an undercoating of purple velvet panties and bra.

'Wow,' Jacob said. 'I don't believe I've ever seen you in *that,* either. Not even when you've been out at the *big* telescope.'

'Tonight I'm dressed for you to do the observing.'

He spun her around, the velvet panties attracting him at once to her velvety ass. He ran his hands over the velvet, and it felt so nice that he was reluctant to move on. But finally he peeled the panties back and gave them a head start down Normandie's legs, so that she could dance them off and kick them away.

45

He caressed the crack of her bottom intimately. With his hands on her ass, away from her pussy, he let her experience her arousal privately for a while, her legs closed, her sex warming and moistening in secret. Then he coaxed her thighs apart, so that he could participate in her wetness. First, he did so with his fingers, teasing and nurturing. Then, when she breathed heavily for more, he dropped to his knees and let his tongue do the walking.

When they moved to the couch, she took the panties with her. She clutched them like a talisman while he fucked her, wringing the velvet undergarment into a taut bundle of erotic energy. When she came, it looked to Jacob as if the panties were having an orgasm, too; and when he came, he grabbed them in his mouth and wrestled her for them, dragging their softness across her nipples while he pounded between her thighs.

'Thanks, Gary,' Jacob said quietly into the phone. 'I'll get this new thing to you as soon as possible. If you feel it doesn't work, you still have the – ugh – rocking horses. But I think you're going to agree that those can wait another month.' He hung up, then joined Normandie, who was posing in front of the Hauser University telescope for Susan Weedon. At Jacob's request, she was wearing her lab coat – this time with more than just sexy underwear beneath it, however.

'This is so sweet of you,' Normandie said, when the photographer was out of earshot.

'What you're doing is important. People should know about it. And it's a way I can help you that goes beyond just proofreading decimal points.'

After Susan had obtained a variety of shots of Normandie, the telescope, and Normandie with the telescope, Jacob ushered his lover to a chair, claiming a stool for himself en route.

'I'm going to switch on my tape recorder now, if that's OK, and you can just officially repeat the stuff you told me the other day.'

46

'In bed, you mean?' She twinkled at him. Susan was twenty feet away, packing up her equipment, but Jacob thought he saw her blush.

'Uh – no. I was thinking more along the lines of the discoveries you're making.'

'I recall making some very *nice* discoveries in bed with you.'

'Thank you. Um – can we talk about astronomy for a while? Just to humour me?' He was delighted that she was having such a good time with this, but her flippant attitude was beginning to make him feel a little silly about the whole thing.

'Oh, *astronomy*! But of course.' Normandie wriggled in her seat and then, miraculously, became quite serious and scientific. Jacob switched on the machine.

'Dr Stephens, I believe you've been making interesting discoveries about the composition of some distant galaxies.'

The scientist took another break, and the pixie returned. 'What's with the "Dr Stephens" shtick? Since when do you call me that?'

Jacob rolled his eyes and switched off the machine. 'Mere professional rigour,' he said haughtily. 'I know that, for now, I'm the only one who will be listening to this tape. But perhaps someday, when you're world famous and they're writing books about you, someone will want to listen to the original transcript of our historic interview. That person, whoever it is, might not wish to listen to questions addressed to Sex-cheeks, or whatever I've been calling you lately.'

Susan was *definitely* blushing now.

Normandie was laughing. 'You're right. OK, let's get on with it.' And she became serious again.

On went the tape recorder. '*Dr Stephens,* I believe you've been making interesting discoveries about the composition of some distant galaxies.'

'Yes.'

'Tell me about it.'

'Most of the galaxies that have been catalogued to date are

47

believed to consist of stars within a certain limited range of compositional matter. However, recently we have been observing some galaxy clusters, new to us, that appear to deviate from this model in terms of ...'

# Chapter Nine

JUNE TURNED TO JULY. Harlan returned from Europe, let Jacob cook dinner for him his first night back, and in the morning began hinting broadly that he'd like the place to himself.

Normandie opined that Jacob 'might as well' move into her place.

'Are you sure that's all right?' asked Jacob.

'No, I'm sure it's perfect,' Normandie replied. 'Just don't describe it as a "date".'

The first out-and-about day that Jacob returned to Normandie's apartment as 'home' happened to be the day he found the July issue of *Hip Hip Horizon* on the coffee table, staring Normandie in the face.

'Well?' he said proudly.

'Oh my God, Jacob.' She burst into tears.

He folded her in his arms. He had never seen her so moved. 'Aw. Pretty good publicity, eh?'

She looked up at him. 'Oh, darling. Do you realise what you've done?'

It was dawning on Jacob that her intonation was not entirely complimentary. 'I – I thought it … Oh, shit. No. You'd better tell me. What have I done?' He sat down.

She began to pace. 'You meant well. I realise that. It's adorable, but … for crying out loud – the *cover*, Jacob!'

'I think it's an excellent likeness.' He stood up again, as if to lend weight to the assertion.

'Yes, all too excellent. There's no chance I can pretend it's someone else.'

'I don't understand. Why would you want to –'

'Jacob. Listen.' She sat him back down on the love seat

and perched beside him. 'I am not front-page news. My work is not of earthshaking significance. I assumed you were going to do – what do you call it, a sideburn?'

'Sidebar. Those are just used in conjunction with longer, related articles. Though sometimes what an editor will do is...'

'Never mind. The point is, I thought I'd have a couple of paragraphs, buried in the back of the mag, with a flattering one-inch headshot of me looking all scientific and sexy.'

'I wanted to do something big.'

'You did something big, all right. "Big" as in a monumental embarrassment. "Big" as in a gargantuan gaffe.'

'Why is it a giraffe?'

'*Gaffe!*' she repeated.

She stood up and began to pace again, shuddering as her journey took her past the magazine on the coffee table. 'No offence to you or those who contract with you ... but what idiotic editor let you get away with this ridiculous puff piece? And don't you dare ask me what I mean by "puff paste".'

'When I told them that what you were doing was immensely important, and that no other major magazine had covered it, they were grateful for the scoop. They, uh, also thought you were better looking than the rocking horse we shot for the other story.'

'Ugh!' On this trip past the magazine, she lingered long enough to turn it upside down, thereby replacing her own smiling face with a vodka ad – which, unfortunately, also featured a sexy woman in a lab coat. She shuddered again before resuming her frenzied walk around the room. 'And the photo spread inside ... making me look like I'm the century's most glamorous and brilliant thinker, as if I had a bouquet of Nobel Prize medals dangling into my cleavage. And the little series of timeline illustrations that maps the history of astronomy from the Aztecs to Copernicus to *me*. Couldn't you at least have put Carl Sagan in there somewhere? Maybe then I wouldn't feel so out of place.'

'I'm sorry.' Now that he understood, he was sincerely

sorry. 'I thought I was helping your career.'

'Sweetheart. I'm proud of what I'm doing. It *is* important. But it's stodgy-little-journal-article important. It's tell-other-astronomers-about-it-at-conferences-and-deduct-the-travel-expenses important. It's *not* hype-it-all-over-the-mass-media-in-a-manner-that-makes-it-look-like-my-mother-has-purchased-the-entire-news-industry important.'

'Gotcha.' They were quiet for a moment. 'So what do we do?' Jacob finally asked.

'Short of driving around the country buying up all the copies and destroying them – for which I doubt there's a grant available – I don't think there's much we *can* do. I'll just have to hope people forget about it before too much damage is done – to my career, to my reputation among my colleagues, to the integrity of science ...'

She was interrupted by a ringing phone.

'Hello?' She listened briefly, then she held the receiver courteously away from her face and shrieked a crisp expletive.

'It's someone from *Insomnia With Rhone Preston*,' she hissed to Jacob, alluding to a ratings-drunk late-night television programme that people promoting themselves in Northern California would do almost anything to appear on.

'Jacob, you remember Professor Passky, don't you?'

'Please, Normandie, it's all right to call me Kate in front of the children. And of course I remember Jacob,' Kate added – though that hadn't been the question. The distinguished professor gave him a glance that Jacob could only have described as raunchy. Fortunately, he saw no reason he was likely to be called upon to describe it.

'Maybe I should wait outside,' he said, hovering as close to the door as he could – which, however, still put him practically on top of Kate's desk.

'Why does he keep saying that?' Kate demanded of Normandie.

'I think we'd both like you to stay, Jacob,' said

51

Normandie.

Jacob noticed the infamous magazine on Kate's desk. He winced.

'I assume you've come to see me regarding *this*,' said Kate, tapping the mag with a noncommittal forefinger.

'Yes,' said Normandie. 'It was really just a mistake. You see –'

The department chair waved dismissively. 'Who cares if it was a mistake. No one has to know that. All that matters is that this "mistake" has put our department on the map.'

Jacob's jaw dropped when he realised that Kate was beaming.

'Cupcake, do you begin to comprehend the prestige … the grants … the faculty this will help us attract? The mind reels.'

Jacob's mind reeled at hearing the department chair call Normandie 'cupcake'.

Normandie swallowed. 'It sounds pretty cool when you put it that way … but I can't help feeling like a fraud. The article makes it sound like I'm second only to Einstein in my importance to modern science. These findings of mine – well, you know as well as I do, they're significant but modest, in the grand scheme of things.'

Again, Kate waved her concerns aside. 'So what! What has the grand scheme of things ever done for us? Can the grand scheme of things write a cheque to fund the tenured position I'm dying to give you?' She tapped the magazine again. 'No one's actually going to read the article, anyway.'

Normandie looked genuinely confused – a rare state of affairs. 'What?' She looked at Jacob.

'What matters,' continued Kate, 'is that it was printed, that it looks like a big deal, that it's on the cover. Right, cowboy?' Jacob had to infer that she was addressing him, despite his notably rodeo-free background. 'Nobody really reads those articles all the way through, do they?' Kate continued.

Jacob made as if to finger his collar nervously, then thought better of it and settled for a shrug of resignation. 'Uh – no, not really. In the business we think people, ahem, kind of flip through these magazines, for the most part.'

Normandie was shocked. 'Why on earth do you bother writing the stuff?'

'I like writing, and I get paid whether or not anyone reads it. Why do you stay up till the wee hours making calculations about bodies of matter that are inconceivably distant from your desk?'

'Touché,' said Normandie graciously, but she was shaking her head semi-despondently.

Kate, by contrast, was beaming more brightly than ever. 'You've done a great thing for us, Jacob,' she said. 'I'd like to do something nice for you in return. Something very nice.' She was licking her lips.

'I think Dr Passky wants to fuck me,' said Jacob that evening.

'That's ridiculous,' said Normandie, handing him a glass of chilled Sauvignon Blanc.

'No, I really think so.'

'Oh, I'm sorry, babe. I didn't mean that the idea that she wanted to fuck you was ridiculous. I meant saying "Dr Passky wants to fuck me"' – here she imitated Jacob's understated baritone delivery – 'was ridiculous. It would sound so much better if you'd drop the formality and just say, "*Kate* wants to fuck me."'

'Right,' Jacob assented, taking a delicate sip. 'So you agree that she may be lusting after me?'

'Oh, I'm positive she is.'

'How do you know? Are there no limits to your brilliance?'

'There may, in fact, be no limits to my brilliance. But I know that Kate wants to fuck you because she told me so, while you were in the men's room. I suppose you feel funny about it, because she's past fifty and you're still a young sex god.'

He put his wine down. 'No. I feel funny about it because I think she's decidedly hot, I don't care how old she is, and I'd love to hear more about this, at your earliest convenience.'

53

The warmth in Normandie's eyes deepened. 'That's the spirit.'

'It's very nice of you to pat me on the back,' he said. Normandie responded by swatting him pleasantly on the ass. 'Or in the general vicinity of the back. Do you really not mind the idea of my screwing one of your colleagues?'

She laughed. 'In the case of this particular colleague, I think it's fairly wonderful. I'm a big fan of hers, you know.'

'Wouldn't you feel left out?'

She laughed again. 'Why would I? I'll be there the entire time, of course.'

She picked up the phone and began to dial. 'She *is* hot, isn't she?' Normandie was actually flushed. Jacob had, to his credit, seen her equally aroused on many an occasion ... but now she looked aroused like an eighteen-year-old virgin. She was giggling as her fingers spelled Kate's number.

'Are you calling to arrange a date for us to hop in the sack with her?' He was not displeased, but this was all happening so fast. 'I thought you couldn't stand dates.'

She stuck her tongue out, prettily. 'It's not a date, it's an appointment. An appointment with my department chair. For cocktails. Here at our place. What happens after cocktails can be spontaneously improvised.'

'Don't forget to circulate a memo to the faculty,' said Jacob.

# Chapter Ten

FROM AN OLFACTORY PERSPECTIVE, Kate was all breath mints from the neck up. But the rest of her had an earthy scent that Jacob responded to with animal interest. There was no one or nothing that could make him forget that Normandie was in the room; but Kate was, like Normandie herself, a personality and a sexuality to be reckoned with. Her hair, handsomely cut and naturally frosty, seemed to frame her as a woman who could be anything she wanted to be. She could be a boss. She could be a colleague. Or, if she chose, she could be a flowering garden of ripe sensuality and erogenous flesh.

Her face glowed with exceptional intelligence and unabashed lasciviousness. She wanted to make you laugh and make you cream. And it was obvious to Jacob that she had always been this way.

'Relax, Jacob,' Normandie was saying.

The three of them had finished their round of cocktails. The late afternoon sun was splashing hedonistically onto the wooden floor of Normandie's bookshelf-and-artwork-heavy apartment. Kate was leaning comfortably into the crook of the sofa, her silver hair kissing her shoulders. She looked magical in a turquoise-trimmed black ensemble of jersey and slacks, with bare feet giving her the perfect bohemian touch. Her nose was proud and her eyes liquid with charm, and Jacob couldn't imagine that the woman had ever looked lovelier – at forty, thirty, or twenty.

He sat tentatively at the opposite end of the generous couch. Normandie stood behind him, her fingertips pulsing excitement onto the back of his neck, making the little hairs tingle.

'So, young man,' Kate said slowly. 'Are you going to

55

handle me, or do I need to let you put me on a goddamn magazine cover first?' And, without waiting for an answer, she leaned forward and began, expertly, to handle him, stroking with calm determination through the stiff fabric of his trouser fly and sending electricity through him. After studying his reaction for a moment and seeming satisfied with it, she leaned in and kissed him on the lips.

*She kisses like a teenager,* thought Jacob. It was a revelation that, just by sitting here, he was making a university chair drool and moisten her panties like the first girl he'd fucked freshman year of college. And this revelation was a serious turn-on for him. He looked over his shoulder to establish eye contact with Normandie, hoping she would see the wildness in his eyes, knowing she would approve.

But Normandie's eyes were closed, and the hand that wasn't on his neck was inside the waistband of her slacks. She was saying something, almost too softly for Jacob to hear. 'Go on …' She said it repeatedly in a staccato whisper, a breath that rode the gallop of her arousal.

He pulled down Kate's clingy midnight-black slacks, and he noticed how powerful her thighs were. He remembered Normandie telling him that Kate was a jogger, and generally in great shape. He wanted to make those strong thighs pump in spasms of uncontainable joy, and, toward that goal, he put a tentative hand on her black lace panties. Her tight, muscular tummy peeked out between the panties and the top, and he kissed her there while continuing to stroke her.

Suddenly, Kate flopped herself face down on the couch, pulling Jacob's hand tightly against her crotch. She kicked her feet up onto the armrest and folded her arms beneath her head. She wiggled her ass for Jacob and squeezed the innermost meat of her thighs against his hand.

Out of the corner of his eye, Jacob saw Normandie lean forward from behind him. She began to pet Kate's hair and breathe into her ear, and he felt Normandie's erotic power combining with his own to pleasure this strong, self-actualised, prestigious woman. The rush that he felt watching her wriggle beneath their harmonised touches was incredible.

With every writhe he elicited from Kate, Jacob was conscious that this was a woman who had been writhing for men and women, and making them writhe in return, since more or less before he was born. He wanted to fuck Kate not only for her potent, in-this-moment desirability, but also for her glorious history. It ennobled and excited him to be part of a long parade of her lovers and her orgasms.

He wanted someone to hold his cock. 'Please – unzip me,' he said to Normandie, quietly, as if Kate's ecstasy were a dream he was intent on preserving. Normandie, still stroking Kate's strands of hair with her left hand, moved forward and unzipped Jacob with the right, retrieving him from his jeans, handling his dancing flesh as only she could.

With the phallic aspect of the situation safely in hand, Jacob assessed the needs of two luscious pussies, one of which currently housed his forefinger, and the other of which was patiently clothed within Normandie's pinstriped slacks.

'I can just reach you if you moon me,' he told Normandie.

She temporarily reassigned the hand that had been petting Kate's hair to the duty of undoing her own jeans, followed by the task of pushing pants and panties to the floor. In one graceful movement, she positioned her ass so that it faced Jacob, bent to receive her pleasure, and resumed stroking Kate. All the while, she continued clutching Jacob's cock.

Jacob began to pat and tickle Normandie all over her glorious bottom, integrating these attentions into the rhythm he was using to titillate Kate's pussy. When his left hand migrated to Normandie's snatch, he removed his right hand from Kate's. Holding Kate by the knee, he moved his face in and tasted her essence.

The department chair banged her face into the sofa cushions, her cries of 'Yes!' almost muffled beyond recognition. Normandie was gasping as Jacob's fingers nurtured her secret spots, and her dexterous interplay with Jacob's prick took on a syncopated quality that made Jacob squirm with delight.

Kate tasted complex. It was a challenge for Jacob to process the sophisticated flavour as she twisted for him and his cock danced for Normandie and Normandie oozed over his fingers. The chain reaction set off by Kate's orgasm left everyone trembling, and the walls echoed with shrieks.

Eventually, the three of them had some supper, and it was over dessert that the tax-deductible portion of the conversation occurred.

'You've accepted that invitation from Rhone Preston, I assume,' said Kate. It was not a question, and it required no answer. 'One little detail I should tell you about. Hube Renkins has been complaining that –'

'Oh, for fuck's sake!' said Normandie. 'Why is he out to get me?'

Kate took another mouthful of coconut cake. 'Be reasonable, Normandie. Renkins has nothing against you personally. He just resents any colleague who gets attention, acclaim, or funding that would, to his way of thinking, be better directed toward his own work.'

It didn't take much mental activity for Jacob to calculate that this Renkins individual must have been the backbiting colleague implicit in Normandie's abstract discussion of backbiting colleagues. 'What, exactly, is his complaint?' he asked Kate.

'He's written to the provost, claiming that Dr Stephens' work has been given exaggerated media attention that detracts from the overall dignity and well-being of the department.'

'I bet he wouldn't be saying that if *he* were on the cover of *Hip Hip Horizon*,' said Normandie.

'Exactly,' said Kate. 'But you have nothing to worry about. I'm doing everything I can to emphasise the importance of your research. Not merely because you and your boyfriend just collaborated to give me the best lick-out I've had since the Andromeda galaxy was formed, but because I really do believe in your value to the university. So what if your current research isn't quite as earth-shattering as the stupid magazine – no offence, Jacob – says it is. We'll build on it, given the right resources … and, who knows, maybe someday it will be earth-shattering. In other words, I'm behind you one hundred per cent.'

'Thank you,' said Normandie.

'Luckily, Renkins doesn't seem to know who author Jacob Hastings is, so at least he's not going to town with the Jacob-Normandie angle. If he had more friends, he'd probably know all about it. But his aloofness keeps him out of the loop most of the time. Still, if he finds out, I'll handle it. I'll use my position of influence and authority to defuse his sordid, if truthful, accusations.'

'Let me get this straight,' said Jacob agreeably. 'The fact that I unintentionally inflated the reputation of the woman I'm fucking will be rendered totally excusable once the department chair, whose pussy we're licking, says it's all right.'

'I don't know,' said Kate thoughtfully. 'It worked for me.'

'Don't you think it could look bad?' asked Normandie.

'What – were you planning on taking pictures of me sitting on your face, with my finger up Jacob's ass, and running them as a follow-up in next week's magazine?'

'Hey, we didn't even do that yet,' Jacob protested.

'Finish your dessert first,' said Kate, gesturing with her fork. 'No, Normandie … personally, I was inclined to keep this aspect of things relatively private. Though, come to think of it, *I'd* like a few of those pictures.'

'I know a photographer,' said Jacob, who was now quite hastily finishing his dessert. 'She'll do anything – even rocking horses. But what does the provost think of all this?'

'Tommy is on our side, the sweetie – for now,' said Kate. 'That's why we have to make sure my vividly depicted predictions of wonderful, federally funded ramifications to all this come true. That's why girlfriend here is going on Rhone Preston.'

'On the *programme,* you mean,' corrected Jacob.

Normandie slithered warm fingers across the back of his hand. 'Let's not rule anything out.'

'You know, when I was a little girl I often fantasised about being on television. Even after I decided I wanted to be an astronomer – I was ten and three-quarters at the time – I imagined going on talk shows, maybe even variety shows, as a glamorous celebrity astronomer. Of course, I came down off my cloud when I noticed that astronomers didn't usually go on variety shows. And that they had stopped making variety shows, anyway. But now it turns out I was right the first time, and I'm going to be a famous television-land astronomer. Whee!'

'Whee?'

'Well, not "Whee" entirely, I guess. Under the circumstances, there's also an element of "Holy fucking crap".'

'Yes, I thought so.'

'You'd think that would be my overriding feeling, in fact. But my overriding feeling has been overridden by the overriding feeling of the person who wants to give me a permanent faculty position. So it's really out of my hands, and I'm trying to get into the spirit of my ten-year-old self. My ten-year-old self would never have forgiven me if I'd turned this down.'

# Chapter Eleven

THE MAN IN THE impeccable, walnut-coloured suit and severe hipster glasses was, if possible, even more officious than the curator of the LMARH had been. He had certainly landed himself a position of officiousness at a higher level of visibility, thought Jacob. He was also considerably taller, which helped him to be not only officious, but supercilious as well. He was brandishing a clipboard – always a bad sign.

'So you are Dr Stephens,' he said, indicating Normandie without looking at her. 'And where is Dr Normandie?' The man looked around, as if expecting another scholar to be paraded out for him, with appropriate fanfare.

'I'm Normandie,' she clarified. 'Dr Normandie Stephens.'

'Oh no, that isn't satisfactory at all,' replied the staffer. 'Our schedule shows a Dr Stephens *and* a Dr Normandie, appearing together, discussing exciting developments in gastronomy.'

'Astronomy,' said Jacob, with surprise.

'Yes, yes, fine,' said the man irritably. 'That doesn't matter. What matters is that we have *two* guest chairs on the set, and we must have two guests to occupy them.'

'But what do you expect us to do about that? Clearly, someone on your staff has just made a mistake.' Normandie's nerves were showing – a rare occurrence, but one that Rhone Preston's staffer had successfully brought about.

The man looked even more condescending than he had before. 'The fact that *someone* made a mistake' – he looked accusingly at Normandie and Jacob, as though it was obvious for all the world to see that they must, somehow, be responsible for the error – 'is beside the point. I need two of you out there, and that's the bottom line.'

'But who?' said Normandie, her annoyance giving way to incredulity.

'Oh, I don't care,' the man whined, as if Normandie were taking up an inordinate amount of his time with trivia. '*Him,* for instance.' He turned to Jacob. 'You have something to do with gastronomy, too, don't you?'

'I –' began Jacob, but Normandie cut him off, a glint in her eye communicating to him that she had regained control of the situation.

'Yes,' she said fiercely, tapping the staffer's clipboard with a note of finality. 'All right. I'm sure *Dr Jacobs* here will be glad to discuss *astronomy* with me on the programme.'

Without even waiting for Jacob to confirm this, the man spun on his heel and, with an air of efficient satisfaction, disappeared.

'That was easy,' Jacob said without enthusiasm. 'Why bother with six years of grad school, when evidently all you really need to become a professor is for someone to switch your first name to your last name?'

'Sorry, darling, but we don't have time for dry wit just now. We need to think. What's your *new* first name, for example?'

'Uh … I don't know. How about Ernie?'

'That'll do. And where are you from?'

'Hmm … Des Moines?' He had always liked the sound of that.

'No, we need the name of a *university* – a non-existent one, so nobody can check on you. And it may be hard coming up with a name for a fictitious university, because chances are there will actually *be* a university by that name, somewhere.'

'Unless the name is really silly,' Jacob said helpfully. 'You know, like "Noodlenoggin College" in Ohio.'

'It's real, only it's in Virginia. Excellent astrophysics group there, as it happens.'

'Oh,' said Jacob. 'Damn. I really wanted to be from Noodlenoggin College.'

'Please don't sulk, Jacob. It looks bad on television.

Maybe you can be from Noodlenoggin College for your next birthday. For tonight, I think we have to take the opposite approach: we should choose a name that's so common that the precise institution that employs you will be for ever obscure.'

He saw what she was getting at. 'You mean like "Mountain College" or something.'

'Perfect! There's probably a Mountain College in Colorado and a Mountain College in Vermont, and a Mountain University somewhere else ... and maybe a University of the Mountains and – well, you get the idea. If one college declines to own you, everyone will just think you came from one of the others. You'll be like someone who crashes a large party, relying on the fact that every guest will assume he came with somebody else. You'll be like a rhubarb pie that nobody wants, or an odd golf ball that doesn't match anyone's brand, or –'

'OK, OK. No more metaphors, please. I don't think my ego can survive it.'

'Anyway, great thinking. This solves everything.'

'I'm afraid I must quibble with your definition of "everything". You seem to be overlooking several factors, such as (a) the fact that someone might recognise me, (b) the fact that I don't know anything about astronomy, and (c) the fact that the show will be starting very soon.' He glanced nervously at a digital clock that was, he thought under the circumstances, much larger than it had a right to be.

But Normandie was impressively quick at dismissing his various concerns, counting them off on her agile fingers. 'A. You're a writer, not a movie star. Yes, your personal friends might recognise you, but if you can't trust your personal friends to keep quiet, who *can* you trust? B. If we weren't in such a hurry, I'd take the time to be insulted that you can claim not to know anything about astronomy after having interviewed me on the subject. Just parrot back some of what I told you, for Pete's sake. And C. –'

The insufferable assistant was at their collective elbow. 'We need to get make-up on the two of you. Now.'

63

The host was affable, charismatic, and all those other television-hosty things. Not only did Jacob feel nervous as hell, but he felt sort of bad that he was about to sit here and lie a blue streak to this guy.

'Dr Jacobs,' said Rhone, 'how long have you been studying the stars?'

'Thirty-seven years,' Jacob said. He had automatically fallen back on his lucky number, without realising that this put him in front of a telescope three years prior to his own birth.

'Really!' said Rhone. 'That's, um, quite some time,' he added pointedly.

Jacob coughed. 'Yes. I'm what you might call the "old guard".'

'You look awfully young for the "old guard".' Rhone got a laugh from the audience, which he acknowledged with a wink to the camera.

'I'm the *young* old guard.' Another laugh, this time for Jacob. 'It's all relative, you know.' The laugh died down, which was the audience's way of telling Jacob that he should have quit while he was ahead and foregone the corollary quip.

'In a minute, we're going to hear about Dr Stephens' work, which has been getting so much attention. But first, tell us about your own research.'

Jacob cleared his throat. 'Well ... there's a lot of stuff out there in space. So I've spent a great deal of time looking it over. Uh ... a lot of it is quite nice. I think you'd like it, Rhone.' Somewhere Jacob had read that if one is ever on a talk show, one should use the host's name a lot.

He realised that more was expected of him, so he forced himself to keep going. 'Personally ... now, personally, um, I have a weakness for those pinkish nebulas – I mean, *nebulae*. I think it's because although I love flowers, I've always been a terrible gardener. So outer space is my garden.' He stole a glance at Normandie, who sat beyond their host in the other guest chair, smiling enchantingly but gripping her armrests as if on a rollercoaster ride.

'That's beautiful, Dr Jacobs,' said Rhone, pretending to wipe away a tear. 'And what have you learned out there in the garden of space?'

Jacob let out a long, low whistle. 'Ooh … where to even begin.' He sensed that he was not performing well. *Just parrot back some of what I told you,* he remembered Normandie saying. 'I suppose I should mention,' he said, 'that the third quadrant of the E997 galaxy cluster is noteworthy for both its asymptotical orientation with respect to the plane of deep space, and its high concentration of neutron-poor gases.' Jacob looked to Normandie for approval, but she seemed unwilling to make eye contact with him.

Rhone succeeded in looking engaged; but that, after all, was his job. And he wasted no time now in shuffling things into Normandie's court, which was a relief to Jacob.

'Now I'm going to talk to Dr Normandie Stephens,' said the host to the audience. '*Normandie* – that's an unusual name, isn't it?'

'I suppose it is – *Rhone.*' The audience laughed. But given how charming Normandie was, Jacob thought they probably would have laughed even if she'd been doing knock-knock jokes.

'If I'm not mistaken, Dr Stephens, you've discovered a new galaxy.'

Jacob wondered what idiot had prepared such blatantly inaccurate notes for the poor host.

'No,' began Normandie, 'that's not –' She stopped in mid-sentence, and Jacob saw something maniacal come over her face. 'That's *not* a mistake,' she said slowly and confidently, to Jacob's amazement. 'I have indeed discovered a new galaxy. Brand new!' She practically sang the last phrase, in a Julie Andrews sort of voice.

'Excellent,' said Rhone, who looked personally gratified.

Jacob could not decide whether he was appalled or delighted. In either case, there was nothing for him to do but stay put and watch her game play out.

'Can you describe your new galaxy? What's special about it?'

Jacob saw Normandie's brow furrow in concentration as she prepared to launch into a repertoire of dry, scholarly information – fabricated but plausible. Then, just as her mouth opened, he again saw something flash across her face – something bright, and intense, and wonderfully mischievous.

'It's funny you should ask that, Rhone.' She touched the host's hand, and for the first time Jacob saw the polished showbiz face waver – presumably from the thrill of feeling her electricity. 'In the eyes of astronomers, there are various special – but rather complicated – things that set this galaxy apart. But what's really interesting about it – and this is something everyone can easily appreciate – is that it looks remarkably like a *rocking horse*.'

'A ... rocking horse,' said Rhone.

Jacob struggled to keep from laughing.

'Yes. You may have heard of the Horsehead Nebula, or the Crab Nebula ... and of course there are many constellations that people have named after the animals and figures they resemble ... Well, this galaxy is shaped like a rocking horse.' She folded her hands in her lap.

'But why do you say a rocking horse, and not just a horse?'

'Because, silly, a regular horse doesn't have wooden runners.' She had just addressed Rhone Preston as 'silly' on his own programme. And it looked to Jacob, from the honest-to-goodness smile the man was sporting and the hint of an honest-to-goodness bulge he thought he spied in the host's honest-to-goodness trousers, that Rhone liked it.

'Are you telling us that you've discovered a galaxy with wooden runners?' the host was asking.

'They're really just clouds of gas, but, yes, they look like wooden runners. Isn't it fun? Mind you, in a few million years they might look like something else. So I say we enjoy them while we can.'

\*                    \*                    \*

66

'*There's a lot of stuff out there in space*?' Normandie teased. She was visibly keyed up after their TV appearance, and she was shifting from one foot to the other out of sheer excess energy. She and Jacob were indulging in a post-mortem, standing by the bar at Kate's favourite martini mecca. Kate was on her way to join them.

'Hey, there *is*. Isn't there?'

'That's not what we astronomers are paid to discover.'

'I'm sorry. Remember, *my* payslip doesn't say "astronomer",' Jacob said, taking a sip of his butterscotch martini. 'I think it says "jackass".'

Normandie bopped an inch closer and patted his cheek, as Kate sidled up to the bar.

'*There's a lot of stuff out there in space*?'

'Shh!' giggled Normandie. 'We did that already.'

'I'm pleased to know that you own a television,' said Jacob drily.

'At any rate,' said Normandie proudly, 'my bit ought to make America happy.'

'A galaxy that's shaped like a rocking horse?' said Jacob.

'Exactly. I told you they were cute.'

'But you just made the whole thing up,' he protested.

'Of course she made it up,' Kate chimed in. 'And even if she hadn't, it would be totally inconsequential, from a scientific point of view. Do you really think scholars get all excited about cosmic phenomena based on how *cute* their shapes are?'

'Well, my mother was an art historian, and she always said that …'

Kate waved a hand, a gesture that served not only to cut Jacob off in mid-sentence but also to summon the bartender. 'That's fine arts. Art is allowed to be cute. Science isn't cute. It's often beautiful, but never cute.'

'What about the biology of wombats and baby koalas and so forth?'

'Why are you arguing with me, Jacob? Do you really want to stand against a streamlined chrome bar debating baby animals at two in the morning? Personally, I think we should focus on drinking, so I can pay for these martinis and you can take Normandie home and give her a nice Wednesday-night shagging.' She turned to Normandie. 'Or do I mean Thursday-night shagging? I always lose track of what day it is around this time of the week.'

'Sorry,' said Jacob.

'The point is, if the seduction of the Bay area television-watching public by the merest hint, delivered in Normandie's breathless, toothpaste-selling voice, that there may be a massive amalgamation of stars 40 million light-years from here that, to our warped minds, suggests a rocking horse ... where was I?' She took a restorative gulp from her recently delivered martini. 'Oh, yes. If that hint is going to translate into federal funding for my programme and salaries for the top-notch scholars I wish to retain' – here she gave Normandie a friendly, unacademic slap on the pert behind of her I'm-going-on-television skirt – 'then I say, "Bring on the rocking horse galaxies."'

'Are you sure the galaxy can't be a teddy bear?' asked Jacob, thoughtfully. 'If it's cuteness you're after, that seems safer.'

'No,' said Kate definitively. 'We already said it was a rocking horse. Besides, there are *two* popular constellations named after bears. We don't want the public to think that astronomers are completely lacking in imagination.'

'Ursa Major and Ursa Minor aren't *teddy* bears,' said Jacob peevishly.

'No teddy bears in my cosmos, and that's final,' said Kate.

'Come on, dear,' interjected Normandie. 'Wednesday-night shagging, remember?'

'Right,' said Jacob, brightening. 'Goodnight, Kate.'

'Goodnight ... teddy bear.'

# Chapter Twelve

ON THE SUBWAY, NORMANDIE couldn't keep her hands off Jacob. And as they walked from the station to her building, she alternated between dashing ahead of him, then back, like an over-eager puppy, and singing sultry lyrics from a Blondie song.

'Goodness,' said Jacob, 'one might think you were a bit keyed up.'

She kissed him without breaking stride. 'Sitting in front of those cameras, it was like my ass was cooking in my seat, my cunt simmering in its marinade. I could hardly sit still, it was so thrilling.'

'It has been quite a night.'

'No. It's been quite an *evening*,' said Normandie. 'When I get you home, then it's going to be quite a night.'

'You are a dynamo,' Jacob said with admiration. 'It's a wonder you don't leave the earth's orbit entirely.'

'I'm too smart to leave the planet while you're on it.'

'You're sweet. And, yes, smart.'

'It's a fact. But tonight, all I want to be is a giggling, hard-nippled creature with a hungry cunt … dripping into panties that have been yanked halfway down my ass. Take me there, Jacob. Make me that creature tonight.'

'I'll do my best.'

'Fuck, I'm hot,' she said as she unlocked the door. 'I hope I can keep my fingers out of my panties long enough to let yours in there.'

She was making him pretty horny, too, and he clutched the nearest bottom cheek through her skirt.

'I know!' she exclaimed.

'You do?'

'The jewelled skirt. Oh, damn, Jacob, tonight can be the night you fuck me in my jewelled skirt.'

'I'll check my calendar,' said Jacob, before she grabbed at his cock, as if his jeans didn't exist. 'Ooh,' he said, appreciatively. 'You know, that was my penis you grabbed there.'

'Yeah, I thought it was probably yours.'

The jewelled skirt had been purchased at a flea market. It was a handmade garment of stiff, lilac-coloured cotton, onto which an assortment of colourful glass jewels had been glued. A dry cleaner would not have liked it.

She had never tried it on before, and Jacob was surprised to see that this skirt – now all that she was wearing – was really designed more like an apron. Normandie, who had examined it before purchasing it, must have realised this all along, he noted. Now, her glorious ass was displayed in a luxurious, six-inch swath where the edges of the apron failed abysmally to meet. And this swath of ass, at the moment, seemed to Jacob to be the most appetising thing he'd ever seen.

'I feel so ordinary compared to you,' he said.

'Then put on a towel or something and be exotic like me,' she said with a laugh.

So he did. He went into the bathroom and selected a handsome, but skimpy, burgundy towel and swapped it for his clothes.

Inspired by her exhortation to 'be exotic', he also grabbed a crisp, navy blue pillowcase. Then he emerged, to parade before her in the bedroom, using one hand to keep the towel in place and the other – with pillowcase – to stroke his cock, which protruded through the gap in the towel. When not stroking, he dangled the pillowcase in front of his loins like a veil.

Normandie was convulsed. 'Oh, baby, that's funny … but it's so sexy. Keep doing it.' Between bouts of laughter, she swayed sensuously, and her jewels glimmered in the light.

He danced slowly toward her, and when he came within

reach, she removed his hand from his shaft and replaced it with her own. Then she spun gracefully around and lined the gap in her garment up with that in his. They moaned together as she pulled him forward and his hot, hard cock made contact up and down the cleft that separated the cool cheeks of her behind.

He dropped the towel as she dragged him to the bed. Normandie lay face down on the mattress, managing to keep Jacob's cock precisely in place in her ass cleft, her cheeks framing his sausage like a bleached white bun. He pressed down gently, and she moved his hands under her chest to explore her naked breasts. Her whole body began to vibrate as he squeezed the soft flesh and teased the nipples, while his cock throbbed cosily against her ass, biding its time.

'Now,' she said, sounding as if she were so distracted that it was an effort to articulate even a single syllable. She slithered onto her knees, then lowered her front half while presenting her bottom, putting her face back down on folded arms.

Slickness was the dominant attribute that Jacob felt as he slid into the warm channel between her legs. 'My favourite channel,' he quipped. He worked his thing wildly inside her and felt her inner flesh respond to every nuance of his movements. Her toes fluttered against his thighs, until they stiffened in pre-orgasmic paralysis. His fingers rendezvoused with hers upon her clit, and the two lovers let themselves through the door of sensory overload. In Jacob's arms writhed the giggling creature of pleasure.

Jacob was surprised to hear the shy, trembling voice of Susan Weedon when he answered his phone.

'Is this Jacob?'

'Susan Weedon?' he responded. Though she'd spoken a minimum of words to him at the museum and at the observatory, she was unmistakable. 'How are you, Susan?'

'This is Susan.'

'Uh-huh.'

'So anyway … I need to talk to you.'

'Oh. OK …'

'About the rocking horse photos.'

That was odd. Though that article had been pushed back to make room for Normandie's controversial spread, it had been signed, sealed, and delivered, with the layout complete and approved and every photo accounted for. He hoped that Gary wasn't taking advantage of the slack in the timetable to rip the whole thing apart and make them produce a new set of pictures. Jacob would definitely ask for more money if he had to spend any additional time at the LMARH.

But he assented to the meeting, and within an hour he was on his way to meet Susan at a café. He deliberately left his copy of the proofs at home, since nobody had officially contracted with him to do additional work on what he'd understood to be a completed project. If Gary needed that, he would have to approach Jacob in the proper fashion. Susan did not constitute the proper fashion; nor, Jacob stated in his inner monologue, did young Brandon.

He spotted Susan as soon as he walked into the café. Whether it was because the light of the afternoon sun was catching her auburn hair just right, or because there was something intrinsically intense about her face or posture, he wasn't sure. He waved, then got himself a coffee before joining her at the table.

'Thanks for coming.' She spoke almost too softly for him to hear, above the low rumble of ambient chitchat and a relatively quiet indie rock album.

'No problem,' he said graciously. 'So what's up?'

'On the phone, I said we needed to talk about rocking horse pictures.'

'Indeed you did,' he said with a sigh.

'I was lying.'

She had only spoken some twenty sentences to him in his entire experience of her, and now she was revealing that one of those sentences had been a lie. Jacob sipped his coffee while he tried to decide how to react to this. What he decided was that he didn't know how to react to it.

'OK.' He really wasn't sure if it was OK, but 'OK' seemed the best response he could come up with.

'I have something else to tell you. Ask you.'

Jacob realised that she was shaking, and suddenly his uppermost concern was that he put her at ease. 'Relax. Ask away.'

'You're not angry?'

'No. I was dreading the trumped-up rocking-horse-related meeting, so I'm actually relieved.' He was instantly glad he'd been candid, because he saw her face relax into a smile – possibly for the first time since he'd met her.

'I enjoyed the rocking horse session. And the other session,' she said coyly, as if she were revealing a secret.

'I'm very glad,' he replied noncommittally.

'I liked seeing you and Normandie together.' She paused. 'Which rocking horse did you fuck on?'

Heads turned as Jacob spattered coffee onto a laminated menu.

'I don't remember mentioning ...' he began when he'd caught his breath.

'A photographer learns to observe things. To read between the lines. To pick up on unspoken cues.'

'I see.'

'So which horse?'

'The biggest one.'

She nodded sagely. 'I thought so. It had a special glow to it.'

'I knew I should have sponged it down,' said Jacob. He couldn't believe he was having this conversation with a woman who had, up until five minutes before, been almost too shy to ask him how he liked the house coffee. He wondered what had gotten into her.

'The two of you have chemistry. Know what I mean?'

He assured her that he did.

'I think of you guys a lot, actually. *Know what I mean?*'

This time he wasn't sure whether he did. 'Think about us?'

Her laugh, like fairy bells, surprised him. 'Do I have to paint you a picture?'

'I thought you were a photographer.'

'I *masturbate* thinking about the two of you.'

Jacob looked around the room, wishing that Susan had not chosen this particular statement as the loudest statement of her career. The indie rock record seemed to have hit a particularly quiet moment, and even the espresso machine had gone silent to make way for Susan's announcement.

'So, I was thinking … maybe we could do another photo session,' she said, very quietly.

# Chapter Thirteen

'WHAT DO YOU THINK?' Jacob asked Normandie.

'What do I think of the two of us as the subjects of an erotic photography session? I think, "When do we get started?" – that's what I think. It's long been a dream of mine to do something like that, to be one of those people in delicious black-and-white tableaux of flesh and pillows and ecstatic facial expressions.'

'So Susan is helping you attain a lifetime goal. That's a talent in itself.'

'What do you think of her?' asked Normandie. They were sitting on the unmade bed, fully clothed, because the bedroom was where Jacob had found Normandie when he'd returned from his meeting with Susan. The bed smelled like Normandie had jilled off after the nap she'd admitted to; Jacob relished the image of her lounging there in an impromptu diddle, working restless fingers in her panties just because it felt so good.

'Susan is a terrific photographer, able to capture anything from the beautiful – that's you – to the inexplicable – those you-know-whats at the museum. I'm sure she'll do a wonderful session.'

'What else do you think of her?'

'What else? Well, she's a little strange, of course … quiet – until she starts declaiming in cafés about her sexual fantasies, that is.'

Normandie ran a finger down the length of his chest. 'Is she sexy?'

'Oh,' said Jacob. 'To me?'

'No,' whispered Normandie with polished sarcasm, 'to "Weird Al" Yankovic.'

75

Jacob reflected. 'Yeah, I guess she is. To me.'

'Tell me about it,' Normandie said, still whispering.

*Tell me about it* was a cue, in their relationship, for the party of the second part to relate or create a sexual fantasy. So he understood now that he was being called upon to spin a vignette with Susan Weedon at its centre.

Normandie reclined on the bed. Her quasi-golden hair was framed by a crimson pillowcase.

'Susan is one of the quiet ones that you have to watch,' he began.

'I would love to watch her.'

'She goes about her business, never saying a word … but she's tuned in to every detail, especially sexual details. She notices where your skirt clings to your ass. She sees when my cock stiffens slightly in my trousers. When your hands brush casually against me, Susan Weedon can detect minute changes in the composition of my perspiration. And she can smell when you're aroused, perhaps even before you realise you're aroused.

'So she goes about her business, and she logs all of this, never saying a word. She records it and takes it home with her, much like her camera records the things that it's supposed to.

'She lives alone. She can strip to her underwear in the living room without anyone noticing. Her underwear is incongruously loud – hot pink thong and lace bra, I believe – and this incongruity is the whole point of Susan Weedon.'

Normandie's hands had moved to just inside the top of her jeans, and her mouth formed a little 'O'.

He continued. 'She's in her living room, but she doesn't settle down yet. She keeps in motion, prowling her own apartment in her underwear, thinking in circles about me and you, replaying everything she's observed. She's alone – she can take everything at her own speed. She's restless between her legs, and her hands repeatedly drift to her crotch.'

'Repeatedly drift,' echoed Normandie. Jacob could see that she was easing herself into masturbation.

'Finally, she's so wound up there's only one place she can take it. So she buries her little bottom in the corner of her living room couch and kicks her legs up and down while she rubs furiously over the thong – and inside it as well – palm squeezing, thumb pressing, fingers dipping, thighs quaking … mind reeling with my cock and your scent and the artist's conception of me fucking you against the wall of the Living Museum of the Goddamn American Rocking Horse.'

'Oh!' Normandie was coming, rocking herself on the bed.

'I want some of that,' Jacob told her, his cock pounding in his pants.

He got some of it.

'While you were out, I got a call from another television show. They've booked me for August.'

'You're going to be the toast of local TV.'

'This one's national. *Gimme Some Science!*'

He knew the programme. A network had ingeniously put an accessible, hour-long science programme in the hands of Priscilla Ray, a former supermodel whose intellect was even more impressive than her pout. They'd added a creative team who could find the glamorous, humorous, or fascinating side of any topic, and the result was a prime-time cash bonanza built out of ratings-risky subjects like insect reproduction and alloy composition.

'You'll be great!' Jacob said enthusiastically.

'Yes, we will,' Normandie concurred.

'We?'

'They want Professor Jacobs, too.'

'Why?'

'I guess they think you're "good television".'

'*Good television?* Good grief. I think I need a cup of coffee.'

'You're drinking a cup of coffee, sweet cheeks.'

He shrugged. 'OK, then. Professor Jacobs I am. Why not.'

'That's the spirit.'

'What about you? You don't mind going on national

television and continuing to lie about outer space?'

'In for a penny, in for a buck,' she said philosophically.

'Do you mean that?' Jacob asked.

'I think so. It sounded good, anyway.'

'Because I have an idea, if you're interested. It's not exactly honest, though.'

'Then it will fit right in.'

'Suppose we brought an image. You know, a slide of your adorable rocking horse galaxy.'

'Wouldn't I love to! But where does one get slides of non-existent galaxies?'

'One asks one's photographer friend to make them.'

'That's asking a lot of Susan, isn't it?'

'We'd have to pay her, I assume – unless she's as turned on by the prospect of Photoshopping whimsical galaxies as she is by the prospect of photographing our lovemaking.'

'You never know. But, OK, I'll keep my chequebook handy.' She thought a moment. 'This means we'll also have to trust her with the secret.'

'We're talking about a woman who's just confided her masturbation habits to me within earshot of an entire café's worth of people. If you can't trust someone like that, whom *can* you trust?'

'Your grammar is better than your logic, Jacob Hastings,' said Normandie lovingly. 'But I believe in your instincts.'

# Chapter Fourteen

IF JACOB HADN'T BEEN reminiscing pleasantly about some of his recent bedroom frolics with Normandie, he probably would have seen the man approaching him as he trudged down the sidewalk.

'Hastings, isn't it?' Both men stopped in their tracks, forcing other pedestrians to sashay nimbly around them.

Jacob recognised the curator of the LMARH. He resisted the impulse to do anything as obvious as rolling his eyes or running away.

Incredibly, he did not know the man's name – for the simple reason that he had refused to give it, despite his extensive appearances in Jacob's article for *HHH*.

'Fine,' Jacob had said. 'We respect your privacy.'

'I don't care about my privacy,' the man had explained. 'But if I give you my name, you'll use it ... and I'd much prefer to be known as the Curator. I'm proud of being a curator, and I want everyone to be reminded that that's what I am.'

'Paragraph after paragraph.'

'Yes.'

So now Jacob, necessarily, greeted him without reference to any name. And he was certainly not going to say, 'Hello there, Curator.' He opted for a simple – and not particularly enthusiastic – 'Hey.'

'Hey, indeed! I suppose it's all in a day's work for you, cancelling articles, robbing worthy institutions of their just publicity.'

Jacob decided not to quibble with that phrase 'just publicity', and tried instead to be conciliatory. 'Oh, no, the piece about your museum hasn't been cancelled. It's just been pushed back a month.'

'Just like I said, then,' said the curator. 'Cancelled.'

'No, really – not cancelled, just postponed.'

'It amounts to the same thing.'

'It does not.' Jacob suddenly wondered how he had become embroiled in this sidewalk game of point/counterpoint ... and how he could escape from it soonest. 'Look,' he said desperately, his eyes roving the immediate area. 'I have to go. I'm late for an appointment to ...' His eyes continued to roam. Bagel place. Newsstand. Liquor store. Nothing much to work with here ... 'buy luggage.'

'Excuse me?'

'No, please ... excuse *me*. I know it's rude, but my luggage consultant has a conniption fit whenever I'm late.' And he sidestepped the curator and bolted, noting in his peripheral vision that the man, thinking he wasn't looking, was giving him the finger.

He ran across the street, through the glass door of a suitcase shop, and into the arms of ...

Hubert Renkins, of the Hauser University Department of Astronomy.

'Sorry!' said Jacob, sincerely, to what he took for an unpleasant-looking but innocent stranger. 'My fault. Are you OK?'

'I'm Professor Hubert Renkins, is what I am,' said the erstwhile stranger. 'Say ... why aren't you back at Mountain College?' he added.

Jacob thought quickly. 'Which Mountain College?' he said cagily. 'I believe there are several.'

Renkins was eyeing him suspiciously, which Jacob theorised was the only manner in which Renkins was capable of eyeing. 'Are you really an astronomer?'

'What a silly question,' said Jacob with a forced chortle. 'Why would anyone *pretend* to be an astronomer?'

'You tell me, *Professor* Jacobs.'

'I'm flattered that you remember my name.'

'I've seen you around the campus with Professor Stephens.'

'I congratulate you on your excellent eyesight.'

'I use a telescope.'

Jacob wagged a forefinger. 'You naughty astronomers.'

'I thought you were an astronomer, too.'

'Er … That's right. Of course I am. I meant to say, *we* naughty astronomers. Naughty, every one of us.' He punctuated this pronouncement with a silly, high-pitched laugh that he'd picked up from some British television comedian.

'What type of telescope do *you* use, Jacobs?'

'I like the kind that makes things look closer.'

Renkins scowled. 'I mean what make, what model, of course.'

'I think it's a Calvin Klein.'

'A Calvin Klein telescope?'

'Would you believe Laura Ashley?'

'What?'

'Look, Professor Renkins … I'm sorry, but I'm just not a label person. I'm much too busy with – um – astronomy things to participate in your rampant consumerism.' He proudly drew himself up to his full height as he said this.

The face of Hubert Renkins contorted into an insinuating smile. 'Of course, Professor Jacobs. Astronomy things. I'm so interested to hear about your research.'

Jacob saw his chance. 'Good. If you let me go now, perhaps I'll get some of it completed.' And he stalked off, pretending – he hoped convincingly – that his fear was instead indignation.

Brandon may not have been the very last person in the world that Jacob wanted to see now, but he would do.

'Dude,' Brandon said concisely, proffering a handshake propelled by exaggerated momentum, all the way from the shoulder. Unlike Renkins and the curator before him, Brandon, in line for a coffee, had been spotted from a distance; but Jacob's own lust for coffee had trumped his aversion to the encounter.

'Hi, Brandon.' Jacob glanced around the café, hoping to find somebody else with whom he could simulate a pressing need to converse. 'What's new?'

'Exactly,' Brandon snorted.

Jacob pretended to be satisfied with this answer.

'You and Normandie should come down to the club some Friday.'

'Thank you.' Jacob was pleased that Brandon didn't consider him too old or too unhip to make the club scene. He felt a little more charitable toward the young man now.

'Yeah, seriously, dude. You shouldn't worry about being old or unhip. We're cool with it.'

At least this wouldn't be one of those occasions when he had nothing to relate when he dropped by Normandie's lab at lunchtime.

'Hello,' said Normandie cheerfully, while giving him a welcoming kiss. 'Did you enjoy your walk from the parking lot? How are the undergrad women's asses today?'

'Actually, I happen to think the grad student women have better asses, on the whole, than the undergrads. Mind you, I'm not *complaining* about the undergrad asses.'

'What about the breasts?'

'Yes, breasts … it's funny, but somehow it feels like more of a time commitment to look at breasts. I'm too busy to look at strange women's breasts.'

'Too busy looking at their asses, you mean?'

With all this talk of asses, Jacob desperately wanted Normandie's in his face. That was it – ass in his face, the ultimate raunchy intimacy. He could get diverted there for endless foreplay.

'Sweetheart?' he ventured.

'Yes?' She had returned to her desk, and she did not look up from her work.

'I'm feeling like I want your ass in my face.'

'Now?'

'No, two weeks from Thursday.' He softened the sarcasm

with a cuddly chuckle. 'You *did* start a conversation about attractive asses. See what happens?'

Her upturned ass was soon situated conveniently upon his lap, seductively framed by a hiked-up miniskirt and a pair of yanked-down panties. Jacob felt that everything he wanted from life at that moment was displayed across his lap. Nothing could be more beautiful to him than her face; but the smile of her bottom was a close second.

He worshipped it with his eyes before he even touched.

A tickle. A soft slap. A finger travelling the crack. A feather-light kiss and a delicate, painless nibble. These cheeks were his playground, and his way of playing made her shiver and wriggle and eventually buck across his sturdy thighs. He knew she wanted more, that he would caress and tease her ass till she became so wet her juices would drizzle down and stain his jeans. Till she was just one clit-stroke away from an ass-shaking orgasm. Till he could clutch the trembling derrière, pressing the cool flesh of his face against a hot cheek, feeling the wildness of her pleasure bouncing against him.

'Yes. My ass.' They both knew how erogenous a zone it was for her. Her round, creamy, cute behind.

'Yes, yes. My ass.' Her compulsive statements emphatically removed any doubt as to whose ass Jacob was attending to.

'Remind me … whose ass is this?' he growled pleasantly. 'Whose ass are these hands grabbing?'

'Oh. Mine … mine.'

They knew how silly it would have sounded to an observer. But in this moment of theirs, the absurd dialogue was not only erotic but absolutely essential.

Over lunch, he told her about the curator. And about Renkins. And about Brandon.

'You social butterfly,' she said. 'And to think I've been hard at work all morning while you've been flitting about the village, chattering with all your friends.'

'You're describing Hubert Renkins as my *friend*?'

'He's certainly not *my* friend.'

'He's not baggage I'm eager to claim, either.'

'Then I suggest you stop hooking up with him in luggage stores.'

'I will make a note of that,' he laughed.

'Come here.' She leaned forward across the eatery table, and Jacob mirrored the motion, to claim his kiss.

'How concerned do we have to be about the fact that Renkins suspects me of being your boyfriend rather than an astronomer from Hilltop College?'

'Mountain College.

'Whatever.'

'He could try to make some trouble. But, fortunately for us, everybody sort of hates Hubert, so people will make a valiant effort to ignore whatever he has to say against us. And it sounds like you managed to brazen it out for the moment.'

'If running away can be considered brazenness.'

'As long as it works.'

Jacob gave some attention to his burrito. 'That odious museum guy actually gave me the finger, when he thought I wasn't looking.'

'East Coast or West Coast?'

'What?'

'Look.' She raised both her hands, flipping Jacob a simulated double bird. He saw that the right hand – the 'East Coast' variant that made him nostalgic for New York – contrasted with the left-hand variant, on which the knuckles surrounding the middle finger rose up like shoulders. He also noticed that the proprietor of the deli was staring at Normandie, as if wondering what the hell was going on at Table 3.

'So that's the West Coast finger,' said Jacob. 'Yeah, I think that's what I got. I'll try to remember to use that one from now on when I flip off the locals. After all, I don't want to come across like an inconsiderate tourist.'

The proprietor looked relieved when Normandie's hands returned to her sandwich.

'By the way,' said Jacob, 'Brandon says we should hit the dance club some Friday night.'

'So?'

'Granted, I don't usually pay much attention to what Brandon thinks we should do. But it would be fun to go dancing with you.'

'Not that I wouldn't like to see you surrounded by hot chicks on the dance floor – I really would, you know …'

'You're counting yourself as one of them, I hope.'

'… but I think one night at the dance club with Brandon was enough for me.'

'Oh! I didn't realise you'd been on that ride before.'

'Remember how you and I met at a party at Brandon's brother's house, and we left together?'

'I do have a vague recollection of that, yes.'

'Well, that wasn't the first party I attended at that house. Or the first one I didn't leave by myself.'

'Ah. So, you and … Brandon?'

'About a year ago.'

'That's fascinating. And – please don't take this as jealousy or competitiveness, because it honestly isn't either…'

'I know, sweetie.' She touched his hand.

'But what the hell did *you* see in *him*?'

'Just what everyone does. Superficial good looks. Energy. A shallow aura of hipness. Freedom from deep thought. I think, speaking for myself, I was feeling old that night, and the attention he was giving me made me feel young. Except he convinced me to drop by the dance club between the party and home, and that did not make me feel young at all, since I felt I was already up past my bedtime. But, when he saw how tired I was, he was considerate enough to agree we should cut that part of the evening short. Or, more likely, it was just that he realised the shagging window was going to close if I fell asleep before we made it to my bed.'

'How'd it go when you got home?'

She shrugged. 'Oh, it was all right for a take-someone-home-to-bed-from-a-party sort of thing. Neither of us showed any interest in pursuing it after that. We really had nothing to talk about. The sex was not bad, but not great. He was pretty good with clits, as I recall – I'll say that much for many of these younger guys – but his chin kept digging into my shoulder, every time he surfaced to kiss me above the neck. Anyway, it was nothing worth making a great effort over.'

She sipped her coffee. 'It's funny. So often, in the past, I've felt that things weren't worth the trouble.' She took his hand again.

# Chapter Fifteen

SUSAN'S STUDIO WAS SET up as the best-lit bedroom they had ever seen.

'How did you get that bed in?' Jacob asked. It was a luxurious, sprawling affair – suitable for luxurious, sprawling affairs – that obviously could not have fit through the door.

'I assembled it here, when I first got the studio,' Susan said softly.

'Aha,' said Normandie. 'So this won't be your first erotic shoot.'

Susan put a hand to her mouth to stifle her already-nearly-silent laughter. Her eyes were pixie-like. 'Not exactly. But it will be my best.'

Jacob, unsure of how to get the proceedings underway, began to unbutton his shirt.

'Would you please keep your shirt on,' said Susan, with a distinctive tone of meek firmness. The combination of her natural timidity and the confidence that came with being in charge, on her own turf, was an interesting one, Jacob thought.

'You mean my actual shirt?' He'd never heard the expression used literally before.

'Jacob is such a he-man,' said Normandie, with a straight face. 'You can't get the guy to keep his shirt on for five minutes at a time. It's very embarrassing at formal events.'

'I have a gradual progression of scenes in mind,' Susan explained. 'I promise you will both be undressed before we're finished.'

'I hope so,' said Jacob, 'or I'm going to want my money back.'

'I'm paying *you*,' Susan reminded him.

'Where would you like us to pose, Susan?' asked Normandie.

'The bed,' said Susan, indicating what was, in fact, the only piece of furniture within the area she had lit. 'Please take only your shoes off and sit on the edge, for now. You can touch, but no orgasms or anything yet.'

'You heard the lady,' said Jacob to Normandie as they assumed their positions. 'Don't go sneaking in an orgasm before she's ready.'

'Damn,' said Normandie. 'I think I'm already having one.'

Jacob now understood why Susan had taken such care over the phone to discuss clothing, reviewing each item in a precise, rabbity voice. His black oxford and grey trousers, and Normandie's cream scoop-necked blouse and ever-popular, ass-perfect pinstriped slacks, were, he now realised, not destined for the studio floor immediately upon arrival.

He sat on the edge of the bed, in a posture that hovered between tentativeness and comfort. Normandie had her knees under her, and her thin, black socks pointed erectly toward the shadows at the bed's edge. She took Jacob's hand and held it against her thigh, the one closest to the camera – near the knee, as if they were romantics on a picnic, with upper thigh contact held in reserve for later in the feast.

'Beautiful,' said Susan, snapping the first shot. 'More like that, if you don't mind.'

Jacob felt self-conscious but happy. Normandie seemed to glow, to be in her element. She mouthed a little pucker-lipped kiss at him, and Susan snapped it. Then, impulsively, Normandie pushed Jacob backward onto the bed. She grinned at the camera, her hand on Jacob's chest, her breasts rounded by Susan's lighting into impish orbs within the blouse.

'I think that's Sequence 1,' said Susan. Jacob sat up, and he thought he saw Susan brush her crotch against her tripod as she wrestled it into a slightly different position. 'Normandie, would you take your blouse off for me?' she said when she'd made the adjustment.

*For me.* Jacob got a kick out of hearing Susan say it that

way, but he couldn't resist teasing the photographer. 'I thought she was taking her blouse off for *me*.'

'You thought wrong,' Susan sang back amiably from behind her tripod.

The beginning of the bare-breast sequence transformed Jacob's romantic, tentative mood into a mood awash with desire. The couple sat in the same positions they'd occupied when fully clothed, but Susan moved the lights so that one breast glowed and the other warmed a slight shadow. The interplay of the texture of Normandie's actual flesh and the illusions of texture rendered by Susan's masterful lighting were fascinating to Jacob.

'May I touch?'

'You may and you must,' said Susan. 'But please follow my instructions. I know what will look right.' He noticed again that Susan was leaning in so as to furrow the front of her black skirt with the hindmost leg of the tripod. She pressed herself subtly against the metal rod as she directed them.

'Cup the bright one with your inside hand,' she said.

He did so. Normandie's breast was especially warm under the lights. It felt like a small, cuddly animal in his palm.

'Normandie, three fingers in your waistband. Like you're thinking about doing yourself.'

Jacob resisted the impulse to stroke his cock through his trousers. Susan Weedon certainly knew how to orchestrate things for dramatic effect, and the dramatic effects were already threatening to break his zipper.

*Snap. Snap. Snap.* 'Kiss it.'

His mouth found a place that he knew was particularly sensitive, and Normandie moaned tenderly, throwing her head back for Susan – or Jacob.

*Snap. Snap.* 'Now the nipple.'

He gently attacked it. 'Normandie,' said Susan, 'would you – oh, good, you're already doing it.' She was evidently referring to the fact that Normandie had dug her fingers deeper inside her pants, and was stroking.

Susan took several more shots. 'I need to see your penis.'

'Oh, God, me too,' said Normandie.

'Thank goodness,' said Jacob. He fumbled feverishly with his button and zipper. Normandie clasped his thigh with her free hand, her breasts bouncing softly in the light.

'Can I hold it?' she asked Susan when the proud cock had been released.

'Please do.' Susan stepped forward to adjust the lights again, putting a virtual spotlight on Jacob's lap. She frowned; then, with a lightning-fast motion that showed a combination of deference and assertion, she touched Jacob's shaft above where Normandie held it, tilting it fifteen degrees toward the headboard – so that it cast a sharp, suitably phallic shadow across his trouser leg. Before it could sink in that she had touched him there, she was gone, across six feet of industrial floor, behind her camera again.

'Rock, please,' she said.

They rocked from side to side, Normandie using Jacob's prick like a lever, her left hand never leaving her pants. Jacob anchored himself by clutching the mattress with his right hand, and he felt close to coming as their miniature world seesawed back and forth with his sex at its centre. Susan snapped away, and each click of the shutter felt to Jacob like the trigger that could send him rocketing.

Susan was beginning to look a little flushed herself; as for Normandie, the wayward fingers in her panties had disappeared from view.

'Black panties?' Susan confirmed.

'Yes,' Jacob and Normandie answered quickly, in unison. Normandie stood up and, for the first time in what seemed to Jacob like hours, removed her hand from her pants.

'Excellent,' said Susan. She stepped forward to claim Normandie's slacks as they slid off. Susan folded the slacks lovingly, and Jacob swatted Normandie's luscious bottom through the black satin before she straightened back up.

'Now you can take your shirt off, mister.'

Jacob sat forward to unbutton it, feeling the kiss of his

rigid cock on his own belly as he did so. As the shirt came off, Normandie massaged his back and resumed her hold on his pole.

'Just like that,' said Susan. *Snap. Snap. Snap.*

'I'm not going to last much longer this way,' Jacob warned.

'That's fine,' said Susan. 'We're almost done with this part.'

'Woohoo,' said Normandie, who had straddled Jacob's thigh and was practically dry-humping it.

'Let's go freestyle now,' said Susan. 'You be natural, and I'll keep shooting.'

'You're not the only one who's going to be shooting,' said Jacob.

'Come here, baby,' said Normandie. She brushed her hair aside with her free hand and went down on him, making Jacob sizzle. Now free to move as he liked without directorial instruction, he slipped one hand into the back of Normandie's panties – he found he could just barely reach the waistband – and nurtured a nipple with the other. Normandie reached for her nexus and began to tug and tease sensuously through the fabric, making herself dance at the hips while her head bobbed over Jacob's ecstasy.

Jacob's orgasmic call was a hoarse, nearly silent one. But from across the room came a high-pitched, feminine echo – the loudest sound he had ever heard Susan Weedon make, an uninhibited shriek of joy. And the most remarkable thing was the way it coincided precisely with a definite click of her shutter, a click that immortalised Jacob's bliss.

Normandie wiped her mouth on a corner of sheet and climbed onto Jacob, ass toward Susan, sweat glistening over her and hunger in her eyes.

'Hey, Ms Ass-in-Panties,' Jacob growled softly, for Normandie's ears only.

'That's *Dr* Ass-in-Panties, if you please. I do have a PhD, remember.'

'For Pete's sake, take those pants off, Jacob,' Susan

interrupted.

Normandie rolled off him and he complied, discarding his underpants in the same motion.

'Let's keep our socks on, I think,' said Susan, who was fully dressed.

So Jacob, naked except for his calf-length ribbed socks, peeled black satin off his lover's ass, but left her feet clothed. The panties were cool and more than a little moist. He rubbed them over his groin and felt his cock begin to come back to life.

Now that she was bare-assed, Jacob went to town on Normandie. A finger glided up and down her crack, then lodged gently within her bum hole. His other hand spread her pussy lips, kneading and teasing and urging, making her even more wet and more wild than she had been.

*Snap. Snap. Snap.*

His face rushed in to kiss and converse with her fragrant, dripping snatch, and her thighs pounded softly against the side of his head.

Susan had given them this, Jacob thought. Susan had worked them into what, even by their standards, was a fucking frenzy.

Normandie sobbed gleefully into a pillow as Jacob's tongue melted her clit and his finger titillated her gyrating bottom. She soaked his face as she came, and Susan's zoom lens made a voyeuristic whirring noise as the photographer turned a mess of thighs and sweat and sex-juice into an art shot of a man's face framed by a triangle of his orgasmic woman's flesh, her quivering thighs only hinting to the camera of the unimaginable delights being lavished on her hidden parts.

When Jacob's face emerged, he saw that Susan was unabashedly grinding against the tripod. Her skirt had ridden up above her bare knees. 'Please fuck her. Please.' This time, it was not the request of a photographer, but of a desperate onlooker. Jacob got the impression that at this point the lens cap could have been on, for all Susan cared. His cock was tremendous now.

Normandie was still slowly writhing in post-orgasmic delirium, stroking her crotch, smoothing her sweat-drenched, blonde pussy hair and churning her ass against the mattress.

He took one of her sock-clad feet in each hand. Then he opened her like scissors and slid home.

'She's watching us,' he whispered into her ear.

'Yes,' said Normandie.

'You feel so ticklish around me,' Jacob continued, emphasising the word *ticklish* by tickling the sole of her foot with his thumb.

'Aaaaaa,' Normandie cooed, mouthing kisses, eyes closed.

He squirmed and danced into her, working her feet like the handlebars of a bicycle, riding her for every bump of pleasure on the road. She clutched his butt cheeks, slapping now and again, and he thought he heard Susan gasp from across the room.

'Aaaaaa,' they told each other, together now, as the pleasure that nestled between them ripened and burst.

The voice that came from behind them was clear and delicate, like crystal. 'Watch me. Oh, fuck, watch me, for fuck's sake.'

'I think she wants us to watch her,' Normandie interpreted, as they struggled via elbows to get up onto their knees.

Susan had unbuttoned her skirt to the waist, so that it hung lewdly around her, leaving her skinny pink legs and her handkerchief-white panties in full view. She was sliding her mound up and down the tripod leg, pressing her chest against the back of her camera, clenching and unclenching her jaw. Her eyes met Jacob's fiercely, then shifted toward Normandie.

Jacob thought the tripod would collapse from the force Susan was using to wrestle herself against it. Instead, what collapsed was Susan, who slithered into a heap at the foot of the camera stand, her hand plunged purposefully into her underwear, her legs splayed on the floor. 'Watch me,' she said just once more, before her face fragmented into a kaleidoscope of libidinous fulfilment and her shoulders shivered inside her dainty cardigan.

She caught her breath, then dissolved into nervous laughter. 'Say *cheese,*' she told Jacob and Normandie, before laughing some more, so hard she was almost crying.

# Chapter Sixteen

FOR WEEKS, JACOB HAD been trying to persuade Normandie to put her work aside long enough to make room for a getaway. Finally, with August upon them, she had agreed.

Jacob, committed to California for the foreseeable future, now owned a car. And Normandie, who was in one of her kinetic moods when they embarked for the weekend, requested the keys.

'I don't recommend using fifth gear on this car,' Jacob advised as they settled into their seats.

'OK. Why not?'

'It only has four gears.'

Her laughter, if any, was drowned out by the accelerator.

Jacob loved routines. More than that, he loved the routine *of* routines, the very existence of quotidian rituals that bonded the two of them. The habits they'd fallen into together these past couple of months – effortlessly, for the most part – were a much more precious commodity than the formalised 'dates' Normandie had resisted for so long. Now, dates were no longer a problem for her; but now, they were largely irrelevant. Now it was about the lunchtime walk they enjoyed almost every day; the extra glass of wine that he brought her in the bedroom on Friday and Saturday nights; the fact that he always brushed his teeth first, while she clipped her nails.

But it was also important to break routines once in a while. Once they'd gotten used to living together, Jacob had begun envisioning a getaway weekend as a way of taking their togetherness into another context. He wanted to feel the little unit that was their partnership travel a short distance through space – if only as far as the nearest seaside hamlet with a one-to-one ratio of inns to inhabitants.

He admired her as she drove. He'd forgotten how sexy he found it to see an alluring woman wearing a skirt and driving, her legs spread to work the pedals like an invigorated pianist. His mind flashed to an outdoor jazz festival he'd attended one summer, where a hard-bopping piano player had stood to take a bow after a sweltering set. The back of her clinging skirt had revealed itself to be streaked in perspiration, as if the sweat had been painted across her ass with a six-inch brush. Jacob had found it inspiring to contemplate the virtuoso grinding her rear into the bench as she hammered out the music, her legs spread and the sweet flesh of her behind cheeks giving up sweat for her art.

He thought about this as he watched Normandie's legs, still fresh with the morning, pumping athletically at the clutch and gas. He wanted to slide one hand under her and grope between her thighs with the other, and he held these thoughts for later.

They slowed down behind a truck that was hauling a sofa. The truck, Jacob estimated, was moving at roughly the speed the sofa would have moved under its own power. Normandie took advantage of the relative lull in the driving to give Jacob's crotch a quick squeeze.

'That reminds me of a story,' he said. 'Do you know that I didn't know how to masturbate properly until I was nineteen years old?'

'No, I didn't know that. I must have missed the day in school where they taught us Jacob Hastings' masturbation history.'

'Have no fear – this embarrassing gap in your education will now be rectified without further ado. As a college freshman, I did not, as I recently said, know how to masturbate properly.'

'What do you mean by *properly?* Did your university make you take a test, or something?'

'I mean that I didn't realise that if you pulled on it long enough, you'd actually get somewhere.'

Normandie guffawed. 'I'm sorry, Jacob.'

'Don't be sorry. It really is funny now, and even then it wasn't tragic. I just didn't realise I could make myself come in waking life. I thought I needed an accommodating orifice for that.'

'So you found somebody who had one or more of those.'

'Yes. But she also taught me what I'd been missing as far as my solo adventures were concerned. It happened almost by chance.'

'OK, now I'm having a hard time imagining how your honey might have jerked you off *by chance*.'

'What I mean is we'd been fucking up and down for weeks. It was only because she was a little sore one night –'

'By chance.'

'No, by fucking. Anyway, before I knew what was happening she was pulling and stroking me so deliciously that I thought I would cream. And, in fact, I did.'

'And the man and his penis lived happily ever after.'

'You have to admit, it does come in handy.'

'Oh, yes. Yes, it does. Come. In. Hand. Eee!' On the last syllable, she grabbed at his crotch again. This time she squeezed it tightly for several seconds before letting go. Then she flashed him a look that said 'Just you wait till later', seized a chance to pass the sofa, and resumed a normal speed.

They drove for some time in silence.

'Do you like it when I wear lipstick?' She broke into his thoughts with an almost random question. This was one of the attractions of long car rides, and one of the reasons he'd been dying to take her on one – or, as it happened, be taken by her on one.

'Do I like *what* when you wear lipstick?'

'Seriously. Believe it or not, there was an actual reason I brought it up. It wasn't just my idea of an alternative to the license plate game.'

'I really wish you hadn't said that. Now I'll be compulsively watching for license plates for the rest of the drive.'

'But we're not playing that game.'

'Which part of *compulsively* don't you understand?'

'Sorry.'

'Forgiven.'

'I was thinking about lipstick recently, after I proctored a summer school exam. I hardly ever pay attention to what my students are wearing – except to the extent that I don't like it if they wear blank expressions at moments when their little countenances are supposed to be lighting up with epiphany.'

'Is that in your contract?'

'But during an exam, I have to walk around and … well, look at them. This has its rewards, of course, because some of them are nice to look at.'

'Can I proctor an exam, too?'

'You'll have to take that up with your own university, *Professor* Jacobs. As I was saying, I look at them. And I notice what fashions are coming and going. I remember noticing, the last few semesters, that few of the women were wearing lipstick. I realised, walking up and down the aisles in my squeaky shoes while they tried to pretend they were concentrating, that I missed seeing lipstick. Now, suddenly this summer, the lipstick is back. And you know what? After one three-hour exam, I'm already sick of looking at it. I suppose there's a lesson in that somewhere.'

'There is, but I think it's that same old "grass is greener" lesson.'

'Oh – so it is. How tedious.'

'But I have no strong opinions regarding lipstick.'

'You'll have to develop some, or this is going to be one long car ride.'

'I thought I could borrow yours.'

'My lipstick?'

'Your opinions.'

'I went shopping,' she said casually, after she'd opened her suitcase.

Jacob knew that shopping was not a casual thing for Normandie. She did it seldom, but always with a serious attitude and a precise focus.

The little pink plastic bag was, in and of itself, enough to give him an erection. Normandie winked at him, all rough-and-ready in her denim skirt and cranberry top, then disappeared into the bathroom, clutching what he knew must be a shopping bag of soft, new lingerie.

Soft, new, *white* lingerie, he learned when she emerged. White stockings. White garter belt. White silk camisole. Soft white gloves that fucked the spaces between each of her fingers.

If there were white panties, she had left them in the bag.

She was covered almost everywhere except her cunt and bottom, creating a sort of reverse panties effect. It was glorious. Then, as if to emphasise exactly where she was unclothed, she walked back into the bathroom, this time leaving the door open. Almost but not quite out of his field of vision, she dropped her ass gingerly onto the toilet seat, and, without having to lift or drop or shed or peel a single article, she peed, freely and nakedly. He admired the perfect smoothness of her hips as she sat, bare-assed and knees together, while the sound of running water echoed beneath her.

His words stopped her in the doorway, on her way back to him. 'You're too lovely for me to touch right away.'

'Are you out of your mind?' she queried.

'Would you … touch yourself, first?'

'Oh,' she said. *'Oh,'* she said again, with rising enthusiasm.

She braced her back against the doorjamb and spread her legs. Jacob sat on the bed.

He licked his lips as she spread hers. He studied the elegant kineticism of her deft strokes, the pumping of her strong thighs, the light bouncing of her ass against the doorframe.

As her flesh loosened, her muscular tightness, paradoxically, built. Moistness drizzled lazily over her fingers; but the way the fingers stretched, pulled, prodded, and penetrated was anything but lazy. Jacob watched as an impossible tension concentrated itself in his lover's sex, until her entire body seemed poised for release. She carried on intently, stirring herself past the boiling point, steering herself up, up, up and finally over the hill. Then she slouched and whimpered.

Without a word, she strutted to the bed, and lay upon it, face down, at Jacob's side. Her bottom was displayed like a precious exhibit above the white stocking-tops. Displayed to him for the squeezing, for the kissing. Ready to be pressed down upon, perhaps, by his full weight, with his rigid cock teasing a cheek, and his desire burning into her firm moon of sensuality until she should squeak in anticipation. The sight was mesmerising.

Her heavy breaths were gradually becoming shorter and shallower. Her little orgasmic aftershocks seemed to grow rather than diminish in intensity, and soon her ass was bobbing industriously up and down, inviting his palm. He caught it on every trip upward, sometimes with a little slap, sometimes with a lingering squeeze; sometimes with one hand, sometimes with both. At the point where her posture revealed her cunt lips, he sometimes ran a forefinger along the slit, making her purr. He could make love this way to her all night, he thought.

But his cock said otherwise. Straining for freedom – first from Jacob's clothes and soon thereafter from its joyful burden of libido – it yearned for Normandie's softest place.

He unzipped, then extricated himself. She remained as he'd left her, waiting for his tactile attentions to return.

'Sweet, sweet cunt lips,' he whispered, inserting a finger. His cock was impatient, but he couldn't resist delaying a little longer.

She rolled over, squeezing his finger so it stayed in place. She spread her arms and legs wide, making a soft, white X of her body, letting him wiggle his finger inside her as long as he wanted.

When he removed it, it was so wet he held it aloft, looking

for a corner of sheet on which to wipe it. But Normandie pulled it to her mouth and sucked it, leaving it sticky with fresh saliva, rather than luxurious with nectar. 'I'm a little juicy.'

Her eyes sparkled, and he wanted to fuck her till they glowed. He pounced on her, pawing at her breasts through white silk; kissing her bare shoulders while her gloved hands flitted over his torso; slowly, heavily working his hips against her naked upper thighs. He groped frantically for his shaft, directing it into her yawning hole, feeling the damp hair of her mound whisper its nakedness to his abdomen, despite all the white lingerie. He was fucking her nude pussy, he emphasised to himself: the raw, naked crotch of the elegant woman in white was splayed around him; and her body, from gloved fingertips to stocking toes, was writhing under him in an elemental stew of arousal, her white pie of an ass anchoring the two of them to a bed of ecstasy.

Her random flailings became more regular, evolving into the familiar rhythm with which she would typically grind her mound against him for a hands-free clitoral meltdown. He synched up to her, answering each grind with a thrust. Together they increased the pace, and when she held herself against him for that one extra second, he knew stars were flying across her sky and comets burning up and down the length of her hard-kicking legs. She hugged him like he was a testosterone-bloated stuffed animal, and he could do nothing but squirt, squirt, squirt his excitement into her ... pumping, pumping.

'I'll have the pound cake with the blackberry drizzle,' Normandie told the waiter.

'And I'll have the peach turnover with the raspberry downpour,' said Jacob.

'Sorry?' The waiter was the eighteen-year-old son of the innkeepers, and not used to fanciful dessert orders.

Normandie snatched Jacob's menu away and handed it to the young man. 'He never eats dessert.'

101

After she ate hers, they went for a walk through the little town, enjoying the mild sea breeze and the various indications that the streets, restaurants, and bars were full of people who were having a good time.

Normandie stepped in a puddle – one of those lingering pools of water whose existence doesn't seem justified by the weather conditions – and Jacob produced a clean, neatly folded sock from each pocket of his sport jacket.

'Since when do you carry socks?' said Normandie, who was grateful but puzzled.

'I put extra socks in this jacket on one particularly rainy day, and I've never had the heart to remove them.'

'Proactive sock-stocking? That's a very "spare light bulbs" way to behave, kiddo.' She steadied herself against him just long enough to replace her wet socks with his dry ones.

'I do have my moments,' he admitted. 'Am I blushing?'

'Becomingly. And you should produce socks more often. It looked strikingly lewd, the way you pulled them out of your pockets.'

'Thank you. I try.'

They went to bed early that night.

# Chapter Seventeen

THE WALL OF PERIODICALS at the downtown bookstore was a broad one, but Jacob could spot the cloying face of his star rocking horse a mile away. He stepped forward – with a mixture of pride and revulsion – to check it out, having learned that *Hip Hip Horizon* was lackadaisical about sending contributor copies. (He had only just received his official copy of the issue with Normandie on the cover; meanwhile, the one he'd brought home from the newsstand on release day was already grey and wrinkled, possibly with grandchildren.)

He had to acknowledge that Susan had somehow managed to find the least objectionable angle, and her cover photo did as much as any photo could to transubstantiate the screaming preciousness of the Victorian era's semi-anthropomorphised animals into something a person might almost be willing to look at over breakfast. Almost. Even with Susan's talent in – and on – the picture, Jacob resolved that he would personally never go near this particular issue of *HHH* before lunchtime.

'Now *that's* what I call a magazine cover.' The whiny voice came from behind his shoulder blades, and both its fussy intonation and the message it conveyed indicated a specific source. Reluctantly, Jacob turned to greet the LMARH curator, while marvelling at the ability of some people to make even expressions of enthusiasm sound peevish.

The man was, Jacob supposed, as close to beaming as he'd ever get – the result being a sort of self-congratulatory, simpering glower.

'Hello there,' Jacob said cordially. 'I imagine you're the happiest man in San Francisco today.'

'Yesterday,' the man corrected.

'I beg your pardon?'

'The magazine hit the newsstands at four yesterday. I would've thought you'd know that, since you work for them.'

'Freelance,' Jacob protested. He wondered if the curator had camped out all week, waiting for the magazine delivery truck to arrive.

'Anyway,' the curator said with a sigh, 'tonight's the big night. They're making me host a party at the museum, to coincide with this.'

'They?'

'Board of directors,' said the curator, in a tone in which one might say 'dickheads'.

'Ah, and you don't want to.'

'I hate having people in there. Still, no choice. Fundraising opportunity. At least running into you here has saved me a phone call. Can you be there at eight?'

'Can I ... what?'

'Well, of course we need you there.' This statement sounded strange, due to its being transmitted in a voice whose personality implied, 'I hate you.'

'But –'

'It's *your* article, after all.'

'Look – I'm afraid you'll have to manage without me,' said Jacob. As far as he was concerned, his contract with *Hip Hip Horizon* did not leave him with any further obligations to cavort with rocking horses, fundraising opportunity or no fundraising opportunity. 'Short notice!' And he bolted toward the front counter with his magazine, not even looking back to see if he was the designated recipient of another West Coast finger.

When he returned from a run later that day, he realised that the curator had gone one step further and had, in effect, arranged to give him a giant-sized East Coast finger by proxy. The message waiting on his phone was from Gary in New York, politely expressing the viewpoint that if Jacob ever wanted to write for *HHH* again, he had better drag his ass to the Living Museum of the American Rocking Horse for their little fête.

'Are you busy tonight?' He had lost no time in phoning Normandie at the lab, because he did not want to face this alone.

'Yes, I'm fucking you till we both scream.'

'I certainly hope so. But I mean before that.'

'Hang on a sec.' Normandie's voice jumped into the background. 'See you later, Kate.' Then her lips were in Jacob's ear again. 'Sorry – I'm back.'

'Kate was there when you were talking about fucking me till we both scream?'

'Sure. It was partly for her benefit that I said it. Don't forget, we're talking about a woman from whose dazzling body we've wrested several impressive orgasms.'

'Nicely put – and, don't worry, I hadn't forgotten. It just took me by surprise.'

'Yes, Kate will do that to you.'

'*Kate* will, eh? That notwithstanding … I called to tell you that I've been collared into attending a shindig at the rocking horse palace tonight. Or do I mean "buttonholed"?'

'Fun!'

'That's one opinion.'

'What time do we have to be there?'

'Darling, you use the best pronouns.' He breathed a sigh of partial relief.

It wasn't that Jacob hadn't done a good job of steeling himself with regard to revisiting the rocking horses. It was that somebody had contrived to put gowns and tuxedos on them, to commemorate the special event. This, in Jacob's eyes, was the immediate problem.

'Lighten up, sweetheart,' Normandie reasoned. 'Even a Victorian rocking horse likes to get gussied up once in a while. *Especially* a Victorian rocking horse, I imagine.'

'But some of them already *had* gowns carved right onto them. Talk about gilding the lily! Furthermore, most of the people here have never even seen what the creatures look like on an ordinary day, thanks to the policy of barring visitors from this fine museum. So what's the point of making such a fuss?'

'As far as I can see, you're the only one making a fuss,' Normandie teased. 'Oh, look – there's Susan.' She manoeuvred around the nearest rocking horse to make eye contact with their friend and wave to her.

Susan hustled over, kissed Normandie on the cheek, and poked Jacob in his firm tummy. 'Didn't think we'd see *you* here.'

'I'm glad you have such a high opinion of my good taste. Unfortunately, good taste is not always the last word.'

Susan turned to Normandie. 'Don't you just want to goose him when he talks like that?'

'Whoo!' said Jacob.

'I thought so,' said Susan. 'You beat me to it by about half a second.'

'Practice,' said Normandie.

'Carnegie Hall,' said Jacob. 'Sorry. Because of that old joke, I say "Carnegie Hall" whenever someone says "practice". Pavlov, you know.'

'Whoo!' said Normandie. 'Oh, dear. Now whenever anyone says "Carnegie Hall", I'll imagine your hand squeezing my butt and I'll shriek. Pavlov, you know.'

'Actually, it was my hand,' Susan confessed. She giggled. 'Whoo!'

'*That* was my hand,' said Jacob.

'I'm glad it wasn't Pavlov's,' said Susan. 'It's confusing enough as it is.'

'Mr Hastings!' The curator was calling to him.

'Crap – I need a drink,' Jacob blurted to his cohorts. 'I'll snag a bottle if I can.'

'He's going to get us drunk,' said Susan hopefully.

'I'm going to get *me* drunk,' Jacob quibbled. 'But both of you are welcome to come along for the ride,' he added graciously.

'He gives good rides,' Normandie volunteered to Susan.

A thundering whine – to wit, the voice of the curator – suddenly came over the PA.

'Ladies and gentlemen, welcome to this special fundraising party in support of the Living Museum of the American Rocking Horse. Please do not touch anything.'

For some reason – possibly politeness, possibly boredom, or possibly just because the speaker had paused – the audience applauded.

'Preserving these delicate creatures is a full-time job. It takes ample resources, and our endowment doesn't begin to scratch the surface.'

The audience, strangely, applauded here as well. Evidently, the speaker had already lost their attention, and they were applauding on autopilot.

'It is our hope that the publicity we've received in the latest issue of *Hop Hop Horizon* ...'

Jacob, who had just returned from the bar with an open bottle of white and three glasses, raised his hand as if to interrupt and correct. But Normandie pulled his arm down. 'Shh,' she advised.

'... and here to persuade you to give generously tonight in support of the museum is the author of that article, Jacob Hastings.'

'At least he didn't call *you* Hop Hop,' Normandie shouted into his ear over the perfunctory applause.

'Here,' Jacob said to her, passing the bottle. He began walking toward the dais with three wineglasses tingling musically in his left hand, but Susan grabbed his wrist and relieved him of these.

'Thank you,' he said when he'd claimed the microphone. 'It's a great problem – er, *privilege* being here on this momentous occasion. It's often troubled me that few people recognise the important contributions that the 19th-century rocking horse has made to our society. But I know their importance is no secret to the people here tonight, and for this I thank you.'

'You're welcome,' said the curator. Jacob gave him a

brief, lateral glance.

'It is my modest hope that by taking the antique rocking horse onto the coffee tables of the 35-to-60-year-old, upper-middle-class, urban professionals who constitute the key demographic of a publication like *Hip Hip Horizon,* that we can ... uh ... what was I saying?'

All eyes were on him. All but two pairs.

'Sorry. The point is that this museum, in order to flourish, requires two things: The first is national exposure, and the second is your ... kissing.'

He'd meant 'support', of course. But he'd been a little distracted.

By Normandie and Susan, who were not watching him.

Because they were locked in the sexiest kiss he'd ever seen.

Normandie's eyes were closed. He'd seen her do this when he himself kissed her, but that was not the ideal time to admire the effect – nor did it provide the ideal vantage point. This situation, by contrast, gave him an ideal vantage point ... and, in spite of everything, Jacob found it to be the ideal time.

Susan's lips pressed against Normandie's with what looked, to Jacob, like the softest pressure imaginable; and yet it was a definite pressure, an engineered melting of one set of lips onto another. Tonight, they were each wearing lipstick, and Jacob imagined that the hues were mixing like promiscuous paint.

When their lips pulled back, he saw that they both looked as surprised as he was by what they'd just done. They were beautiful.

'Kissing?' asked the curator. His eyes followed Jacob's into the crowd; but Normandie and Susan had now broken apart, and all the curator saw was an attentive audience.

'Uh ... yes,' improvised Jacob. 'In New York, when you make a donation to a worthy cause, we say you're giving a kiss. It's sort of like "show me some love".'

'Oh,' said the curator. He did not look convinced, but the audience, perhaps for lack of anything better to do, once again applauded. Jacob leapt upon this as an indication that his speech had concluded, and he headed back toward Susan and Normandie.

Normandie welcomed him with half a glass of wine, which Jacob gulped unceremoniously. He noticed that his hand was trembling.

'You were good,' said Susan.

'Really?' said Jacob. 'I was a little distracted, you know.'

'He has a touch of ADD,' Normandie explained.

'I do *not* have ADD,' Jacob protested. 'Not tonight, at least. Tonight I had an episode of YKBMM.'

'What's that?' asked Normandie.

'Your Kiss Blew My Mind.'

She took his hand.

'Now, why don't we just –' he began, but he was interrupted by the curator. The man had snuck up behind them. He looked as if he'd really wanted to tap Jacob on the shoulder, but had never learned how to do it.

'You're not leaving, are you?' he asked.

'Now why would I do that?' He could, off the top of his head, think of a thousand things he'd rather be doing than hanging around the LMARH – every one of which involved both Normandie and Susan.

'Good,' said the curator. 'People will be wanting to talk to you about your article.'

'Do you really think so?' Jacob was annoyed but slightly flattered.

'I don't care if they want to or not. I'm going to push it,' the curator admitted. 'Anything to keep them from touching the horsies.' He darted away to greet a potential big spender.

'Just tell them not to touch me, either,' Jacob called after him. 'Whoo!' he added, in response to Normandie's well-applied squeeze to his rear. 'Present company excluded, of course.'

Normandie refilled his wineglass. 'Here. Let's drink to the horsies.'

'No one told me I was going to have to *talk* to people,'

Jacob complained.

'Now, now, darling,' said Normandie. 'Drink your wine and relax.'

'At this rate, I'm going to be drinking more wine than I'm used to,' he warned.

'Maybe that's for the best, tonight.'

'Maybe it is,' he acknowledged.

Susan giggled.

The curator was steering the big spender their way. He successfully navigated her within conversing distance of Jacob, then darted efficiently away again.

'I'm Gladys Gilroy,' said the customer. She was an elegant – if daunting – middle-aged woman who wore her jewellery like clothing and her clothing like jewellery. 'I'm so fascinated by your rocking horses,' she informed Jacob in a monotone that suggested she was anything but. He wondered who had dragged her here tonight, and he reflected that affluent individuals with generous dispositions must have to put up with a lot of evenings of this type.

'Thank you,' he said, noncommittally. 'They're really not mine.'

'I know,' said Ms Gilroy with a thin smile. 'You just work here.'

'What a revolting thought,' Jacob said under his breath.

'Jacob's a little shy,' said Normandie smoothly.

'And he has ADD,' Susan said in Jacob's ear. He wanted to goose her again, but that could entail an explanation for Gladys Gilroy – who might possibly want to be goosed, too.

'Jacob came all the way here from New York because he was the only writer in the country who was qualified to do justice to these exquisite creations,' proclaimed Normandie. As she made this grand statement, she gestured around the room, sloshing only a small quantity of wine on Ms Gilroy. 'Oh, yes, a lot of talent and effort has gone into getting this museum, and its contents, the recognition it deserves.'

'I can see that,' Ms Gilroy grudgingly agreed.

'But, as you know, it takes more than talent to secure the

future of an artistic heritage.'

Normandie was amazing, thought Jacob. He wouldn't have been surprised at this point if she had fished Ms Gilroy's chequebook out of her clutch and offered to make out the cheque for her.

'I'm *sure* I can help you,' said Ms Gilroy. She looked relieved to have it over with. She nodded a goodnight to Jacob and moved toward the pledge kiosk, which was placed strategically near the refreshments.

'Uh-oh,' said Normandie, cocking her head in another direction. 'This one's not going to be so easy.'

She was indicating a white-haired, jolly-looking man who was ambling toward them. Apart from the fact that he generally gave the impression that he *had* recently been goosed, what Jacob noticed about the man was that he had an open copy of the dreaded magazine in hand – open, presumably, to Jacob's article.

'Now that's not fair,' Jacob hissed.

'Sorry, baby,' said Normandie, giving his arm a reassuring nudge. 'But I'm afraid he's all yours.'

'Tremendous, tremendous,' he heard the man gushing, almost before he was within earshot. Jacob wondered if he had been saying 'tremendous' all the way from the other end of the building.

'Thank you,' said Jacob.

'So much more I want to know.' It was as bad as Jacob had feared.

'Correction,' the man continued. 'So much more I *have* to know.'

It was worse than Jacob had feared.

'Tell me about *her*,' the man said lovingly, jabbing at one of Susan's photos with a stubby, over-enthusiastic finger.

'Cindy,' said Susan helpfully.

'Wait a sec,' said the man. He scoured his pockets for a pen. When he found one, he wrote carefully in the magazine: 'Cindy'.

'Yes,' Jacob sighed. 'She was named Cynthia Rosalind by

the Baltimore craftsman who created her in 1874. She was the last horse he carved, and, according to connoisseurs, she's the finest one known to have survived in good condition. There are still a lot of these things hidden away in attics, fortunately.'

'Excuse me?' said the jolly man.

'I said that *un*fortunately, many of them are still in people's attics.'

Susan giggled, and Normandie nudged her with a discreet elbow.

'And where, exactly, is Cindy?' said the jolly man, spinning himself around like a top to take in the whole room. 'I don't see her here.'

'She couldn't make it tonight,' Jacob said conclusively. 'But the pledge kiosk is right over there.'

'Oh yes,' said the jolly man. 'Tremendous, tremendous.'

'This is excellent wine,' said Jacob, after another generous gulp. 'Much better than the last glass I had.'

'It's from the same bottle, Jacob,' said Normandie.

'You're cute,' said Jacob.

'You're tipsy,' said Normandie.

'I don't care, you're still cute. I hope the two of you are going to kiss again.'

'Maybe later,' said Normandie, giving Susan a shy, conspiratorial look. 'I feel a little conspicuous, now that you're no longer holding the crowd rapt, all eyes up front.'

'You don't look conspicuous at all. You look ravishing.'

'That doesn't make any sense, but I'll accept the compliment.'

'Who says compliments have to make sense, anyway,' Jacob answered. 'You don't, Susan, do you?'

Susan, whose attention had been diverted by a passing tray of canapés, was confused. 'I don't what?'

'Say compliments have to make sense.'

'I don't remember saying it. Why, was I quoted somewhere as saying that? I could say it if someone really needed me to. But I really don't like speaking in front of crowds.'

Jacob polished off the wine in his glass, then refilled it. 'That's OK – I'll do it.' He meandered back to the dais and helped himself to the microphone.

'Ladies and rocking horses,' he began. 'I've been asked to say a few words. Unfortunately, I don't have a few words, because I used them all up writing an article about this museum.' He hesitated, and the inevitable applause kicked in.

'As my worthy opponent has testified, the horsies need to be polished. And his endowment doesn't begin to scratch the surface … of the varnish. That's a little joke.'

Again came applause, this time as a convenient substitute for laughter.

'This notwithstanding,' he continued, 'you're beautiful. Not the horsies – *you*. More beautiful than you know. More beautiful than I know. And you can tell that's a compliment, because it doesn't make any sense.' More applause.

'Well, I just had to get that off my chest. Don't forget to tip your rocking horses on the way out.'

'This is an unusual man,' Susan said to Normandie when Jacob rejoined them.

'Yes. Let's take him home to bed, shall we?'

'I was hoping you'd say that,' said Susan.

'So was I,' slurred Jacob.

# Chapter Eighteen

THE THREE OF THEM clattered into the apartment in a collage of chuckles and deep breaths.

'I hope Jacob's not too tipsy to be any good in the bedroom,' said Susan.

'Jacob is sobering up nicely, thank you very much,' said the man himself. The fresh air had done a great deal to clear his head of what had not, after all, been such a large quantity of alcohol. True, it had been considerably more than he was accustomed to these days – and consumed with impressive haste – but the effect on him was proving to be quite transient.

'Actually,' said Normandie, 'I could use some more to drink myself. I was too busy watching the floor show to have much at the museum.'

'Girlfriend,' said Jacob as they all moved toward the kitchen, 'as far as I'm concerned, you *were* the floor show.' He felt the beginnings of an erection tingle as he cast his mind back to the Susan-Normandie kiss. And perhaps it was a lingering effect of the wine that he'd used the incongruous word *girlfriend* to address his girlfriend.

Susan was frowning. When she spoke, her voice seemed to recapture some of its former wispy diffidence, which no longer usually characterised it in the presence of Jacob and Normandie. 'This isn't an erotic photo session, now. This isn't a kiss at a party. This is real. This is your home, not my set. Do you really want me here?' She almost stammered the question.

Jacob saw Normandie's face light up with kindness. She put down the wine bottle she'd been about to open. 'Let's show her,' she said.

She squared herself up to Susan, flashed a smile at her,

then pulled the other woman into a very physical kiss.

'Oh,' said Susan, looking happy.

'Your turn,' Normandie said to Jacob.

He mimicked Normandie's tactics. The approach, the smile, and the kiss that engaged the whole body. Though Susan was almost as tall as he was, she clung to him like a monkey climbing a tree, and it was impossible for Jacob to keep his erection from throbbing against her long, cool belly, which moved invitingly beneath a lightweight cocktail dress. She tasted sharp to Jacob, pleasantly acidic like lemonade.

When the moment ended, Susan looked back and forth at the two of them. 'Yeah?' she said hopefully.

'Yeah,' said Jacob and Normandie in unison.

'What about your wine?' Susan gestured toward the kitchen table.

'I think we'll get to that a little later,' said Normandie.

Jacob thought that Susan looked a tad unreal, sprawled expectantly on their bed, still fully clothed. She was of slight build, certainly; but it was her personality that made her seem especially ethereal. Even when passionate and determined, she moved like a deer.

She squeezed a hand between her legs. 'I'm in your bed.'

'Technically,' said Normandie, 'you're *on* our bed, at the moment, the bed being still made up. But this won't be the first time this bedspread has been stained.' Normandie's ass hit the bed with a solid bounce, and she leaned forward and tickled Susan. Jacob couldn't see exactly where the tickling was directed, but Susan's thin squeal of delight told him it was someplace good.

'I've wanted to tickle you since I saw you behind that camera, poised like a horny little flower,' said Normandie.

'More,' said Susan.

Normandie's little black dress rode up her ass as she leaned in for the second instalment. She was on her knees between Susan's legs, and already Jacob could see the moist patch beginning to appear across the epicentre of her lilac panties.

115

The tickling was vigorous but brief, just enough to make Susan kick her legs and clasp Normandie's waist, in a touching expression of sexual hunger. Normandie began to kiss Susan's throat, on one side and then the other, wiggling her ass in a way that made Jacob moan. Standing there with his pulse in his dick, he thought about how good Normandie was with a woman, and how very, very lucky he was that she had chosen to be with a man – to be with him.

She came up for air and called to him. 'Darling, I'm positively dripping.' She reached inside Susan's skirt. 'Mmm, so are you, dear. Help me out, Jacob.'

He tossed his jacket and tie on a chair, unzipped and climbed out of his trousers, and decided the rest of his clothes would have to take their chances. Almost without the assistance of his hand, his cock emerged from the slit in his boxers, pointing intelligently toward the hub of panty-moistening activity on the bed.

'Maybe Jacob could tickle my feet a little,' Susan suggested politely, while rocking her head from side to side to accommodate Normandie's kisses to her neck, chest, and shoulders.

'Yes, maybe I could,' he said hoarsely. He titillated between Susan's toes while using his other hand to slide Normandie's panties down. He licked fresh juice from Normandie's slit, steadying himself against her kinetic ass. When Susan had had enough toe tickling, she retracted her foot, leaving Jacob both his hands free to attend to Normandie's pussy.

Now he could really get to work. With Normandie occupied in groping, squeezing, and generally devouring Susan, Jacob could do justice to the tender cunt at his fingertips.

He stroked the outsides of the outside lips.

He stroked the insides of the outside lips, and he watched the lips spread further for his fat fingers.

He delicately, so delicately, let his fat fingers tease and caress the inner lips … dipping in, sliding wetly out, dragging trails of her wetness across her buttocks and thighs. Hearing her voice answer him in the beautiful language of feminine moans. Then, touching her with his tongue, right where it mattered the most.

Normandie's cries became ascendant, superseding the other woman's carpet of giggles and coos to attain sonic pre-eminence in the room. Jacob accelerated his routine … faster laps with his tongue, faster strokes and dips with his fingers, faster friction from his palm against her delicious bottom and her bucking mound. A cameo appearance of his pinkie in her smart little anus … then tongue to clit like ice cream, till Normandie shrieked in staccato ecstasies.

Beyond and beneath Normandie, Susan's legs were active like a swimmer's, and Jacob knew she needed to be touched – touched, that is, below the waist. He was about to reach under Normandie and find Susan's crotch … but Normandie was too quick for him. Back on earth and resuming her nibbling kisses all around Susan's face, she grabbed Susan under her skirt and soon had her dancing with sensation. Susan, like Normandie, was still dressed, and Jacob was fascinated by how she looked more naked, writhing in her floral cocktail dress, than many women looked when they were actually naked. She was entirely wedded to the experience of being handled by Normandie; and, even with tight panties between the flesh of Normandie's hand and the heat of her own cunt, every nuance of her posture, every feature of her face was that of a woman being gloriously fucked.

'You're so wet,' Normandie informed her.

'Mmm,' drooled Susan. 'Maybe your boyfriend would like to smell my panties.'

'But I'm still using them,' Normandie said. 'Doesn't it feel nice to be stroked through panties, by someone you like?'

'Mmm,' said Susan. 'Oh! Right there, yeah.'

'How would you like to come in those panties, sweetie?'

'Ahh …' said Susan.

'I can make it happen.'

Susan was practically crying with pleasure now. She held

117

Normandie's head, compulsively petting her hair, while Normandie slowly but surely carried her up a spiral staircase of arousal … until quiet Susan exploded with crazy joy.

Jacob had no idea where the fuck Normandie had learned to deliver an earthmoving female orgasm across a pair of panties, but he knew he'd never forget what he had just witnessed.

'Oh God,' said Susan, 'oh God. Will somebody please peel these panties off me now? Would do it myself,' she explained telegraphically, 'but … too busy … writhing.'

'I'll take care of that,' said Jacob, eager not to miss his chance.

Susan's aroma tickled his nose – and by extension his cock – as he slid the damp knickers down her slender legs. He enjoyed his first view of her pleasure-saturated snatch, a neat landscape of womanhood that lay lazily between pale thighs and below a trimmed patch of pretty red-brown hair.

Normandie was virtually on top of him, and she breathed in his ear while he brought the panties up to his face and inhaled. The impact of Susan's fragrance and Normandie's hot breath made Jacob forget that he was practically sober now.

'Suppose Jacob were to fuck you, pretty girl.' Normandie grasped Jacob's hard-on as she made this offer on his behalf. 'While I watched and drank Merlot,' she added, lending picturesque detail to the scenario.

'Well,' said Susan, 'if you're sure it's Merlot.'

Normandie sat comfortably on a chair, cradling the bottle between her thighs. Her dress by now had given up the game of modesty and hung listlessly around her bare pussy. She sipped sensually at the wine and trained her eyes on Susan and Jacob.

Susan took Jacob's face and began kissing him wetly and repeatedly on his mouth, his cheeks, even his nose. With Susan still in her floral dress, he felt like he was on a picnic. And when Susan swatted the rear of his boxers and laughed, he felt like he was at an amusement park.

'Give it to me?' She made it a question.

He gave it to her. With one hand on her right shoulder and another on her left hip, where her dress, like Normandie's, was lewdly riding up, he slid into a cunt that was so ready for him he almost slipped right out again.

Susan's sigh sounded like the splash of a jumping fish in the clear, cold water of a mountain stream.

Her little breasts were still packed snugly into the dress, but Jacob wanted them. And, since Susan was braless and the fabric was thin, he was able to squeeze and mould them while he fucked her. She clutched at his back, bolstering his efforts both on her and in her. Her nipples scraped against the dress, and the dedicated thrusts of his cock worked her like a pump, making her wetness stew and seep around him.

He glanced at Normandie, who was composed but intent. 'Fuck her, Jacob,' she said helpfully, in a stage whisper.

'I'm on it,' he assured her.

'Hahaha,' Susan added. She looked to Jacob like an ecstatic mess, like arousal and pleasure had stirred her into the human equivalent of a sloppy joe.

'Hahahahaha,' Susan continued, and Jacob realised that her laughter was an orgasm, and that he and Normandie had led her to this by posing and goosing and kissing and tickling and stroking and, at last, at last, fucking her into another world.

They were both so moved by Susan's display of fulfilment that they slipped into a reverent silence. The only sounds in the room were Jacob's heavy breathing; more wine being poured into Normandie's glass; and the lingering laughter that rippled through Susan as she came down from heaven.

'Wine, please,' she finally said.

Normandie gallantly passed her the full goblet, then left the room to get herself another glass – and another bottle.

They all sat on the floor, between the bed and the chair, like teenagers 'hanging out'. Normandie remained quiet as she enjoyed her wine, but her face glowed and her hands played in Jacob's lap. The second bottle had been opened, and, with Jacob done wining for the night, Susan and Normandie claimed it.

The more wine Susan had, the more inclined she was to talk. She spoke quickly, pausing only to gulp Merlot.

'I love couples,' she said. 'Couples know how to fuck. You guys have been practising on each other – don't deny it, now – and then I come along and, well, I come along, all right. I'd sleep with couples all the time, if I could. Some of them don't want me to, but at least I can take their pictures.'

She poured more wine for herself, refilling Normandie's glass as well.

'One or three,' she continued. 'If I can't go to bed with a couple, then I'd just as soon do it solo. I'm good at it, you know.'

'Yes,' said Jacob. 'We've seen you.'

Susan waved her hand dismissively. 'What, at the studio? I was just getting warmed up. You should have seen what I did for myself after you left. Tried some new positions that made me feel like both halves of a Kama Sutra pic. Thought my fingers would never want to leave my hole that night. Sore for days afterward. No complaints.'

She emptied the bottle into her glass, then sniffed the air. 'Mmm, that's me, isn't it? I smell nice. Unless …' she reached over and touched Normandie's cunt, as if this were as natural to her as picking a piece of lint off a friend's sweater. 'Different,' she said, bringing her fingers to her nose. 'Equally nice, my friends, but different.' She thrust her fingers toward Jacob's nose. 'See what I mean?' She set her wine glass down and, with the hand that had been holding it, groped herself. Then she swapped this hand for the one at Jacob's face. 'Different – see? Hey, where's my wine?'

Normandie handed Susan the glass she'd set down, mouthing '*She's drunk*' to Jacob.

'*No shit*,' Jacob mouthed back.

Normandie dissolved into giggles. '*Me, too*,' she mouthed.

'You're laughing,' Susan said, 'but you guys are awesome. I could piss my pants from how awesome you are.'

'You're not wearing pants,' said Jacob.

'I bet I know your whole life story. Both of you. Two life stories. Count 'em. You –' she touched Normandie's knee – 'grew up in a small town and talked all the time. Like I'm doing now. Am I right?' She didn't wait for an answer. 'Small town girl. Big mouth. Big brain. Big, big orgasms, later on … but I'm getting ahead of myself. This guy –' she jerked a thumb toward Jacob – 'spent his whole life on a boat, rocking, rocking. One day – he's about twenty-five, let's say – he gets off the boat … maybe he wants a burrito … and he sees this big-mouth-big-brain-big-orgasm chick. So he forgets all about the burrito, and all he can think about are orgasms. Day and night. Orgasms, orgasms, orgasms. Orgasms for breakfast, orgasms for lunch, orgasms for dinner with extra orgasm sauce and more orgasms for dessert. And the rest –' she looked back and forth at the couple, with eyes almost as full of meaning as they were full of alcohol – 'is history.'

Jacob applauded. 'Don't look now, Dee, but I think we should buy the film rights to that story.'

He thought it was a clever remark … but his lover, he soon realised, had drifted off into a drunken sleep.

He looked back at Susan to find that she had now closed her eyes, too. Her toes touched Normandie's, cutely, on the bedroom carpet.

# Chapter Nineteen

JACOB PRIDED HIMSELF ON making good, strong coffee, and on mornings like this, it was especially appreciated. Doubly appreciated, on this occasion, because the kitchen held, not one, but two sex-satiated women, fresh from their showers in adorable terry cloth robes – and, through the miracle of large quantities of water consumed before they'd relocated from the floor to the bed, each sporting a hangover-free disposition that made the coffee a robust delight rather than a remedial potion.

After breakfast, Normandie and Susan chose to lounge in terry cloth for a while; and it came as no surprise when Jacob, having reached an impasse with his crossword puzzle, leaned over to Normandie's side of the love seat and nibbled briefly on her thigh. When he returned to the puzzle, he saw that Susan, sitting across the coffee table from them, was shifting in her seat, and he got a glimpse of borrowed blue panties.

'Susan,' said Jacob. 'As long as you happen to be lounging here in our apartment, wearing a fetching terry cloth robe and a nice little pair of blue panties, chilling out after a night of Merlot and – and so forth … Normandie and I have a proposition for you.'

'I'm tired,' Susan laughed.

'This is something you can do by yourself, at home,' said Normandie.

'Did I talk about that last night? I seem to have a vague memory of it.'

'You did talk about that,' said Normandie, 'but this isn't that. This is a photography commission – and not even an erotic one.'

'You're not going to ask me to do pet portraits, are you?'

'In a way,' said Normandie, 'I guess I am. You see, *my* pet

– my hobbyhorse, if you will – is a galaxy shaped like a rocking horse.'

'How nice,' said Susan. 'What do you feed it?'

'I feed it hot air.'

'What?' Susan looked into her mug, as though the coffee might elucidate.

'Susan, I've invented a galaxy.'

'Discovered it, you mean.'

'No, *invented* it. If I'd discovered it, we would already have a picture of it. However, since I've only invented it –'

'Don't say "only", darling,' said Jacob, 'as if there were nothing to it. I bet you've gone to more trouble in fabricating the Rocking Horse Galaxy than some astronomers go to in discovering real ones.'

'I get it!' Susan almost shouted her epiphany. 'You need a picture of the Rocking Horse Galaxy, which doesn't exist, and therefore you need me.'

'Exactly,' said Normandie.

'Hohoho,' said Susan. 'I hope you weren't thinking of paying me.'

Normandie explained to Susan what photos of galaxies generally looked like, and showed her a few samples online.

'I like the purplish ones,' said Susan.

'Go wild,' said Normandie. 'Just make sure it looks like a rocking horse.' Normandie gave her an encouraging pat on her terry cloth behind.

'Promise to do that again when I bring you the image?' asked Susan.

'Are you sure you don't want us to pay you?' said Jacob.

'No. Little swats to my behind will suffice, thank you.'

'This could displace the dollar, if it catches on,' Jacob remarked to Normandie.

'Invest now,' said Normandie.

He decided to take her advice. Normandie dashed playfully away as he rushed toward her, but she soon let him catch up. As Susan looked on, Jacob carried Normandie to the couch, where he set her down, rump upward, lifted the hem of her robe, and gently but enthusiastically slapped her naked bottom till they were both laughing too hard to continue.

Eventually they all got dressed, and Susan thanked them for their hospitality, not to mention (as she put it) all the great fucking.

Normandie and Jacob had agreed that they'd spend some time prepping for the *Gimme Some Science!* appearance. Specifically, both of them were of the opinion that 'Professor Jacobs' needed a crash course in astronomy patter if he was to make a better showing than on the previous occasion.

'I've been studying the interview you gave me for your magazine article,' he now told her. 'At this point, I've practically got it memorised.'

'Excellent,' said the expert. 'Why don't we try a dummy television interview.'

'Under the circumstances, I'd prefer we find another term.'

'OK. Let's try a *simulated* interview. I'll pretend to be Priscilla Ray. Do you think you can imagine for a little while that I'm a super-intelligent, super-sexy, super-beautiful woman?'

'*Imagine* it? No. *Observe* it, yes.'

'I like the way this interview is going already.'

'Good,' said Jacob. 'I'm on a roll. Keep 'em coming.'

'Professor Jacobs,' began Normandie in a television-host sort of intonation, 'what part of space has your group been focussing its attention on?'

'Our attention doesn't get focussed. That's only the telescopes,' quipped Jacob. 'Say, shouldn't you have a laugh track or something rigged up to simulate uproarious laughter?'

'Consider it uproared. Please proceed.'

'Er, we've been looking at an area of space that is roughly over *there*.' He pointed toward the hall closet. 'Depending where we are in the Earth's daily rotation and annual revolution, of course. Anyway, I think that's about where I last saw it.'

'Jacob ...' said Normandie, without the television-host voice.

'Am I being too technical?'

'Why don't you try using the stuff I gave you for the magazine. You know, the stuff you supposedly have memorised?'

'Oh. Right.' He cleared his throat. 'What we're finding is that galaxies in this area have a compositional make-up that is unusual, given their presumed age. We're at a point in the science at which we have a good idea what to expect from a certain type of galaxy in a certain place; and yet here's a corner of the universe that seems to have its heart set on surprising us at every turn.'

'Perfect,' said Normandie.

'It should be. You said it on pages 22-23 of *Hip Hip Horizon* – though I took out the page break, of course. I especially like the "seems to have its heart set on" bit. Great human interest stuff.'

'Thank you. Just stick to that kind of thing, and you'll do fine.'

'What if she asks me a question that wasn't covered in our article?'

'Then you improvise.'

'I think I'd better rehearse my improvising. Ask me something surprising.'

'What colour underwear are you wearing?'

'Rocking-horse red. But seriously ...'

'All right, all right. What would you say has been the most important discovery in the field of astrophysics in our lifetime?'

'Um ... Stephen Hawking?'

'Not who,' Normandie whispered, '*what.*'

'Damn,' said Jacob. 'If I can't fall back on famous names and faces, then I ...' He stopped short.

'What's wrong?'

'I just thought of something: famous names and faces.'

'I thought you were in favour of them.'

125

'Not when they're me.'

'What?'

'Look – when I played "Professor Jacobs" on the local show, we figured the chances of my being recognised were slim, or at least small-shouldered with no ass to speak of. Even so, you've seen what a problem it's caused with Hubert Renkins. But now, we're talking about national, supermodel-hosted TV. I know I'm just a relatively obscure – if handsome and charming – writer. But, believe it or not, there actually are quite a few people in New York who have the pleasure of knowing what I look like. Not to mention people from back home, people I went to college with, diner waitresses who fell for me on road trips and will never forget my face …'

'OK, I get the idea,' said Normandie. 'Though I'd like to hear more about the diner waitresses sometime.'

'Sure, hon.'

'I was forgetting that you're not just my private treasure.'

'Never fear – my family jewels are all yours,' he said generously. 'Except when we share them with some of our special friends, of course.'

'Family jewels!' said Normandie, brightening.

'At your service,' said Jacob, reaching for his zipper.

'No – I'm thinking not so much of the jewels, at the moment, as the family. Professor Jacobs' family.'

'Huh? But we just made him up.'

'Exactly. So we can make up his brother, too.'

'What?'

'I told the producers that Professor Jacobs would appear with me. Little do they know that Professor Ernie Jacobs' research team at Mountain College also includes his brother, Professor … um … *Sinclair* Jacobs.'

'*Sinclair?*'

'The fact that Sinclair arrives to do the show with me, instead of Ernie, reflects a minor misunderstanding. Or something. I explain that the two brothers are virtually interchangeable, as far as their work is concerned, and, *voilà,* the tape rolls without you.'

126

'I would question the ease with which you can expect to jerk around a network television programme ... but I'm too happy to be relieved of my role to rock the boat.'

'We just need to find somebody to be Sinclair.'

'Yes, a co-conspirator. We're accumulating quite a few, aren't we?'

'You mean Kate and Susan. True.'

'Could Sinclair be a girl?'

'It's a little late for that, Ernie. You should have worked on your parents before the pregnancy.'

'Seriously ... it sounds like it would make a good androgynous name these days. Why can't Susan be Sinclair?'

'Aside from the fact that she's practically paralysed by shyness when she's in public, you mean?'

'Right,' said Jacob. 'I keep forgetting that – probably due to the contrast she provides when she's alone with us.'

'And since Kate is far too prominent, we're left with no choice but to recruit another crony.'

'At least we still have a few weeks. Maybe a crony will drop from the heavens.'

'I'll check the extended weather forecast,' said Normandie.

# Chapter Twenty

THE DAY KATE CALLED and asked them to meet her at her office was a particularly lovely one. Even the students looked especially lovely as Jacob and Normandie walked across the campus green. Jacob especially noticed the couples – for example, the Pre-Raphaelitish redhead who studied a textbook while her beatniky boyfriend sat beside her on their blanket, caressing her legs under her peasant skirt. Jacob found himself hoping that the woman was free of panties. It was no direct concern of his, of course; but Jacob was the type who was frequently thinking of others. He went so far as to hope that the boyfriend could smell his woman's cunt in the summer air.

This thought had a predictable effect on Jacob, and he soon found himself trading in his clasp of Normandie's hand for a guiding palm on the back pocket of her jeans.

'I wonder what's up,' said Normandie.

'My hand is on your ass.'

'No, I mean I wonder what's up with Kate. It's a busy time of year for her, so this can't be a spur-of-the-mo social invitation. Or even a mere sexual one.'

'I challenge your use of "mere". And maybe she's *really* horny. It's been a long time since we had our hands all over her.'

'Remember, we're not the only ones on her dance card. Kate gets around. I'm not saying she won't welcome the opportunity to party naked with us again someday … but any fear that she hasn't been getting any is, I'm sure, unfounded.'

'Gotcha.'

'No, this must mean some urgent piece of business.'

'I guess we'll soon know what it is.' They had arrived at

the relevant building. Normandie opened the stair door, and they clomped their way to the fourth floor.

Kate's office seemed even smaller than Jacob remembered.

'Hey, sexy,' said Kate, without looking up from her desk.

'Hi,' said Normandie and Jacob, in unison.

Kate now looked up and gave them an approving smile. 'Sit down ... uh ...' she looked around '... on the edge of the desk.' She cleared about two inches of space at each of the far corners of her desk, allowing a modicum of perching room for her guests' firm, respective asses. Jacob and Normandie did their best to swivel their upper bodies so as to maintain eye contact with Kate, and with each other.

'I need to talk to you about my conscience,' said Kate. 'And, please, no witty, speculative remarks regarding the existence or non-existence of said conscience.'

'I didn't say a thing,' said Normandie, smirking.

'Said conscience,' Kate continued, 'has been troubling me over the little matter of present company conspiring to fabricate galaxies on national television.'

'Said conscience didn't mind us doing it on *local* TV?' asked Jacob.

'Said conscience is a little slow to kick in sometimes,' Kate confessed. 'Rhone Preston is water under the bridge –'

'Yes,' said Normandie, 'that's how the critics sometimes describe his screen presence.'

'... but I'd really prefer it if we could find an alternative to lying about rocking horse galaxies on *Gimme Some Science!*'

'Your conscience is a good egg,' said Jacob. 'But what alternative do we have?'

'To begin with, there's always the alternative of backing out of the appearance, and trying to let this die a quiet death.'

'I see,' said Jacob. 'And if anyone asked us about the galaxy we'd supposedly found, we could just claim that we'd lost it again. Easy come, easy go.'

'Something like that,' said Kate.

'That's going to look just wonderful on my CV,' said

Normandie sulkily.

'We might even – to quote my conscience at one of its more fanatical moments – elect to admit to the university, and possibly even the public, that we're a bunch of fakes.'

'Not that that doesn't sound like tonnes of fun,' said Normandie, 'but did you and your conscience discuss any alternatives that wouldn't involve throwing my entire career down the toilet?'

'As a matter of fact,' said Kate, brightening, 'we did. Here's my thought: Just because you made up a galaxy shaped like a rocking horse doesn't mean there *isn't* a galaxy shaped like a rocking horse, out there somewhere in the visible universe. One that's shaped at least a little bit like a rocking horse, I mean.'

'And?' said Jacob.

'And so … Normandie, as your department chair, I'm directing you to get your rear –'

'Her *luscious* rear.'

'Yes, thank you, Jacob … I'm directing you, Normandie, to get your *luscious* rear over to our great big telescope and start looking for one.'

'Start *looking for one*?' Normandie looked startled at first, then impressed with Kate's ingenuity. 'You mean actually try to find a rocking horse galaxy?'

'I've arranged for you to have exclusive access to the observatory for a week. I figure that's long enough for a gifted astronomer who's searching specifically for any galaxy that looks like a rocking horse – even just a little bit like a rocking horse – to find one. Besides, it's all the time we have. If I'd blacked out the observatory schedule for you for any longer, Hubie Renkins would have had a temper tantrum on my office floor … and, as you can see, I don't have room in here for that.'

'Renkins,' Jacob said, with an evident lack of enthusiasm for the man's existence.

'I have to tell you,' said Kate, 'if it weren't for him, my conscience might still be napping. He's really been pestering the provost, you know. The more I heard about Renkins' uninvited appearances at Tommy's office, the more I began to question whether we were behaving in a perfectly upright and academically exemplary manner.'

'I commend you on your integrity,' said Normandie.

'OK, OK. So we're all corrupt and dishonest. Now let's move on to something more interesting. Can I check and see if your breasts feel as good as they look today?'

Normandie shrugged, with mock indifference. 'I had a feeling it would eventually turn into *that* kind of meeting.'

Jacob knew that Normandie was braless today, but only now did he see her nipples poking against the fabric of her scarlet blouse.

Kate cocked her head toward the door. 'Would you lock it, boyfriend?' He hopped off the desk to do so. 'Just make sure you stay on the inside. I may need your help groping this TV star.'

Kate climbed onto the desk, navigating among folders, index cards, pens, a calculator, a plastic tray of sticky notes, and other items of bureaucratic or academic significance. By steering herself carefully toward Normandie's corner, she managed to avoid kicking her keyboard and monitor onto the floor.

Normandie unbuttoned the top two buttons of her blouse, giving Kate a nice view of her cleavage.

'Lovely,' said Kate, giving each globe a soft squeeze. Then she ran a finger along the crack that separated them, beginning at the base of Normandie's throat and finishing deep within the blouse.

Normandie smiled, untucked her blouse from her jeans, and unbuttoned the remaining buttons from the bottom up.

'Oh, you're delicious,' said Jacob. He felt strangely private and intimate with Normandie, admiring her smooth torso in front of Kate, amid all the unglamorous inconvenience of a tiny, cluttered office. As he watched Kate lean closer to Normandie, squeeze both her breasts at once, and lick sensuously along her neck, he felt as if he were being given

131

the gift of a special show.

Normandie touched the front of her jeans and flickered her eyes at Jacob. He came out of his voyeuristic trance and – rather than contending with the desk – knelt on the floor, reaching up to unsnap her. He took his time moving from snap to snap, enjoying the pace of her breathing, the cool texture of pink satin that revealed itself behind the snaps ... and the warm sensitivity that lurked just within the satin.

She had kicked her sandals off, and he let his fingers fuck her teasingly between her toes while his other hand progressed slowly but surely into her jeans.

When all the snaps had been unsnapped, he traced the border between satin and flesh and slipped a dexterous finger inside the panties. He felt her squirming for him. He felt her heat and, extending his finger a little further, her wetness. When he finally slipped the finger inside her, she sighed heavily; and when he looked up at her face, he saw that it was rocking from side to side in a languorous ecstasy, as if she were already in the grip of an orgasm – one that was developing at a geologic pace.

Kate was tweaking and sucking Normandie's nipples and, as time permitted, tickling under her arms with her tongue. Despite earlier claims that she wouldn't, Normandie appeared to have left the planet's orbit as she rode all the sensations, as the events playing out cosily inside her pussy and wetly upon her nipples and intimately under her arms lifted her increasingly higher on a carpet of pleasure.

Suddenly, the pace accelerated. The foot in Jacob's palm could not hold still, and a self-interested hand grabbed his wrist to ensure that the finger in the relevant snatch moved *exactly* like that, and touched the local flesh *precisely* there. He saw that Normandie's other hand was on Kate's neck, and that Normandie's breasts were flushed from the attention they were receiving – pink and round and happy, with nipples that looked practically orgasmic in and of themselves.

Her climax expressed itself through gyrations and moans and juicy, sticky seepings around his finger and into her

132

panties, a classic *come in your jeans, my dear* moment. Kate tickled her one last time under her arm; Normandie shrieked and bathed Jacob's finger with another serving of feminine joy.

'Look at her coming for us,' said Kate, beaming. 'You must be so proud.'

'In more ways than one,' said Jacob, glancing down at an impressive ridge in his trousers.

'I'm a busy woman,' Kate continued, 'but I've never regretted making room in my schedule for a pair of sensational breasts. Holy fuck, look how alive they are, how buoyant.'

Kate was right. Normandie was breathing hard, and her beautiful, nude chest moved like the ocean.

'And now,' said Kate, 'we all have work to do.'

'Just a second,' said Jacob. 'I don't think I'm going anywhere, with this iron bar in my trousers.'

'OK,' said Kate, 'I'm itching for it, too, and you've talked me into it.' She turned politely to Normandie. 'You don't mind if I sit on your boyfriend's pole for a minute or two, do you?'

Normandie shook her head.

'*You* don't mind, I trust?' Kate said to Jacob.

She hopped nimbly off the desk – again Jacob was reminded that the department chair spent a lot of time at the gym – and reached into her herringbone miniskirt to retrieve a fine pair of black panties, which she laid on top of her computer keyboard. Then she pushed Jacob gently onto the floor.

'Oh,' said Kate, pulling a thick textbook out from under the desk and blowing the dust off it. 'For your head.' She handed it to him, and he got situated on his collegiate pillow.

'Now then,' said Kate. She unzipped Jacob, helped herself to his cock as if she were pulling a flashlight out of the middle drawer under the stove, and positioned him for her descent. Then she lowered herself, taking him in thoroughly and efficiently. She wriggled on him for a moment, and when she looked Jacob in the eye, he knew that satisfaction was on the way for both of them.

She held on to his sides and slid up and down him with finesse. Jacob looked up and around to see Normandie watching, fascinated, as Kate brought matters to where they needed to be.

'This is just a quick workaday fuck, OK?' said Kate, speaking in a laboured voice.

'Uh-huh,' Jacob grunted.

'Oh, fuck …' Kate growled, and Jacob felt her lingering on an up stroke, then sliding, with a wallowing luxury, into the slowest yet down stroke, her inner muscles constricting rhythmically against his sensitive tool all the while. The pace and sensations were impossible for him to absorb without losing his control. The charisma of her pussy's orgasmic gymnastics pulled his own bubbling release out of him like a rabbit from a magician's hat.

As the two of them wailed together and their pelvises danced a lewd perpendicular dance on the floor, Normandie applauded.

# Chapter Twenty-one

'SO,' SAID JACOB AS they ramped onto the freeway with the sun low in the sky. 'Thus begins the first instalment in our week-long galactic goose chase.'

'And remember, whatever it lacks in excitement, it promises to make up in tedium,' said Normandie. 'But I prefer to think of it as a scavenger hunt, rather than a goose chase. A goose chase implies futility.'

'Sorry,' said Jacob. 'The implication of futility was unintentional.'

'Also,' said Normandie, when the sun had taken another definitive dip, 'we won't necessarily have to spend a whole week on this. A rocking-horsish galaxy is just as likely to reveal itself to me on the first night as the seventh.'

'If I were a galaxy, I'd reveal myself to you as soon as galactically possible.'

'You're better than a galaxy.'

'Thank you. I'm also more conveniently located.'

Normandie squeezed his knee, as if to confirm this, while keeping her eyes on the road.

'Say,' said Jacob, 'are you going to call Susan and cancel our order for "one nicely shaped galaxy, hold the authenticity"?'

'Your brief stint as a short-order cook is showing. And, no, I wouldn't have the heart. She was so excited about the whole thing.'

'But what will you do with the image?'

'I'll probably re-gift it to my Aunt Stacie. That's usually what I do with things of that type.'

They were nearing their exit when Normandie squeezed Jacob's knee again.

'If you're groping for the stick shift,' said Jacob, 'it's slightly to the left. If you're looking for something else, it's slightly to the right. And while we're on the subject – have I mentioned that the first thing I want to do when we get inside is peel your little panties down and get my hands on your sweet behind?'

She laughed. 'That sounds approximately lovely. But I have to tell you, I really need to pee. So the first thing I plan to do when we get inside is peel my little panties, as you poetically call them, down, and get my sweet behind, as you term it, onto the official Hauser University Observatory toilet seat for thirty seconds.'

'Fair enough,' said Jacob. 'I shall stand outside the official Hauser University Observatory lavatory door and scoop you up promptly as you exit. I shall then do various delicious things to your official Hauser University astronomer's ass and, in the due course of time, plunge my unofficial faculty hanger-on meat into your –'

She cut him off. 'Oh, Jacob. Yes and yes … but you'd better shut up before I wet myself.'

She'd been scouring space for about two hours. Each time she saw something remotely promising, she would give Jacob a glance through the lens; but he could tell by the half-heartedly optimistic manner in which she offered these views that she held no serious hopes for them.

Early in the proceedings, they'd decided to keep themselves amused by discussing what each of the not-rocking-horsish-enough bodies more convincingly resembled. It was just the old inkblot game; but at least, unlike the games Jacob and Normandie usually played, it kept them focussed on the task at hand.

'I think that's more like a yak than a rocking horse,' Jacob now said about one such object. 'And I certainly don't see any runners.'

'You're right,' she agreed.

'Could we offer them a yak?'

'I don't think I can change animals at this point, without my credibility suffering.' She took another look. 'Besides, I think even a yak is stretching it. It's really sort of like a misshapen animal cracker – the kind where you're not sure which animal it's supposed to be, and you eat it out of pure politeness.'

Jacob switched on the radio. Classical music somehow felt appropriate to this project. Why Haydn was a good match for absurd astronomical treasure hunting, Jacob couldn't have said. But it just seemed to work.

'Anything?' he asked, after a while.

'Nothing with runners, I'm afraid … Oh!' she said suddenly. 'Look at that one.'

He stepped up to the eyepiece. 'You need a break, Dee. That's a smudge on the other lens.'

'Damn. That smudge looked more like a you-know-what than anything I've seen all night.'

'Yes, smudges have a way of doing that.' He grabbed a lens-cleaning cloth. 'At least I'm useful for something. You'll let me wash those bottles yet.'

'Jacob, there *aren't* any bottles.'

'So you keep saying.'


The nights that followed yielded only the assortment of curiosities that you'd get from a set of inkblots – a blob that looked a little bit like trapeze artists, a lump that sort of evoked a pita full of falafel, etc. On their last night in the observatory, Normandie noted a gas cloud that resembled, as she put it, 'a smeared sled', and then admitted defeat.

'Too bad we couldn't cosmically hybridise the sled thingy with the yak thingy,' Jacob said on the long drive home.

'Yeah,' said Normandie.


Kate looked at the no-nonsense watch she forced herself to wear. She didn't like anyone or anything, even Time, interfering with her doing things her own way. The watch was a concession to the fact that Time was going to have the last word on that one.

She had cut it as close as she could. Tommy Nibs, the university provost, might be a buddy of hers, but it wouldn't do for Kate to be tardy for a meeting called in Tommy's office – particularly a meeting that also included Hube Renkins. Renkins would certainly have arrived early. By the time Kate had finally locked up her office, Renkins had probably been pestering Tommy's secretary for a good ten minutes.

She navigated the campus maze with a confident, athletic stride. She didn't want to arrive with resentment percolating under her collar, so she forced herself to find something more pleasant to think about than the trouble Renkins was making for her. Tommy himself was a pleasant subject. She had spent some very nice times with him, though today's meeting would certainly not be one of them. Had it really been five years since their last single-sleeping-bag camping trip? The realisation shocked Kate. In general, realisations related to the passage of time were about the only thing that could.

Tommy was a big, huggable teddy bear, she reflected. She liked men of that type – among many other types, of course. Tommy was both comforting and comfortable, and yet he had an industrial-strength animal charisma. Once you got him into a sleeping bag, his behaviour definitely ceased to resemble that of a teddy bear.

His face glowed warmly for Kate when he stuck his head out of the little conference room and saw her waiting in his outer office – where she was sitting as far from Renkins as it was possible to sit, without resorting to the windowsill.

'Hello, Kate,' Tommy said in a tone from which, Kate noted, a casual observer would never gather that (a) he was expecting her, and (b) she was in trouble.

But she was prepared – Kate was always prepared. As much as it rankled to have to do it, especially in the presence of a petty onion like Hube Renkins, she was ready to admit that Normandie's purported discovery of the Rocking Horse Galaxy had been the result of a 'misunderstanding'. The precise details of how she would describe this 'misunderstanding' had not yet formed themselves in her mind; but she could come up with something later and relay it to Tommy via a memo. The important thing this morning was to accept the embarrassment and be done with it. If Normandie had succeeded in coming up with something real to pass off as the RHG, Kate would be using a different strategy today. But Normandie's phone call last night, after her final session at the observatory, had ruled out that possibility.

'Come on in,' said Tommy. 'You, too, Hube,' he said with a hint of sourness, and almost as if it were an afterthought.

They settled themselves around the conference table. Kate always felt silly sitting around a ten-person table with only one or two colleagues. She would have been more at home sitting cross-legged on the floor. Or open-legged, for that matter – but this wasn't that kind of meeting.

'I've called this meeting, Kate, because Hube has shared some concerns with me regarding Professor Stephens' big discovery.'

She braced herself. 'Look, Tommy. With all due respect to both you and Professor Renkins –' she gave Hube a curt, formal nod – 'I think people are making too much out of what Normandie said on that television programme.'

'*Insomnia With Rhone Preston,*' Renkins supplied helpfully.

'Thank you. I actually did know the name of the show,' said Kate. 'As I was saying, there's too much being made of that. In fact, I want to tell you –'

'Nonsense!' Renkins banged a chubby fist on the table. 'It's a big deal, and it deserves to be treated as such.'

'I have to disagree, Hube.' Kate wanted to yell at him, but she was shrewd enough to see that the time had come to be soothing. So she spoke softly. 'You know how those media people are.'

Renkins ignored her. 'Tommy, is the university going to allow some interloper from a rival institution to steal the most

139

important discovery in the history of Hauser University?'

Kate was confused. Interloper? Rival? Hauser U. didn't even have a football team.

But Tommy had obviously been put in the picture. 'Hube happens to have observed an – ahem – association between your Professor Stephens and the astronomer from Mountain College,' he explained gently.

Kate didn't become an astrophysics whiz by not being able to put two and two together. Suddenly, she found herself faced with the daunting task of suppressing her own laughter. Hube was priceless. Hube and his toy telescope, 'happening to observe' Normandie and Jacob holding hands as they walked across the quad. Kate liked the image, especially the part her imagination created where Normandie goosed Jacob right outside Hube's window.

'It's a serious concern,' Hube insisted to Tommy, who appeared irritated by such a statement with regard to something he was, obviously, already convinced of. 'By now, this guy from M.C. has probably offered her a tenure-track position – and maybe even marriage – if she'll ditch us and bring her galaxy over to their team.'

Kate wouldn't have known where to begin in critiquing Renkins' crazy scenario. From the idea of tenure being offered in tandem with marriage, to the concept of Normandie pulling her galaxy down from the sky and end-running it over to a 'rival institution', the whole thing was ludicrous.

But that wasn't what mattered. What mattered was that Tommy had bought it. And Tommy's having bought it suited Kate fine.

'I am concerned about this, Kate,' Tommy said. A minor roll of his eyes followed when he heard Renkins' smugly mutter, 'As well you should be.'

'OK, Tommy,' said Kate.

'There's only one solution,' said Renkins. 'You've got to transfer responsibility for the Rocking Horse Galaxy to someone more reliable.'

'*What?*' Kate had not anticipated this leap of chutzpah,

and it was all she could do to keep from blowing up at him.

'It's obvious,' Renkins said. 'I have tenure, and I'm not about to elope with strange astronomers.'

'Too bad for us,' Kate said, *sotto voce* – but not quite *sotto voce* enough to escape a stern look from Tommy. 'It seems to *me*,' Kate continued, 'that the obvious solution would be to make Normandie's position permanent. That, of course, is a budgetary matter.' She looked at Tommy with big, innocent eyes.

'I'm sorry, Kate, I can't commit to anything like that just now.'

'Well I certainly can't commit to reassigning Normandie's piece of space to *someone else*.'

'No, and I wouldn't ask you to,' said Tommy.

'But –'

'Please, Hube,' Tommy said with firm diplomacy. 'Kate, all I want you to do is ensure that the university gets maximum publicity out of the Rocking Horse Galaxy while we can, and that all the publicity be as much about Hauser as it is about Professor Stephens. I want her big break to be our big break – and the bigger, the better.'

'I think I can go along with that,' said Kate.

# Chapter Twenty-two

SUSAN WAS GIGGLING GIRLISHLY when she arrived with the photo.

'I realise I could have just e-mailed the file. But I wanted to see your faces when I unveiled it. And a print is so … dramatic.'

'Of course,' said Normandie.

'This is exciting,' said Jacob politely.

When Kate had told them to go full steam ahead – explaining that the provost had virtually instructed her to have Normandie lie wildly on national television – Normandie and Jacob had been very glad that they hadn't cancelled the commission they'd given Susan. Nonetheless, they couldn't help feeling more ambivalent than they had at the outset.

'Just because Kate's conscience has clocked out for the day doesn't mean nobody else around here has a conscience,' Normandie had told Jacob.

'I know what you mean,' Jacob had said. 'I thought Kate's conscience was kind of cute, though. I'd like to see more of it.'

'We may have to get her drunk first,' Normandie had advised.

Susan was clutching her manila envelope, grinning maniacally.

'OK,' said Normandie. 'I'm ready! Let's see it.'

'Now I'm shy,' said Susan.

'You silly person,' said Jacob kindly. 'You came all the way over here to show us that photo.'

Susan giggled.

Normandie got a mischievous glint in her eye. 'You know what I think, Jacob? I think maybe Susan's not going to show us that photo unless we show *her* something first.'

Susan giggled.

Normandie walked dramatically toward Jacob, like a game show's prize-flaunter. With a graceful motion, she laid one hand on his shoulder. Then, with great flair, she undid the button at the waist of his trousers.

Susan giggled.

Jacob stood very still.

Normandie slowly unzipped him. Then she teased his cock out from the billowy coyness of his boxers. She gestured toward it like a magician's assistant as it rose – as if by magic.

'Oh, fuck, yes,' said Susan with a reverent hiss. She carefully placed her envelope on the coffee table. Then she approached Jacob.

'May I?' Her eyes moved back and forth between Jacob and Normandie.

They, in turn, made eye contact with each other, breaking into broad smiles.

'Help yourself,' said Jacob to Susan.

'Oh,' she said quietly.

With a trembling, tentative motion that belied the fact that she'd been unequivocally intimate with the couple before, Susan began to stroke Jacob. He felt his smile freezing into a grimace of tense, incipient bliss, and he looked again at Normandie, to make sure she was watching his face. She certainly was, and he saw her eyes shift into a libidinous focus and her tongue lick discreetly at her lips. Normandie's thighs were pressed tightly together, a sign that she was cherishing a special feeling between them.

Susan dropped to her knees, and Jacob enjoyed the sight of her rose-coloured panties pouting under the awning of a miniskirt. Then his eyes closed, as the shy mouth taking in his exposed meal of flesh sent a wave of indescribable sensation straight up his spinal cord.

'Oh … oh *dear,*' he said with a mildness steeped in quivering pleasure. The truth was that he was too overcome to say anything stronger. All he could do was dance gently against her face and treasure every moment. He ran his fingertips lightly through his own hair, the effort of reaching down to Susan's head being more than he could manage.

He couldn't stand it any longer, this all-consuming bath of pleasure coursing through him. So he let go – pumping, shouting, dancing, giving up and giving it up.

But Susan and Normandie were not ready to give up. As Jacob sank onto the couch, it looked like they were just getting started. He was prepared to pitch in – as soon as he caught his breath – but, then again, it didn't necessarily look like they needed his assistance.

Susan had stood up, and she and Normandie were facing each other, each with her left hand at the waist of the other's skirt, as if they were about to dance.

They were.

Without losing eye contact with her dancing partner, Normandie eased her right hand into the other woman's panties. Susan followed her lead, preserving the symmetry by reciprocating.

Now they began to turn, actually dancing around the living room, stepping to an unheard rhythm. Fingers dancing in each other's panties.

Jacob watched in awe.

The pair had his full and most intense attention, naturally, and he took in every detail of their interaction. The way Normandie subtly led the dance, though their motions were almost identical. The way Susan was making a soft, unbroken sound – a cross between a moan, a hum, and a hint of below-the-surface laughter. The way the circular motions of Normandie's hand in Susan's panties were clockwise, while Susan's reciprocal circles were anticlockwise.

Soon the twitching of their groins began to fight against the smooth, consistent movement of the dance. Spasmodic motions broke in upon their display of poise – and ultimately tore it apart. The elegant, circular dance was derailed, superseded by the bawdy, jiggling partnership of two women fucking each other's cunts to juicy heaven with their fingers.

They bobbed left and right, shuffling their weight and banging their asses against the air, each embodying an involuntary expression of her impending female explosion. Their bodies struggled to hoard the ecstasy as long as they could, until they cried pleasure like two trumpets, pulling themselves together into a wet, vibrating black hole of orgasmic energy where their pussies and fingers all blurred together.

Normandie staggered to the couch, joining Jacob. She kissed him briefly but passionately. Then she looked at Susan, who had slumped into a chair.

'*Now* can we see that picture?' she asked.

Susan picked her envelope off the coffee table and brought it to the couch, where she squeezed in on the far side of Jacob. She handed the envelope over to Normandie.

'It's the top picture,' she said.

'Are you sure we can't offer you a cheque or money order?' said Normandie, before opening the envelope. 'I keep thinking about how you would normally get paid for this type of thing – I assume quite handsomely.'

'That expression always makes me visualise currency with Cary Grant's picture on it,' said Jacob.

'I do like Cary Grant,' said Susan. 'But … no. My treat.' She squeezed Jacob's knee.

'Thank you, Susan,' said Normandie. She pulled the top picture out of the envelope and glanced at it.

'Um,' said Normandie.

'Oh,' said Jacob.

'Hmm?' said Susan.

The image certainly suggested a deep-space object, if one judged by the hazy, pinkish-purple aura that bled into a jet-black emptiness at the photo's periphery. The problem, however – as quickly noted by both Jacob and Normandie – was that the object at the centre looked not so much like an amalgamation of stars clustered vaguely into the shape of a rocking horse, as like an actual, operational rocking horse that stood ready to accommodate a child.

'That's Betty,' said Jacob.

'What?' asked Normandie, who seemed so stunned as to be grateful for the opportunity to say something as simple as 'What?'

'Elizabeth Marjoram, aka Betty, property of the Living Museum of the American Rocking Horse. I'd know her anywhere.'

'For crying out loud,' said Normandie. '*Elizabeth Marjoram?* Do they all have names like that?'

'I warned you about that place,' said Jacob. 'Betty represents the craftsmanship of an artisan named Charlie Lippman.'

'You have such a good memory,' said Normandie.

'Perhaps,' said Jacob. 'But Charlie's signature is visible in Susan's photo.'

'Isn't this what you wanted?' Susan looked like she was about to cry.

'Yes … and no,' Normandie said carefully. 'It's my own fault – I should have made it clearer that I didn't actually want the image to actually incorporate an actual photo of an actual rocking horse. With, um, the actual craftsman's signature.'

'You don't like it,' said Susan, hanging her head.

'Hey,' said Jacob, 'what about the other photos in that envelope? Maybe one of those will be more … er … more … er …' He gave Normandie a panicked look.

'More … different,' said Normandie decisively.

'The other photos are the ones of you guys in bed,' Susan explained.

'Well,' said Jacob, 'that *is* different.'

Normandie suddenly seemed to have an inspiration. 'Susan. Darling. It's terrific. Really it is. But we're in a position now to take a more… *subtle* approach.' She walked to her desk, and pulled something out of a folder.

'Look. This is an object that Jacob and I have affectionately nicknamed the "smeared sled".' She handed the picture to Susan.

'Hello, smeared sled,' said Susan. 'Cute,' she declared to Normandie.

146

'Yes,' said Normandie agreeably. 'It's cute. And it's *real*. Of course, it's not shaped like a rocking horse. Not much like a rocking horse, anyway. But it could be, couldn't it? With your help?'

'Oh, yes,' said Susan. 'I'm an old hand at this now.'

'But let's try something less dramatic this time. Let's try just extending the shape and colours that are already there, to give only a *suggestion* of a rocking horse. No real features. No wood tones. No craftsman's signature. Just a slightly less sleddy and more rocking-horsy smear. Maybe with some pinkish-purple highlights around the edges, since you're so good at that. Can you do that for us?'

Susan grinned.

'I'll e-mail you the original image tonight,' said Normandie.

'Wanna look at some pictures?' said Normandie seductively, after Susan had gone home. She dropped the envelope onto Jacob's lap, where it teased his groin with promise.

She suggested they get undressed and spread the photos all over their bed.

Jacob felt sacredly naked with Normandie as they communed with the images Susan had created. He fondled her derrière as they leaned over to study the session, which Normandie had laid out in chronological order, left to right and top to bottom.

Their erotic journey, as orchestrated and captured by Susan, paraded before them. Jacob could taste the tension in the earliest shots, in which he and Normandie were clothed, barely touching, but alive with an electricity that flickered across the lights and darks of the photographer's black-and-white palette. His hand upon her warm bottom became urgent as they relit and relived the particular passion of that moment.

'Is it possible to be nostalgic for something that just happened a few weeks ago?' Normandie asked.

Jacob didn't have to speak to indicate that he understood. He let the play of his fingers along her rear crevice transmit his accord with the sentiment.

Sometimes it seemed as if his whole world centred on the crack of her ass.

She shifted on her feet, aimlessly, her motion merely an expression of a developing itch. He kneaded her cheeks and teased the nestled anus, sensing the yearning between her legs. It beckoned him.

She pressed her ass against him, causing his stiff cock to embroil itself in the cleft of her cheeks. She pointed at a particular photo and said, simply, 'That.'

The image showed Normandie's lovely greyscale derrière pointed prettily toward them, with Jacob's face wedged securely into the creamy nook where, were his head not in the way, her cunt would be smiling for the camera. The angle was such that Normandie's face was visible in the background, and the immortalised ecstasy it showed was – more than an echo – an amplification of the congress taking place at her underside.

Jacob hastily cleared the photos away, taking pains to keep his roving prick from licking any of the prints and glazing them with precum.

Normandie had climbed onto the bed, hunching down to give him full access to her hindquarters. 'If I felt any sexier, I think I'd burst into a thousand sexy pieces,' she whispered.

Jacob, too, was sailing high. He gripped himself in one hand as he knelt behind Normandie to kiss her cunt, knowing that his cock was nearly beyond the point of patience.

She tasted sweet with passion, her liquid a precious pool within her lips. With his free hand, he messed around with her buttocks as if he were shaping pastry, driven by an animal compulsion to handle her, handle her, handle her back there. All the while, he licked her, making her ooze, spreading her over herself with his tongue, as a chef might paint hot butter over the dough he will raise to orgasm.

She moaned low and long, as if she had sailed away from the dock of time and would float forever on self-sustained pleasure. But his tongue became Morse code on her clit, signalling her to plunge off the edge of her bliss and land, sated and wetly joyous. The hot rain of his irrepressible climax spattered onto her thighs, and Normandie's lips mouthed, 'I love you.'

# Chapter Twenty-three

'WE NEED A PROFESSOR Jacobs.'

'Who doesn't?'

'I'm serious, Jacob.'

'I know, I know. But where on earth are we going to find one? Or were you thinking of looking in a different solar system?'

'Forget it. I'm not paying that kind of gas money. No, I think we want someone right here in SF. Someone we can coordinate with.'

'You don't mean "coordinate", you mean "conspire".'

Normandie shrugged. 'Whatever you say. You're the writer.'

'Hmm ...' said Jacob. 'Let's see. Whom do we know who's fundamentally dishonest?'

'I don't think we want someone *fundamentally* dishonest. Just a little dishonest around the edges, when the occasion requires. Most important, it has to be someone who's charismatic.'

'And someone your colleagues won't recognise.' He suddenly laughed. 'Ha – I have half a mind to suggest Brandon.'

'Jacob! Yes.'

His jovial laughter turned to a hollow rattle. '"Jacob, *yes*"? Don't you mean, "Jacob, *no*"? Or even, "Jacob, *are you out of your tree*"?'

'Not at all. You're very much in your tree, in my opinion.'

'But ... he ... Look – for one thing, he hangs out with grad students.' Jacob felt that this would settle it. 'Those big parties at his brother's place, and all that.'

'Grad students, shmad-students,' said Normandie

collegially. 'It's the bigwigs we have to worry about, and they're never invited to those parties. I'm lucky I get invited, with my PhD in tow.'

'I think *everyone's* lucky you get invited, with *all* your attributes in tow – me in particular, considering that's how we met. But getting back to Brandon ...'

'Yes, let's. Let's get to him right now.' She looked at her watch. 'Eleven on a Friday night. That means we know where to find him.'

'But ... OK, sure, he's charismatic. But don't we want somebody a little more articulate, and maybe a little less, er...?'

'Stupid?'

'Stupid. Thank you. That's the word. And, remember, if he says something stupid during the show, you're the one who'll be on board the Stupid Train with him.'

'I'm not sure he's as stupid as we think. Remember, he's very adept with oral sex.'

'Meaning that if he gets flustered during the taping, we break in and suggest he go down on Priscilla, rather than answering her questions?'

'It is a thought. The man does have a very capable tongue.'

'Maybe so ... but what if he gets tongue-tied during the interview? Then he won't be any good for cunnilingus, either.'

'Now you're just quibbling,' said Normandie. She kissed Jacob on the nose. 'Let's go.'

The dance club seemed more magical to Jacob when he didn't have to sit through the mid-evening transition from its alternate identity as a boring pub. Granted, it was still a pretty bare-bones dance club ... but the throb of the bass and the jolt of the strobe went a long way toward making the place seem alive. And, he noted, the whirling young women in their playtime nightlife clothes didn't hurt the atmosphere, either.

Brandon was at his post, holding his own on the floor. He raised an eyebrow in greeting when he saw Jacob and

151

Normandie slide in and seat themselves at a small table near the tiny dancing area.

'Aren't you going to talk to him?' Jacob asked.

'Yes, but I don't want to drag him off the dance floor to do it. That's OK for fucking, but not for business propositions.'

'Good point. Then how about a drink?'

Jacob fetched a martini for Normandie and a tonic-and-lime for himself. When he rejoined her, he placed his hand on her thigh and began stroking her through the sexy thinness of her tights.

They were waiting for a break in the music, but the DJ seemed to be engaged in one of the longest unbroken mixes in Western history. Jacob occupied himself by watching the strobe-kissed bodies of the dancing women, while he continued to pet and squeeze Normandie's leg.

Her hand made an exploratory tour of his package, and she made eye contact to show that she not only understood, but endorsed his fascination with the dancers. 'Enjoying yourself?' she asked.

He nodded and kissed her.

'Let's dance,' she said, jumping up.

He felt conspicuous with a half-hard item in his pants; but he reasoned that nobody would notice unless intent on studying his crotch ... and that anyone who wanted to study his crotch might as well do so, for all he cared. He was not ashamed of his lust for life.

He and Normandie began dancing together. But as the fluid group shifted around them, Jacob soon found himself in the midst of a complement of young women, while Normandie engaged in a polite boogie with Brandon. Jacob felt self-conscious, moving in such close proximity to these creatures of another generation. But they didn't seem to mind, and he decided that if Normandie could hold her own with a creature like Brandon, he could make it through the mix without unduly embarrassing himself among these women.

The first time he made eye contact with the tall brunette, it was an accident. While swaying to the music, he became aesthetically interested in her little mod cap with its pinwheel design. As he looked at the cap, he realised she was looking at him. Their eyes met, and she smiled indulgently. She smiled as if he were a welcome curiosity, and he felt his hardness get a little harder.

Then she began imitating his movements, and Jacob became completely self-conscious. He found himself imitating her imitations of his steps, with the result that the two of them ended up revolving in a circle that was slightly too large for the space they had to work with. Luckily, the person Jacob unwittingly backed himself into was somebody who loved him very much.

'Gotcha,' said Normandie, hands around his waist.

The DJ was finally taking a break to talk to another DJ on his cell phone, and Brandon followed Normandie and Jacob the short distance to their table.

'How's it hangin', Jake?' said Brandon.

'Hello, Brandon. Has anyone ever told you that you have a rather antisocial way of being sociable?'

'No,' said Brandon.

'Brandon,' said Normandie. 'How would you like to be on television?'

'As what?'

'An astronomer,' said Jacob.

'Like, I'm not in the union,' said Brandon.

'Astronomers don't have a union,' Normandie explained.

'Dude, I mean the actors' union.'

'Ah,' said Jacob. 'You wouldn't exactly be acting, you see.'

'Whoa – I can't sing.'

'Not a problem,' said Normandie. 'The world does not need singing astronomers at present. Really, it's a *kind* of acting. But not exactly. You see?'

'Um,' said Brandon. Confusion seemed to deprive him of his swagger, and the young man appeared to be desperate for a hint.

'What Normandie's trying to say is that she'd like you to

impersonate an astronomer.'

'Huh?'

Normandie filled him in. 'We take you on *Gimme Some Science!* and introduce you as eminent astronomer Sinclair Jacobs, brother and inseparable crony of equally eminent astronomer Ernie Jacobs.'

'That's me,' Jacob explained. 'Hey,' he said to Normandie, 'if we're inseparable, how do we explain the fact that we never appear on TV together?'

'Union rules,' she replied briskly.

'But you just said astronomers don't –'

'Not *your* union. The viewers' union.'

'Do I need a telescope for this?' Brandon wanted to know.

'No,' said Normandie. 'Don't worry.'

'Actually, I was hoping you'd give me one.'

'We'll be paying you, Brandon,' said Jacob irritably. 'You can buy a telescope with the money.'

'OK, hang on a sec. Let me just think about this,' Brandon said, screwing up his face into what passed for a thoughtful expression. 'I'm supposed to pretend I'm an astronomer, and talk to Priscilla Ray.' His face suddenly lit up. 'Hey, couldn't I just talk to her without the astronomer deal? That I'd even do for free – no telescope, no perks. She's pretty hot, y'know.'

'Yes,' Normandie informed him, 'we know. But your interest in chatting up the luscious Ms Ray is, I'm afraid, tangential to our object here.'

'Oh.'

'Well?' asked Jacob.

'Look,' said Brandon. 'I don't know about this, y'know? It feels kind of, I dunno, dishonest.'

Jacob had been prepared for all sorts of snags, but it had never occurred to him that Brandon would have bona fide, card-carrying scruples. It left him speechless … and a little ashamed.

'You know,' he finally said to Normandie, 'I keep forgetting to think about how dishonest this is. I was going to think about it last Tuesday, for example, but I ended up doing a little vacuuming instead.'

'I won't deny that it's dishonest,' said Normandie. 'And, by the way, the carpet looked wonderful after you vacuumed it. But I don't think we'll really be doing any harm. It essentially doesn't matter one way or the other whether the universe comprises a galaxy shaped like a rocking horse ...'

'A what?' said Brandon.

'... or whether the universe comprises one, or two, or zero handsome astronomers named Professor Jacobs. You see my point?'

'Yes,' said Jacob. 'I'm handsome, and I do a good job with the vacuum cleaner.'

Normandie looked a little troubled. 'I didn't set out to fool all of the people some of the time, or – damn, how does the rest of that go?'

'Some of the people,' said Jacob helpfully, 'people who need people, are the luckiest ...'

'Never mind. I'm generally honest, as you know. I usually only lie about things like my intention to phone my father's distant cousins when I'm visiting their fair city. But this all happened by accident. We're committed now; it won't hurt anybody; and I think it will be sort of fun.' She was very sure of herself by this point, and Jacob could hear the crisp, oral semicolons with which she laid out her argument like silverware.

'Well, if you really think it's cool,' said Brandon hesitantly. Then he brightened. 'Man, I wish I could get credit for this. I'm minoring in drama.'

'Yes,' said Jacob, 'but you can't buy a telescope with college credits.'

'Thank you, Brandon,' said Normandie. 'We'll be in touch.' She pulled a pen out of her pocket and scribbled on her napkin. 'These are the dates you'll need to be in LA with us.' She handed him the napkin, which Jacob noticed had a sexy martini-and-lipstick stain at its corner.

'You're a good guy, Brandon,' said Jacob.

'Yeah, dude.' The words dripped off him like perspiration as he floated back to the dance floor.

# Chapter Twenty-four

IT WAS A DAMP, unsociable evening outside, and Susan entered the apartment as if she planned to hibernate there – or at least spend the rest of the weekend. Water beaded up on the plasticised envelope she'd insisted on bringing to Normandie and Jacob – who by now understood that e-mailing the image would not hold the same thrill for Susan.

When the photo and photo specialist had been duly dried off, the threesome squished onto the love seat for the unveiling.

It was a work, not only of art, but of admirable shrewdness. This time, Susan had clearly made subtlety her watchword, and the 'smeared sled' had been transformed into the 'Rocking Horse Galaxy' through a combination of colour, shadow, enhancement, extension, and omission that was hard to identify and harder to question. The vague, pinkish-purplish shape looked just enough like a rocking horse to lend credence, and not enough to look implausible. It was a classic celestial object, a thing of nebulous beauty and chaotic composition.

It was clear that Normandie was deeply impressed. 'Now I'm glad all over again that we're going through with this.' Then she laughed, and explained to Susan that the plan had had some ups and downs.

In this atmosphere of reverence for the ludicrous, glorious print, Jacob felt that anything any of them could say on another subject would be anticlimactic. But Susan proved him wrong.

'I think about the two of you all the time.'

Normandie took Jacob's hand, and she smiled warmly at Susan. 'You're so sweet. We think about you a lot, too.'

157

Susan looked intense. 'I see every piece of your body …' she turned to Jacob '… and your body. Interweaving, in all sorts of positions, in my dreams when I sleep. And before I go to sleep. It's like the session we did was just the tip of the iceberg. I can see the two of you from every possible angle. Fucking. Fucking from every angle. I can see the texture of your skin in every conceivable lighting.'

Normandie didn't blush easily, but this had done it. 'Darling,' she said to Jacob, 'isn't that beautiful?'

'Mmmnh,' said Jacob.

Susan continued her expository speech. 'I want to crawl under the pair of you – or on top of you – between you – fuck fuck fuck you. Straddle you, have you both.'

'Haven't we done that?' asked Jacob.

'Every fantasy. Every single fucking fantasy. Both of you. Every time I come.'

Normandie put down Susan's print, which she'd been holding all this time. 'Come here, Susan.'

Since the three of them were seated on the same love seat, there wasn't much distance between Susan and 'here'. But Jacob was in the middle, and Susan lost no time in climbing over him. Her stiff skirt and warm-thighed tights fondled his lap for a second en route to Normandie's embrace.

'Baby,' said Normandie, as Susan fell into her.

Jacob was again struck by how potently Normandie and Susan could kiss, as he had been at the LMARH soirée. Their mouths and faces seemed to blend like two juices in a smoothie, and he was almost tempted to watch their faces only. Yet there were also their bodies to consider. Susan was pawing like an animal at Normandie's turtleneck breasts, while manoeuvring her legs into a straddle that bunched her skirt between Normandie's tummy and her own urgent nexus. Normandie bounced her strong thighs in echoes of the ravenous kiss, giving Susan what looked like the ride of her life. Who needs a fucking rocking horse, thought Jacob.

Pieces of the women's clothes began to come off like the flaky outer layers of two oven-warm croissants. Normandie's

158

breasts bobbed for Susan, and the photographer licked and squeezed them like she'd never tasted flesh before. Susan, who had shed her skirt, tights, and thong, squirmed from one of Normandie's bouncing thighs to the other, leaving wet marks here and there on her jeans. Jacob wondered what you'd call this treatment. The jeans had been stonewashed before they were purchased, but now they were – the term formed itself in his mind – *cuntwashed*, too.

Susan raised herself up, bringing her feet to the cushions and squatting above Normandie's lap, inviting the other woman's hands into her desperately wet crotch. When the fingers reached her, she hovered and swayed, looking like her intention was not only to receive pleasure in her cunt but also to look as lewd as possible while doing it.

Jacob wanted them both. Most of all, he wanted to shower them with affection – his sweet, generous woman and the impassioned, adoring friend who was so hungry for them. He ignored his erection long enough to stroke their heads, kiss their cheeks and their ears, and generally lend his blessing to the proceedings. Each of them kissed back at him, turning their heads to mouth and slobber at his face, kindly dolloping morsels of their arousal onto him, letting him participate in their liquid abandon. When Susan rattled into orgasm, her clenching cunt a flushed, fussed-with mess in Normandie's hand, Jacob felt her teeth against his cheek.

Normandie's nipples, meanwhile, were dancing beneath Susan's fingers, and Jacob saw Normandie's entire body dance with them. Her hips, tight in jeans, sashayed on the cushions, and Jacob knew that someone had better peel and fuck her at his or her earliest convenience, before Normandie burned a hole through the seat of her pretty pants.

Her jeans came off more easily than he'd thought they would, complete with pussy-soaked blue panties and pink ankle socks that looked practically edible. Susan cleared out of the way for the fucking – but she didn't clear far. She stood behind Jacob, and made haste to get his pants down while Normandie unbuttoned his shirt and ran her hands over his

159

chest.

Normandie and Jacob swivelled so that he could enter her in classic style on the love seat. His ass bucked up just a little as he penetrated, and he felt it meet with warm resistance – Susan's mound, frigging his buttocks.

Normandie was still in a state of acute nipple erogeneity, and, once Jacob's cock was nicely situated up her snatch, she directed his hands to her respective breasts. He knew this mood of hers, the mood in which she wanted to writhe from the chest downward, while writhing also from the pussy upward, letting herself be skewered below and fondled above till pleasure exploded from her centre in every direction.

From behind, he felt Susan find a rhythm and a path by which she could hump herself against his hipbone, in such a way as to transfer pressure to her clit – a manoeuvre he recognised. As she slithered sensuously from rubbing herself against his butt to shocking herself against his pelvis, her breathing became ragged, and it was punctuated by squeaks.

Normandie's heels were kicking against the sofa cushions, and her wetness was swirling around Jacob's pounding cock. Something had to give … and the something was all of them. Normandie's thighs banged against his own, and her hands froze his in their exact, nipple-delighting posture of the moment. Susan's thin hands squeezed him urgently around the waist, while her pubis climbed spastically up and down his hip-line like velvet sandpaper. Jacob simply lost control, pumping into his lover like a huge dog drinking from a water bowl.

Normandie had to give up the fight to persuade Susan to accept money for her work. She seemed adamant about making a gift of any and all concocted astral rocking horse images.

'How about this, then,' said Normandie. 'We take you to LA, as our guest, and bring you to the taping. We can say you're our nutritional adviser or something. You'll get to see the slide of your creation when it's first unveiled, to many an

160

"ooh" and "ahh", no doubt.'

 'Will I get to stay in a hotel with you?'

 'Of course,' said Normandie.

 'Deal,' grinned Susan.

# Chapter Twenty-five

THE HAPPY NOISES OF a street fair woke them on Sunday morning. Sunlight mingled with their good-morning kisses and cuddles, then danced for Jacob in harmony with the cheerful, efficient sound of Normandie brushing her teeth.

Where they had left Susan the night before, there was now a small plastic bag in a luminous shade of blue. They had given her dinner and she had fallen asleep in the living room, cosy as a bunny after fucking like a rabbit. This morning, evidently, she had woken early, nipped down to the street fair … and dropped off a gift before leaving again, identifying it as such by a sticky note on the bag: 'Thanks, guys.'

It was, in fact, two gifts. Two pairs of groovy, striped socks. Thick purple and black stripes adorned one pair, while the other sported stripes in lime green and yellow.

'I'm not sure what I can wear these with,' said Jacob, as they examined their presents.

Normandie looked sly. 'Do you really think she wants us to wear them *with* anything?'

Normandie was kinky and delicious in just the lime and yellow socks. Jacob alternated between looking at her beside him and looking at her in the full-length mirror, which they had crowded in order to check themselves out. He noticed that his cock, still flaccid, looked particularly fleshy in counterpoise to his purple and black footwear.

'We look very *anatomical,* don't we,' said Normandie.

It was true. Her hips flared femininely, and her breasts were vivid. The brief dip of her groin into its female conciseness made Jacob's flaccidity now morph into readiness. She looked, in a word, fuckable.

She turned to face him, grabbing his shoulders so that he,

162

too, pivoted away from the mirror. 'Rock my socks off, baby,' she challenged.

She took his hand and led him to the bed. She sat on the edge, spreading her legs. Her pussy winked and wafted for him. In her socks, her feet looked like comic-book boots, arching their sexual tension into the floor the way a buttress channels architectural stresses. Jacob could trace the path of the stresses all the way up the arced pillars of her legs, where they converged and flowered into the pouting anticipation of her centrepiece.

He knelt at her cartoon feet. This had to be slow, he knew, to do justice to the concept. One sock at a time. One stripe at a time. One half-inch at a time. Lowering cotton down here and raising the heat and moisture up above. He knew she would love it, would cream for it.

'Socks before pussy,' said Normandie, echoing his thoughts.

After each stripe was folded down, he glanced up, monitoring her wetness. By the time he was nearing her ankle, the sparkle of sunlight on her womanly glimmer was almost too bright to look at. The honey dripped and pooled lazily on the bed.

When he finally and deliberately, with all the patience he could muster, eased the sock across her sole and off the cliff of her toes, he knew he had to have her without further delay.

'How about we leave the other sock on?' he queried.

'Oh, God, yes,' she replied.

The two of them became a three-socked monster of skin, with Jacob's fingers, mouth, and cock virtually fighting each other for access to her succulence. His mouth got the prize, while his fingers went to work stroking the territory that ran from her outer lips to the uppermost flesh of her thighs. His fingers became a web of interactive lingerie, teasing and delighting the soft, special places that silk panties might have the privilege of groping beneath the shade of an elegant dress.

As she absorbed his tickles, she could barely keep herself on his mouth; but he followed the nectar. When she was titillated to frothy perfection, he moved his hands to her outer thighs, and poured his face into her like he was eating watermelon. He relished the nuanced shades of her flavour, treasuring the differences between the taste of her clit, that of her puffy lips, and the core essence his tongue found when it went deep into her pot. He was sure he could have passed a blind taste test arranged along the living map of her vulva.

'Oh, I'm happy,' she chattered as he licked her out. 'Lick my happy cunny.'

'Thth ngxnkly wttm dnnug,' Jacob explained.

She laughed with a merry, orgasmic irrelevance and washed more happy juice onto him.

Jacob now had the distinction of being a naked man in socks with an enormous, stiff penis. He lay down on the bed beside Normandie and displayed himself to her.

She sat up and assessed him. She scooted around, taking up a position between his legs and bending his knees up. She clutched his socks, getting a solid grip on each ankle … and leaned in to suck him into heaven.

She didn't need to take all of him into her mouth, and she did not do so. Instead, she painted his shaft with an impressionistic brush, letting her mouth slide up and down, straight or at an angle, with an eclectic but always effective addressing of his need. He soon felt the spiny inflexibility of his member decompressing into a turbulent tube of fungible sensation, and all that was solid gave itself up into his passionate liquid – matter into energy.

'I took your advice and went to see the editor of the *San Francisco Inveigler* today. I thought I'd just introduce myself, and see if I could talk her into giving me some feature assignments.' Jacob paused to sip from the water glass that the waiter had just delivered.

'And?'

He could tell that Normandie was as invested in her advice proving successful as she was in her boyfriend proving successful. 'I'm sorry to say your advice backfired,' he said with a wince.

'*What?* But that was excellent advice.'

'Yes, it was. But nobody told the editor that. She thought I was an unscheduled appointment, and you know how editors feel about those.'

'Hmph,' said Normandie. 'You don't look anything like an unscheduled appointment.'

'You say the nicest things. Anyway, it just goes to show … something. I'm not sure what, but it *definitely* goes to show.'

'What about the other editors you were going to visit?'

'Mm,' he mmed. 'I neglected to visit them today, out of – well, out of negligence. Maybe next week.' He reflected for a moment, looking into Normandie's approving eyes. 'I wish you could come with me. Everyone seems to behave better when you're around. Nobody wants to disappoint you.'

'I could sneak in when an editor is at lunch and hide in a filing cabinet.'

'Yes, but if the editor didn't know you were there, it would defeat the purpose.'

'I never realised how complicated the publishing business was.' She sipped her water. 'Hey, look! Kate's over there in the bar.'

Jacob craned his neck. 'So she is. Looks like she's with a friend.'

Normandie laughed. 'Undoubtedly. The question is, was he a friend thirty minutes ago, or another stranger that Kate has quickly turned into a friend?'

'I can't see his face.'

'Me neither.'

'Oh, well.' Jacob turned back to face Normandie. 'Deprived of another cheap thrill.'

'Or maybe not. Kate's getting up. I think she sees us. Unless she smiles that way at everyone. Which she might. But, no, she's waving. It's definitely a "hello-there-Normandie-and-hello-there-back-of-Jacob's-head" sort of wave.'

'So what does the guy look like?'

'I still can't see him. We're going to have to wait until he steps closer to – eeh!' She had cut herself off with a shriek. Now she was stifling giggles.

Jacob craned his neck again, just in time to see Kate walking toward them, along with her companion – the curator of the Living Museum of the American Rocking Horse.

'Oh noes!' whispered Jacob, who sometimes had a tendency to pick up more Internet slang than he would care to admit. His discomfiture was due not only to the fact that he had always found the curator to be an unpleasant little pimple, but also to the fact that he *still* did not know the man's name.

But Kate made things easy – as she always did. As soon as she and her friend had helped themselves to the vacant chairs at Jacob and Normandie's table, she made what passed for an introduction. 'Jacob, I know that *you* know Chummy. How about you, Normandie? Have you met?'

'Not officially,' Normandie said.

Jacob reluctantly made eye contact with the man now identified as 'Chummy'. He was about to offer a dry 'How are you?' when the curator smiled and slapped him jovially on the back.

'Very nice to see you,' he surprised Jacob by saying. 'Kate and I have just been having drinks,' he proceeded, unnecessarily, to explain.

'Normandie and I were about to have dinner,' Jacob hinted.

'Excellent idea,' said Chummy effusively. 'You always were a clever one. After you left our fundraiser, the donations poured in. People kept telling me how funny you were, what a good time they'd had. Personally, I didn't see it … but I'll take the cash. As far as I'm concerned, I owe you one.'

Jacob wasn't sure he wanted one of whatever Chummy owed him; hopefully, he would never have to call in the loan.

'Oh!' said Kate. 'If we're going to have dinner with you, we'd better bring our drinks over.' She and Chummy toddled back toward the bar on this errand.

Jacob leaned toward Normandie. 'Interesting the effect that alcohol has on some people.'

'And money.'

'I've seen this before, though – a person stepping out of his panjandrum outfit and undergoing a drastic transformation.'

'Huh? When was he wearing pyjamas? Did I miss it?'

'What I want to know,' said Jacob, 'is do *we* call him Chummy, too?'

'What do you mean?'

'I mean, I have no idea if it's his first name, his last name, a nickname, or a term of endearment. If it's the equivalent of her calling him honeybuns, I'm not on board.'

'Maybe his name is really Cholmondeley. Don't the Brits say that like Chummy?'

Jacob shook his head. 'No, that's Chumley.'

'Damn,' said Normandie.

'Besides, as far as we know, neither Kate nor Chummy is British.'

'You don't seem to be having any trouble calling him Chummy.'

'This is different. It's third person, and I'm talking to somebody who regularly sees me naked. I'll say just about anything to you.'

'Do you want to call *me* Chummy?'

Jacob flinched. 'Do you want me to?'

'Maybe later.' She kissed him, then cocked her head to indicate that their friends were approaching again from behind his back.

'What are we having for dinner?' asked Kate.

'We actually haven't ordered yet,' said Normandie.

'Good thing I'm here, then,' said Kate. 'You kids clearly need someone to get you on track. Lemme see that menu, Jacob.'

# Chapter Twenty-six

'I THINK THIS MAY be the party we've been waiting for,' Normandie said as her eyes scanned her e-mail.

'Have we been waiting for one?' said Jacob.

'I have,' she reminded him.

It was true, he realised. Ever since the *Insomnia With Rhone Preston* appearance, they had avoided the various shindigs within the Hauser University community, for fear of additional Hubert Renkinses coming out of the woodwork and saying 'boo' to the so-called Professor Ernie Jacobs – in front of other people who knew him as Jacob Hastings.

Now, Normandie was looking at an invitation from a buddy of hers named Glenda, who taught at a small college in redwood country. It was close enough for Normandie and Jacob to get to, but far enough that she was unlikely to run into any of her own colleagues there.

Nevertheless, since Rhone Preston's San Francisco-based show could presumably be picked up in Glenda's neck of the woods, Normandie wisely suggested that Jacob pose as Professor Ernie for the duration of the party.

'Does that mean we can't engage in public displays of intimacy and affection?' Jacob worried.

She considered the question. 'I don't think so,' she finally answered. 'As long as they *only* meet you as Ernie, it doesn't matter if we're an item. I'll just fill Glenda in on everything, because she knows I'm shacking up with a wonderful guy named Jacob, and I don't want her to think I've left you for you.'

'I appreciate that.'

'I appreciate *you*.'

'Come here.'

'So now I'm impersonating an astronomer at a party. My, the shenanigans we get up to.' Jacob smiled at Normandie as she drove them partyward. 'Say, how come you can't have just one shenanigan?'

'*You* can have one,' she said. Without taking her eyes off the road, she gave his groin a squeeze that was somewhere between affectionate and lascivious. 'There. A shenanigan with your name on it.'

'That was a shenanigan?' asked Jacob.

'Didn't it feel like one?'

'Yes, I guess it did.'

They laughed at this for the next mile, savouring the space and intimacy of amusing themselves together in the confines of a moving car.

Normandie laughed a little longer than Jacob, so he had the opportunity to calmly study her face as it glimmered with mirth. Seeing her this way filled him with a desire to feel her beneath him, rolling from side to side with pleasure. But, since this probably wasn't going to be *that* kind of party, he prepared to wait till their return home to pounce on her.

Glenda was a sturdy-looking botanist who always seemed to have a sardonic remark hanging on her lip. She hadn't seen Normandie in a year; and soon after the couple arrived, she began talking to her friend with a making-up-for-lost-time dedication, navigating her through the house as she did so. Meanwhile, Jacob introduced himself as Ernie to a kitchenful of wine-drinking academics. He fervently hoped that none of them were astronomers – or at least that any of them who *were* astronomers had already had enough wine to render them harmless. He tried to break the ice in a non-astronomical fashion by mentioning the drive in from San Francisco.

'So how're things in San Fran, Ernie?' asked a tall, quavery-voiced professor of undetermined specialisation. He wore the sort of thin, long beard that Jacob associated – rightly or wrongly – with bluegrass musicians. Jacob wondered if the quaver was natural, or affected for the purposes of bluegrass singing.

169

'Things are windy and urban.'

'I reckon they are,' said Professor Bluegrass. 'So you're a friend of Glenda's?'

'Only in the sense that we've never met, or otherwise interacted,' Jacob explained.

'Sounds like a beautiful friendship.'

'Very little strife, certainly.' He raised his glass of wine in a jaunty toast. 'Actually, I'm here with Normandie.'

'You lucky animal,' said Bluegrass, with a quaver on *animal*.

He felt a tap on his shoulder. Since boyhood, his reaction to this sensation had been to expect nobody to be at the shoulder that had been tapped, and a waggish comrade to be present at the other shoulder. But, in this instance, the tapper tricked him – she was posted where the tap had originated. She was a very bespectacled, cheerfully tipsy scholar who looked like she had been lecturing on Joyce and Woolf since before they'd even begun writing.

'Hullo,' she said with exaggerated bonhomie. 'You're Normandie's friend, aren't you?'

'He'd better be,' Professor Bluegrass piped in. 'They're sleeping together.'

'Quiet, Seymour,' Professor Joyce-and-Woolf chided playfully. 'These economists are always underfoot,' she said, ostensibly to Jacob. 'So where *is* Normandie? I haven't seen her in months.'

'She's around somewhere,' Jacob said unhelpfully. 'She's wearing a bright red sweater.'

'Impossible,' Joyce-and-Woolf argued. 'She's far too interesting to wear a bright red sweater. Carmine maybe … crimson possibly … scarlet … but *never* bright red.'

'Come to think of it, it was a blue sweater,' said Jacob. He decided to find her. He loved watching her around groups of people, and it had been a while since he'd had the opportunity.

He followed the sound of her laughter from around a corner. It was a sound that lent intensity to all the colours

170

around him, even when heard from an adjoining room. He could visualise the way she'd be tugging at her sweater hem, laughing out of sight around the friendly wooden corners of a house in full party.

When he found her, she was telling a story.

'… and I only got a glimpse of the cover, because I was hurrying through the bookstore – presumably en route to a pressing cappuccino.'

The group around Normandie echoed her laughter.

'But I had to ask myself: If the market can bear an entire book about maraschino cherries, then why can't I get tenure?'

'I don't get the connection,' said one of her listeners politely.

'The connection,' said another, with more sass than politeness, 'is that Normandie's response to *everything* is "Why can't I get tenure?".'

'Maybe so,' Normandie admitted. 'But only because I've never been given a satisfactory answer.'

'It's a matter of budgets, isn't it?' asked a serious young man whose shirt collar looked like it would be spending the entire evening wrestling with his crewneck sweater.

'I said I wanted a *satisfactory* answer,' Normandie replied, 'not the same old tedious one. If they would just give me a different answer once in a while, then I wouldn't complain. I might throw myself on the floor and have a hissy fit – but I wouldn't complain. As it is, every time I try to …'

Jacob didn't hear the rest of her response, because suddenly there was an insistent voice coming from behind him. 'What kind of astronomy do you do, Ernie?' it asked. He turned to see that Joyce-and-Woolf had followed him into the living room.

'What kind? I don't know … what kinds are there?'

She laughed at his apparent witticism, not realising that the ignorance was unfeigned. Normandie, responding to some peripheral awareness of the developing situation, quickly took charge.

'Ernie mostly does research. And right now, if he doesn't

171

mind, he's going to get me another drink.'

'Why can't you get your own drink?' asked Joyce-and-Woolf.

'They taste better when he gets them.'

As he walked toward the kitchen, his train of thought – an awestruck consideration of Normandie's ability to steer clear of a touchy subject – was interrupted by the sound of a familiar voice resounding from the vicinity of the front door. Somebody was arriving, apologising unconvincingly to Glenda for being late and, in the same breath, expressing the hope that she hadn't run out of drinks. It was, in fact, Hube Renkins.

Jacob spun around and retraced his steps to Normandie's side. 'Is there more than one bathroom in this house?' he whispered.

'I think so,' she stated through a haze of confusion.

'Let's find one,' he said, grabbing her elbow and pulling her toward the far end of the room, where, he had surmised, the egress would take them out of the path of Renkins' inevitable trajectory from coat closet to drinks table.

'Jacob!' said Normandie. 'What the –'

'Renkins,' he explained.

'Eep,' she concurred.

They snuck up the stairs and located the bathroom that would likely be off the beaten path as far as other guests were concerned. Jacob locked them in.

'We can't stay in here all night, you know,' said Normandie.

'Do you think we could lower ourselves out the window to our car?'

'I refuse to lower myself to that.'

'What right does your friend Glenda have to know Hube Renkins, anyway?' said Jacob sulkily.

'I'm sorry. Honestly, she used to be so reliable.'

'But wait a second …' said Jacob. 'Why are we afraid of Renkins? He already thinks I'm Ernie, as does everyone here. He already suspects that you and I are an item, and that I take

172

every opportunity to visit you, thereby neglecting many of my responsibilities back at dear old Mountain College. So what's the problem?'

'Oh!' said Normandie. 'You're right.'

'I guess I just panicked,' said Jacob.

'And you panicked me,' said Normandie.

'Yes. That's because "panic" is a transitive verb.'

'Unlike "picnic".'

They were giggling inanely but happily by now.

'So we can go back down,' said Jacob.

'Not so fast,' said Normandie. 'I haven't picnicked you yet.'

She wrapped her arms around his neck and kissed him lusciously, tickling his mouth with a few residual giggles. He felt her warmth, her giggles, and the glass of wine he'd consumed collaborating to create a very pleasant effect.

He rubbed the sides of her hourglass through the cosy blue sweater. Making out with a sweater-clad Normandie in the bathroom at a party made Jacob feel more infused with the classic collegiate spirit than any number of professorial impersonations ever could.

Good old-fashioned making out, thought Jacob. The kind that knows no limits.

Soon she was in only sweater and panties, a lapful of huggable, kissable, gropable cuddliness. She unbuttoned his shirt and, as she reached to access the buttons that trailed into his jeans, he stroked the little wet spot on her undies.

She growled, urging him to stroke with more resolution. The wet spot spread, and her delicate aroma began to fill the bathroom.

'Believe it or not, I've never been fucked at a party,' she whispered. 'After a party ... before a party ... instead of a party ... but never during.'

Jacob was too busy peeling panties to reply with more than a libidinous grunt. He tossed them aside, then took in the sight of this bare-assed lover in a blue sweater.

'My love for you is bottomless,' he said.

173

'That makes two of us.'

Fucking Normandie in the sweater felt different from the countless other fucking-Normandie scenarios Jacob had had the privilege of experiencing. The contrast between the pale, cool flesh of her naked ass and the friendly cotton bulk of the top made him feel wonderfully lewd. He was fucking her naked cunt in a bathroom, wedging his hands between her bare bottom cheeks and the fuzzy bathmat. She would probably end up with lint clinging to her behind, and he would have a mouthful of yarn from having nibbled at her breasts through the crewneck. And he knew they didn't care about the lint or the yarn or the taste of sweater because they were fucking fucking fucking fucking …

# Chapter Twenty-seven

'I KNOW A GOOD car game,' said Normandie as she drove them home.

'It's too dark to scout licence plates,' said Jacob.

'This is even better. This is where I tell you a sexual fantasy.'

'Then again, the licence plates *are* illuminated.'

'Jacob!'

'All right, all right,' he teased. 'If you insist. Roll the fantasy.'

'The *sexual* fantasy.'

'Is there any other kind?'

'Point taken.' She cleared her throat. 'My Sexual Fantasy. By Dr Normandie Stephens, age 30.' She cleared her throat again.

'Is the throat-clearing part of the fantasy?'

'The throat-clearing is an optional bonus.'

'Got it.'

'And you shutting up now and listening is a mandatory proviso.'

He nodded, smiling. She twinkled at him.

'I've always thought it would be very sexy to be played like an instrument. I mean, *really* like an instrument. For example, let's say I'm on stage at the Symphony, on a bed – centre stage, of course –'

'Of course. Oops – sorry, I wasn't supposed to talk.'

'Enthusiastic interjections are all right,' she reassured him. 'So anyway … the orchestra surrounds me. But there's an instrument missing from their ranks. A solo instrument. A violin.'

'Too bad. The patrons will probably all want refunds.'

'They will not,' said Normandie. 'Because *I* am appearing in lieu of the violin. And a handsome man with very adept fingers – you, for instance – is appearing in lieu of the violinist.'

'How does the conductor feel about this?'

'In the fantasy, she's the one who has suggested the whole thing.'

'Ooh, I like your female conductor already.'

'Yes. She looks a little like Susan.'

'What happens next?'

'You've been to classical concerts ... people check their coats and take their seats, study their programmes.'

She swallowed, then looked over her shoulder to change lanes before resuming. 'Finally, the house lights dim and the chatter devolves to a murmur. The conductor makes eye contact with me for a brief but intense instant, then with you. Then she turns to the rest of the orchestra and cues them to begin.'

'Who is the composer?'

'I think it's Mozart. Mozart tickles so nicely.'

Jacob could hear the cheerful flow and surge of a Mozart score, and he was beginning to experience the excitement of what was to come.

'They play for quite a few measures without you. You and I just look at each other, calmly, without touching. We are very confident on stage.'

'What are we wearing?'

'Really! You are so shallow. I take you to the Symphony to hear great music, and all you're interested in is what people are wearing.' She sighed in mock resignation. 'If you must know, you are wearing your tux; whereas I am entirely naked, except perhaps for some suitable piece of symphonic jewellery.'

'You're always over-dressed,' said Jacob, with a forced sigh of his own.

'Your first solo happens around my right nipple.'

'Is that ordinary right, or stage right?'

176

'The nipple closest to you. With an expert feel – as it were – for every nuance of Wolfgang Amadeus's rhythm, you greet and tease it, playing me note for note as the absent violinist would do upon his or her instrument.'

'Clearly, I have the finer instrument.'

'Thank you. Perhaps that's why the violinist didn't show up.'

'My solo continues?'

'No, it's back to the orchestra now. You remove your hand.'

'Aww.'

'Well, let's say you rest it on my hip.'

'Which –'

'The hip closest to you. We listen to the glorious music. My nipple is still tingling. It misses you, but Mozart has ensured your speedy return. I'm wet,' she added, squirming in her seat.

'I can tell.'

'I'm wet in the fantasy, too.'

'How convenient.'

'I can feel my wetness beginning to pool – I'm naked except for the jewellery, remember – '

'I hadn't forgotten.'

'– and I know my juice is glistening under the lights. And now it's time for your next solo. This time, you bring me both hands, and so both your old friend the stage right nipple and the shy little virgin stage left nipple become part of the score. Staccato tweaks … with legato strokes to my breast-flesh in counterpoint.'

'Violins don't do counterpoint.'

'I'm a special violin. And every *dumdedumdum* in the piece is a sensual adventure for me and my little breasts. By the end of the solo, I'm writhing.'

'Me, too,' said Jacob. 'I'm not sure I'm going to make it through the whole movement.' He unzipped his trousers.

'There you go,' she said approvingly.

'I feel bad, though. I get to *come* to your symphony, while you have to keep driving.'

'Don't worry. I'll get mine.'

'I promise it,' said Jacob.

'So do I. Now, this time we don't have to wait as long for your next appearance. You tap neatly on my belly ...'

'Your *sensuous* belly.'

'I'll accept that. You tap neatly on my *sensuous* belly, as we wait out the few measures. You're holding me at the ready, as a violinist might hold the violin, itching to play. Then ...'

'Yes?' he hissed eagerly.

'It's time. And now you get to really show your talent. Upon my breasts, yes; but the melody doesn't confine you to that. Not this time. One hand flutters down to where I'm wet, bringing the pulse of the music to those lips. The other hand travels freely as well, finding harmonics at the back of my knee ... on the tip of a toe ... oh, God, places only a great composer could imagine. And I ... I ... I need to pull over.'

Jacob never stopped stroking himself while Normandie concentrated on availing herself of the present exit, which offered them a deserted rest area. When she brought the car to a stop, she cut the engine and turned the dome light on. Then she undid her seatbelt.

'Yes, you're playing me like an instrument, bringing discrete moments of pleasure to every sensitive place on my body, then moving back and forth between them in ticklish glissandos, until I'm completing resonating with the music, my body singing with pleasure.'

Jacob had never heard such an erotic mouthful.

He was getting close, and he saw that Normandie had a hand in her pants. Judging from the motion of her wrist, her fingers were moving furiously.

'You're all over me, but, inevitably, your music hovers over my cunt. Your fingers pluck, then hold, controlling the tone, vibration, sustain, and duration of each note. You become slick with my resin.'

'Ohh,' said Jacob.

178

'I'm buzzing from my ears, which have become flushed little tuning pegs, to my smooth, warm ass, which vibrates with every tone. Then, as the genius of Mozart brings all our senses to a peak, you, maestro, provide a masterstroke, finishing me off with one perfect, climactic quarter-note on my clit, and …'

She didn't need to say anything else. They just sat there in their respective seats, a well-lit exhibit of abandonment. They rocked and jiggled cartoonishly, letting their own hands take them where Normandie's vividly related fantasy had pointed.

'Oh, fuck!' said Normandie.

'I'm coming,' moaned Jacob, stating the obvious as his cream shot onto the dashboard.

'Yes. Me … me … ahhhh!' The car shook with her scream.

When they arrived home, Normandie undressed for bed while Jacob fussed with the stereo. Soon the room was brightened by an unseen orchestra.

'You just lie there,' said Jacob. 'I need a minute to get into my tux.'

# Chapter Twenty-eight

'EXCUSE ME.' THE WOMAN smiled at Jacob as if she believed that her status as somebody's grandmother entitled her to filial loyalty and indulgence from everybody under forty.

'I'm sorry,' said Jacob. 'I don't work here.' He was used to being mistaken for various types of retail managers. Normandie had hypothesized that he must have a 'retail face,' though she'd graciously, hastily added that *she* didn't see it.

'I know you don't work here, silly,' said the grandmother. 'You're the young man with the rocking horses. From the party at the museum. Jacob Hastings.' She said his name as though only she could be trusted to remember it, as though Jacob himself might have carelessly lost track of it.

He winced. 'It's very kind of you to remember me. But I'm in a bit of a hurry right now, I'm afraid. I'm going out of town tomorrow, and I need to get some condiments.'

The woman looked around them, at the shelves of drugstore products that filled this drugstore. 'Condiments?'

'Sorry – I meant *toiletries*. I always get those words confused.' He tried to cover his embarrassment. 'Don't you?'

'You are never to cook for me, young man.'

'Deal,' said Jacob. 'Now, if you'll excuse me …'

'I'm so glad I've run into you,' continued his interlocutor, who evidently had not excused him at all. 'I'm Sylvia Hodgeport, and – though I say it myself – I have one of the most interesting collections on the West Coast.'

'What type of collection?' He had, for the moment, given up on escaping from Sylvia.

'Rocking horses, of course. Naturally, my collection can't compare with that of the museum …'

'Is *yours* at least open to the public?'

'Oh, no,' said Sylvia solemnly. 'Why, think of the mud.'

Jacob, obligingly, considered the mud. Then he remembered where he'd heard the name 'Sylvia Hodgeport' before. She was the person that the curator had alluded to as doubting his legitimate claim to that title.

'You're from Denver, aren't you?' She was now looking at him in a way that could only be described as 'peering'.

'No, I am not from Denver,' he said irritably. 'Nor do I have any plans in the foreseeable future to be from Denver. At present, I'm much too busy.'

'Hmph,' snorted Sylvia. 'Too busy shopping for *condiments,* I suppose. Well, you certainly *look* like you're from Denver.' She really gave the impression that she thought he was lying.

'What does that mean? Is it my altitude or something?'

'Don't be a dickwad.' That was one thing his real grandmother had never said to him. 'You look like Osbert.'

'I see,' said Jacob. 'I look like Osbert. Of course I do. Um … *Osbert?'* He tried to make the question sound like a polite one, though he had doubts as to whether 'Osbert' was even a real name.

'Osbert is from Denver.'

He'd had just about enough of this. 'This has been a very educational experience, Ms Hodgeport. But now I'd really better –'

'It was Osbert who named my first rocking horse, as a matter of fact.'

Jacob wondered whether letting someone who was himself called Osbert name *anything* was such a good idea; but he kept this thought to himself.

'Dear Mary!'

This seemed like a mild oath for somebody who'd just called him a dickwad. 'What's wrong?' he asked solicitously. If Sylvia had suddenly realised she'd left the water running in the bathtub, he'd be glad to call her a cab.

'Nothing's wrong. I was just allowing myself a sentimental moment to reminisce about Mary.'

181

'Mary?'

'The rocking horse. The one Osbert named. Are you not paying attention, young man?'

So, it had taken every ounce of the prodigious talent of Osbert from Denver – whoever he was – to come up with the name Mary. 'I'm sorry,' said Jacob. 'Perhaps you'd like another sentimental moment or two to yourself. I could go shop, or, you know, leave the neighbourhood or something.'

'Ridiculous! I haven't even told you about Dr Peach-Bottom Yum-Yum McGillicudy.'

Jacob blinked, as if he'd been hit in the head with a pillow. 'Is she from Denver, too?'

'Dr Peach-Bottom is another one of my horsies. That one I named myself,' she said proudly. 'I found her in the back of a barbershop in 1959. And what I was doing in the back of that barbershop is another story.' She laughed salaciously and slapped Jacob on the shoulder. Then she abruptly regained her stiff demeanour. 'I tell you, it's a relief to be able to talk to someone who understands horsies,' she said earnestly. Jacob felt as if he might, at any moment, be expected to retrieve a sugar lump from his pocket.

'The twins came later, of course,' Sylvia continued.

'Of course.'

'Derek and Tibbits, I mean. Not Cakebox and Lesser Humphrey.'

It occurred to Jacob that 'Lesser Humphrey' sounded more like a typeface – or possibly an English hamlet – than a rocking horse.

'I like you, Jacob Hastings,' said Sylvia, though her demeanour had largely implied the opposite. 'You're easy to talk to. We must go somewhere where we can *really* talk.' She smiled possessively.

Oh, good lord, was she actually trying to pick him up? Visions of Sylvia and her lovers spending abandoned nights among the likes of Dr Peach-Bottom Yum-Yum McGillicudy and 'the twins' sent his head spinning.

It was not, strictly speaking, courteous of Jacob to

deliberately upset an entire display of toilet paper in order to create a diversion and make his exit.

But it was what he did.

'How'd the errands go?' asked Normandie.

Jacob bristled but reminded himself that it wasn't her fault. 'I decided to do it tomorrow morning, instead,' he explained calmly. Then, turning to her for solace, he related his adventures with Sylvia.

Normandie sympathized, laughed, and patted his shoulder. Perhaps unfortunately, she then began to give expression to a train of thought that his narrative had prompted.

'I gave my rocking horse a silly name, too,' she remembered. 'Ginger Crabgrass Crescendo.'

'And you raised an eyebrow at "Elizabeth Marjoram"?'

She ignored this comment. 'I used to imagine that Ginger and I were in the opera together, or working as gardeners.'

'I don't see the connection.'

'Didn't you ever have a rocking horse?'

'No. But lately I seem to have made up for lost time.'

'Ginger and I spent countless hours together after school.'

'Which one of you was in school?'

'She was better than milk and cookies.'

Jacob settled in for a long evening. He couldn't deny it, though –'Ginger Crabgrass Crescendo' had a certain ring to it.

# Chapter Twenty-nine

KATE REALLY HATED THESE receptions. Really, really hated them. The department heads and administration had to mingle and pretend to be buddies, when the reality was that most department heads were strangers to each other, and most of them were afraid of the administration – for whom cutting budgets seemed to fall right behind breathing, eating, and sleeping as regular activities. Kate, of course, wasn't afraid of anybody; but she wasn't particularly interested in any of them, either. The exceptions were the people, like Tommy the friendly neighbourhood provost, who actually *were* her buddies. But those people she'd rather interact with in a bar – or a bed – than here at the Hauser University reception garden. And, hell, Tommy wouldn't even be here, Kate reminded herself. The brat was on vacation.

'Well, *you* must be proud as a peacock, Kate.' Jim Donning from Engineering.

'I'm always proud as a peacock, Jim,' she rejoined. 'But what the hell are you talking about?' She thought it best to play dumb.

'Your Dr Stephens. Your –' He fumbled in the air for the next word, as though the cosmos could coalesce around his fingertips. 'Your galaxy, or whatever it is.'

'Oh, it's not really mine. I think the university owns any galaxy we discover using their telescope.'

Donning laughed at this. Would he leave her alone now? Kate was relieved when he raised his plastic beer cup in a salute to her and removed himself, sacrificing her company for that of a rapidly diminishing bowl of potato chips. But, unlike the potato chips, there were more where he came from.

'*Kathérine!*' said Livia Farmer from Romance Languages,

masquerading, as usual, as someone of vaguely European birth. 'Not too uppity to speak to us, with a *galaxy* under your belt, I hope?'

'Uppity yours, Livia,' said Kate, pretending that she meant it in fun. 'So, how's the language racket?'

'Can't complain, dear. Of course, I haven't been around much this semester – as you know, it's my sabbatical, and I've been spending most of my time in Chicago, doing work at *Matthieu Grève's* institute.' Kate noticed that the name of the prominent structuro-semiologist was dropped with the usual clatter.

'So I hear. And I hope the union is blessed with many micro-structuro-semiologues. But who's running your department in the meantime? Keeping the faculty from putting gum under the chairs, I mean. Did you leave Lewis in charge – or is his little plagiarism boo-boo too recent a memory?'

'Excuse me, Kathérine, but I must speak to the dean before she leaves.'

Kate congratulated herself. Decades of associating with annoying colleagues had certainly not left her devoid of tactics when it came to ridding herself of them.

But now, she wasn't sure what to do. There was nobody she wanted to talk to, and she was especially wary of fielding questions about the delicate matter of the Rocking Horse Galaxy. Yet she couldn't, alas, leave quite this early without meeting with administrative disapproval. She wasn't hungry – and what little food had been offered was mostly gone by now. After all, they were twenty minutes into the party.

This left one option, and she exercised it.

The scotch went down smoothly, and it hit the spot.

'You guys are bluffing, aren't you.'

The quiet, confident baritone surprised her, and she almost spilled her second scotch as she spun around to face him. 'Hi there, Julius.'

'Kate, Kate, Kate,' said Hauser University's token poet.

'Is that some new kind of blank verse?' teased Kate. She

liked Julius French, the big, walrusy bard – liked him even when he was holding her dirty laundry up before her eyes. She didn't know he was going to be here – she'd forgotten that the English Department chair had passed to him, more or less by default, last semester.

Julius put his tongue out. 'Shows how much *you* know. *Kate* rhymes with *Kate* rhymes with *Kate* ... so it's rhymed verse, not blank verse. You'd better stick to discovering non-existent galaxies, young lady.'

Two scotches and a boyish seventy-year-old poet on her ass, and Kate Passky was going pleasantly wet in the knickers. 'Whaddya mean, 'non-existent'?' She poked him in the ribs.

He chuckled the type of deep, resonant chuckle that Kate imagined the jollier sorts of poets had been chuckling since time immemorial. 'You're forgetting, my dear ... I used to be a scientist, until they threw me out for excess creativity.'

She would take this kind of jibe from him, as from few others. And how she preferred his insinuating 'my dear' to the icy 'Kathérine' she'd fielded just a few minutes earlier from Livia.

'I know how discoveries of this type come to light, in the normal course of events.' Julius was one of the few people who could get away with saying things like 'in the normal course of events,' Kate observed to herself. 'Yours is fishy.'

'You might like to know that the last person who hassled me about this was our esteemed colleague Hube Renkins.'

Julius laughed so loud that heads turned. 'Good for Hube,' he said quietly. 'It just goes to show how far a little pettiness can take you.'

'Personally, I wish it would take him farther. Much farther. New Zealand would be nice, for example.'

'Anyway, we don't have to talk about this.'

'No,' Kate said pointedly, 'we don't.'

'And rest assured I won't say anything to anyone else. I wouldn't dream of jeopardizing whatever it is you naughty scientists are up to. I just wanted to tease you a bit. I'm bored here, and you're the only person it's any fun to talk to.'

'You can be a pain in the faculty ass, Julius, you know that?'

'See – you're fun to talk to even when you're cranky.'

She couldn't resist his charisma any longer, and they laughed together this time.

'Won't you take me home with you, Kate? I promise to wipe my feet on the way in.'

She gave it serious consideration. It was, from a sexual point of view, appealing … and, even aside from the sex, she could certainly do worse than to spend a chunk of her evening bandying words with Julius. But she felt she really didn't have the energy to be that sociable tonight.

'Rain check,' she finally said.

'That's what you said last time.' He was pouting.

'OK, so I owe you *two* rain checks. Or, if you prefer, one snow check.'

'Call if you change your mind. I'm always up late.'

As Kate walked home, she was looking forward to a bath, and some private time in bed.

In the bath, she thought about Julius, and she chuckled retroactively at his mischievous behaviour. Her soapy fingers found her pussy lips as she relished a vision of his boyish face in her mind's eye.

Should she have taken him home? Maybe … but it was so nice to be alone. And Kate Passky didn't need a man to get off. She was going to get off tonight, unassisted, and damn nicely, thank you very much. She was already so wet inside from anticipating the pleasure she planned to bring herself that she decided to slow things down, to better savour a nice, slow build-up.

Fresh from the bath, she spread out, face up, on the bed. She let her hands reach for the far corners of the mattress and her heels anchor things at the bottom. Her juncture breathed in the refreshing night air, which tickled across the moisture left by the bath – and prompted an answering moisture within. Wallowing in her privacy, she gyrated her pelvis to drink in these sensations. For the moment, she held off on touching herself, basking prefatorily in her consciousness of Kate Passky's bed as Kate Passky's own place of pleasure. How luxurious it was sometimes to lie waiting for her personally delivered ecstasies, with no collaborating man or woman tangled up in her privacy.

With studied languor, she brought one hand down to where her hunger was simmering. Lightly, she tested the texture of her delicate lips, assessing the degree to which they'd begun to bloat themselves with arousal. A dribble of juice giggled into her hand, and she sensuously ground her smart, sexually empowered ass into the bed, preparing to take possession of herself.

At first, the two fingertips that edged just inside did so tentatively, bringing a light, exploratory pressure to bear – like fingers running along the rim of a glass of water. Kate bucked into herself, playing a two-sided game of tease and respond, asking herself for more.

She gave it to herself.

The fingers entered in earnest now, connecting liquidly with her yearning and ever-more-awake inner walls. The bucking motion morphed into a riding posture, as she giddyapped raunchily upon her digits and used the heel of her hand as a clitoral saddle horn. Her derrière bounced athletically, and the mattress springs answered her equestrian fucking with an asinine *heehaw*.

She became a rocking boat, a tight little one-woman dinghy splashing about in her own wake. In private, she could make herself come like nobody's business. God, it felt good. It was crazy how good one woman could feel in a bedroom at ten o'clock at night.

*Ten o'clock*. Only ten o'clock. The figure danced in Kate's head as the orgasm receded from a tidal wave to a bathtub-size current. Maybe she'd give Julius a call, after all. Just because she'd been great in bed without him didn't mean she couldn't share the wealth a little bit.

# Chapter Thirty

JACOB FELT, ABSURDLY, LIKE a dad when he got behind the wheel of the car, with Normandie beside him and Susan in the back seat.

The clear weather and miraculous near-emptiness of the highway seemed to give a blessing to the adventure that was the journey to Los Angeles. Jacob was ambivalently excited – the combination of publicity and deception was, if nothing else, a stimulating prospect to consider, and the fact that he would not personally be under the studio lights this time gave him additional leisure to enjoy bouts of anxiety and trepidation from a more objective perspective.

He also welcomed the excursion for its own sake, for the sheer romance and recreation it provided. They had plenty of time – they'd all arranged to pad the excursion with several extra days, to take full advantage of the change of scene – and there was no reason that the next few days couldn't be very pleasant ones.

'Who, exactly, is this guy you're getting to be the astronomer this time?' Susan asked.

'His name is Brandon,' said Jacob.

'Sharp guy?'

Normandie and Jacob looked at each other.

'We're going to give him plenty of coaching,' said Normandie.

'Eek,' said Susan softly.

'He'll be fine,' Normandie insisted.

'If you say so,' Jacob concurred.

'The main thing we all need to remember,' said Normandie calmly, 'is that the host, the studio audience, and the viewers *want* to believe in rocking horse galaxies. And, being lay people rather than snotty astronomy colleagues like Hube Renkins, they have no reason to doubt that, when we tell them about a rocking horse galaxy, we're on the level. Why would it even occur to anybody – anybody other than Renkins – that we'd made the whole thing up?'

'When you put it that way, it almost makes me question my belief that we *did* make the whole thing up.'

'Trust me, we did. But don't forget that we've since halfway redeemed ourselves with the bona fide Smeared Sled Object … as enhanced by Susan, of course.'

'Yay!' said Susan from the back seat.

'Add to that the fact that Hube, for what it's worth, is now on our side, and one can almost feel like we're operating from a position of great leverage.'

'You think one idiotic astronomer cheering us on from his living room couch gives us leverage?'

'Let's call it a psychological leg-up. The show is taped, though, so we'll have to visualise Hube's cheering as a future event.'

'If it's all right with you, I will personally try to avoid visualising Hube at all.'

'To be honest,' said Normandie, 'the only thing I'm worried about is keeping the host's interest long enough to really make the most of this opportunity. I've watched the show a few times, and if Priscilla Ray senses that the audience is bored – or that *she's* bored – she'll go to a commercial, and you'll find yourself out with the vending machines by the time the ad's over.'

'Eek,' said Susan.

'Will you please stop saying "eek",' requested Jacob, with a hint of testiness. 'You're going to use up all the "e"s.'

'Sorry,' said Susan.

'Jacob,' said Normandie. 'The fact that you happen to be driving doesn't give you the right to be bossy.'

'You're right. Sorry, Susan. You can say 'eek' as much as you like.'

'Eek,' said Susan, calmly, trying it on for size.

They had begun with only a quarter tank of gas, and Jacob elected to take an exit and replenish. 'This looks like an "easy on, easy off",' he said.

'Easy to get it on, easy to get off,' Susan echoed.

She and Normandie got out to stretch their legs while Jacob procured the gasoline. The landscape was dull at this particular turn-off, and Normandie was a bright spot in her raspberry-sherbet T-shirt and aqua-tinted jeans. Her breasts looked especially like fruits today, thought Jacob. The subtle but seductive flare of her hips drew his eye as she loosened her limbs and blinked in the sunlight, and he developed his first erection of the day.

'I'm going to run into the restroom,' she said. 'How about you, Susan?'

'I'll wait,' she said.

Susan was dressed like the complete California traveller, smart in a vintage mini-dress, sandals, and sunglasses.

'Look!' She pointed across the parking lot, where the driver of some sort of tour bus was standing by as his customers re-boarded the vehicle.

Jacob saw why the bus had attracted Susan's attention. The customers were all women, and each of them planted a kiss on the bus driver's cheek as she embarked.

'How quaint,' said Jacob. 'I wonder what type of group that is.'

Normandie was just rejoining them, and they directed her attention to the ongoing attraction.

'Do you think they're all his aunts?' asked Normandie.

'I think maybe he's getting married tomorrow, and those are his ex-girlfriends,' Jacob theorised.

'I think we should kiss *our* driver,' said Susan.

They moved back to their car. Before Jacob got in, Susan dashed around and gave him an enthusiastic kiss on the cheek.

'Me, too, then,' said Normandie. She sauntered slowly over and kissed him fully on the lips.

'Wait a second!' said Susan. 'No fair.' She approached Jacob again. 'I only did this.' She repeated her peck.

'Whereas *you* did *this.*' She dipped Jacob back for a full-force, ten-second lip lock.

When they came up for air, Normandie tapped Susan on the shoulder, in the time-honoured tradition of cutting in. 'No, I didn't. If I'd meant to do *this,*' – here she gave Jacob a dip of her own – 'then *this*' – she did it again – 'is what it would have looked like.'

'Fair enough,' said Susan. They all got into the car.

'I've never been to LA,' Susan remarked after a while. 'Do people have hot sex in LA?'

'It's a possibility,' said Normandie. 'What did you have in mind?'

Susan's laughter was slightly wild. 'Oh no. I'm just along for the ride, right?'

'I think that's probably up to you,' Normandie answered. 'Remember, you're our guest – and guests usually get what they want.'

'I may hold you to that,' Susan said quietly.

Normandie glanced into the auto club guidebook she'd brought along. 'You're in luck, Susan. It says here that people have hot sex in Los Angeles.'

They spent much of the next hour eating shards of pitta bread with dollops of baba ghanoush, all of which had come out of Normandie's tote bag along with the guidebook.

'All right, I have to pee now.' Susan announced it as if she were announcing her impending marriage. Jacob took the exit.

'I hope you're coming with me,' she said to Normandie from outside the car.

'I don't have to.'

'Please just come in and talk to me from the sink,' Susan pleaded. 'That's half the fun of a road trip.'

Normandie made eye contact with Jacob and shrugged.

'I'd offer to take your place,' said Jacob, 'but ...'

Normandie got out of the car. 'No worries,' she said. 'I'd hate to miss out on *half* the fun of this entire trip.'

'Race you!' said Susan. And she dashed into the service plaza.

'What did you talk about?' Jacob asked when they returned.

'The girl's quick,' said Normandie. 'We barely had a chance to break the ice.'

'Hee,' said Susan.

Jacob wasn't sure if his energy level could accommodate four days of accommodating Susan, on top of Normandie (or Susan, on top of him … or under him). Travelling was fun, but exhausting in and of itself. Normandie was on record as being 'frisky in hotels'. And then there was that little matter of a television appearance to survive. All told, Jacob felt that vitamins were in order.

'Hotel room,' said Normandie with relish. 'Just the phrase makes me horny.'

She sat on the bed nearest the door, testing it out. An instant later, Susan followed them into the room and threw her bags onto the other bed.

'You're sure?' said Susan. 'About just one room?'

Normandie smiled. 'Saves money, you know. Unless you're uncomfortable?'

'Hee,' said Susan. She then, without further ceremony, slipped out of her skirt and top.

'I'm going to take a rest,' she said. Judging by her body language, Jacob decided it was very important to Susan that they see her private ass sliding in between her solitary covers with nothing but panties on it.

He embraced Normandie. 'I could go for a "rest", too.'

Normandie whispered in his ear. 'Did you like seeing Susan get into bed, Mr Horny-Pants?'

He whispered back. 'Yes, as a matter of fact I did.'

'I have panties on, too,' came Normandie's return whisper. 'Would you like to see them?'

Susan sat up in bed. 'I would!'

'Yes, we would,' said Jacob, taking in Susan with a courteous nod.

Normandie peeled her jeans with a neat efficiency,

193

revealing raspberry-sherbet bikini panties that matched her top. The raspberry bottom drew Jacob's eye as Normandie crossed to a chair to deposit her jeans.

'Do something, Jacob!' said Susan.

This all-in-one-room set-up was going to be interesting, he thought. And he didn't hesitate to 'do something'.

His hand was inside the raspberry panties before she'd even straightened up. He kept it there as she stood and turned, using it to guide her toward the bed.

He let go of her long enough to pull back the covers and shed his jeans. He let his cock wait inside his boxers for now, eager to feel it grow and strain as he rolled around with her. They got under the covers, and he sent his hands everywhere at once to grab and fondle her.

'I can't see!' complained Susan.

Normandie reached for the covers and threw them off, onto the floor.

Jacob went after her pussy, pawing and sniffing at the panties and giving Susan a perfect view of his boxer-packaged male butt.

He had to assume that the playful slap he felt there, moments later, came from Susan – as both Normandie's hands were around his neck.

Normandie's eager motions were so frantic that they prevented Jacob from sliding her panties down. Letting instinct lead the way, he pulled her gusset to the side, released his machine through his underwear slit, and entered her, solidly and crudely – thereby creating a union of two animals, fucking in their nice human underwear.

As they turned each other into pleasure stew, a third animal rode Jacob's ass, howling with glee, her hot pussy in her own hand.

# Chapter Thirty-one

JACOB HAD BEEN WARNED about traffic on the way to the airport – about traffic on the way to anywhere, in fact – so he left himself a ridiculous margin for error when he went to meet Brandon's plane. The result was that he was considerably early. He didn't mind. It not only allowed him to feel self-satisfied about his prudence and punctuality; it also allowed him to stroll aimlessly through the terminal *qua* shopping mall, admiring the colours and lighting and layout, if not perhaps the merchandise itself. And if it so happened that there were plenty of beautiful women walking through the terminal ... well, Jacob could deal with it.

At around the expected time, a familiar face came streaming through the 'beyond this point' exit. But it wasn't the familiar face he'd been expecting. Instead of shaking the hand of Brandon, he found himself embracing Kate.

'What are you doing here?' she said unceremoniously.

'The TV show, remember?'

'I don't mean what are you doing here in *Los Angeles,* cupcake. I mean what are you doing here greeting my plane? I didn't even decide I was coming until this morning, and I thought nobody except my secretary knew.'

By way of a reply, he pointed at Brandon, who was just now coming through. 'I'm here to meet *him.*'

'That movie-star-of-tomorrow airhead guy who kept calling the flight attendants "dude"? Good luck. What if he isn't interested in meeting you?'

'No, I'm here to *pick him up.* Oh, damn, let me rephrase that...'

'Skip it,' said Kate. She turned to Brandon, who had just joined them. 'Kate Passky, Hauser U. Astronomy.'

Brandon permitted her to grab his wrist in a handshake. 'Whatsup. I'm –' he turned to Jacob. 'Hey, what was that name again?'

'Professor Sinclair Jacobs – and please try to remember it from now on, Brandon. But Professor Passky ...'

'Kate,' she corrected.

'Kate is part of our, um ...'

'Deception,' said Kate. 'So this is the guy who's standing in for you, eh? Yeah, he'll probably look all right on television.' She licked her lips.

'I've been, like, thinking,' said Brandon, who looked concerned. 'This isn't one of those shows where you have to hit a buzzer or whatever before you answer, is it? I'm a total spaz with buzzers.'

'No, Brandon. No manual dexterity will be required. All you'll need are the talking points that Normandie's going to give you. And your common sense,' he added hopefully.

*'What* is *that?'* said Susan, when Jacob arrived with Kate and Brandon. She had opened the door when Jacob knocked. She had been – and was – wearing only a towel.

'What is what?' asked Jacob.

Susan cocked her chin in the direction of Brandon.

'I think you need a pair of glasses to accessorise that towel,' volunteered Kate. 'It's not a "what", it's a "who".'

'That's what I meant,' said Susan.

'Kate, this is Susan. Susan is our friend and personal photographer.'

'Very,' said Susan. 'But enough about Kates and Susans.'

'Hey, I'm Brandon.' He smiled at her.

'Hey.' She glowed at him.

'Speaking of hay,' said Kate, 'I'm about ready to put on the feed bag. Does that toy restaurant downstairs actually work, Jacob?'

'Unless somebody's broken it since we had breakfast.'

'I'll unpack my Crazy Glue, just in case. See you down there in about ten minutes?'

Jacob nodded, and Kate headed around a corner to settle into her room.

'Where's Normandie?' he asked Susan.

'Shower.'

'Brandon, do you think you can find your room?'

'Dude,' said Brandon, with a delivery that implied Jacob was underestimating his intelligence.

'Good. See you at lunch.'

'Me, too,' said Susan. She lingered in the doorway as Brandon headed down the hall.

'Is he *really* that handsome?' Jacob asked, when they were both inside.

'I didn't stop to notice,' said Susan. 'Too busy thinking of ways to eat him up.'

The topic of Brandon's evident charms did not hold infinite interest for Jacob, and he was quickly distracted by the sound of Normandie's shower water running. This was more like it. He put his ear to the door and knocked. 'May I join you?'

'Mmm,' came her voice.

Jacob didn't really need another shower, but this shower was too tempting to resist. Warm, wet, steamy Normandie. 'Frisky in hotel rooms' Normandie.

The stall might have been designed for exactly this – it held the two of them snugly but comfortably, and the water and steam enveloped them perfectly.

'I got a head start,' said Normandie. She brought his hand to her crotch as she kissed him, and he could feel what she meant. She was open. Slippery. Ready. She put her tongue in his mouth, and he felt himself quickly catching up.

The water seemed to help rather than hinder his grip on her ass cheeks as he lifted her up, forward, and finally down, onto his prick. They hadn't fucked in this position – standing up, face to face – in quite a while, and Jacob found that his legs craved it as much as his cock. There was something so satisfying about staggering in place with Normandie split onto him, about letting his knees tremble gently as he thrust up into

197

her. He felt her clenching around him, and he felt the power of feminine legs that could not keep still, due to the intense pleasure radiating out of their juncture.

He kept his friction slow and thorough, scraping himself through her while pulling her body up and down against his lower abdomen – where he knew her clit could take each stroke to heart.

Her arms gripped him, her tongue went wild in his mouth, and her legs lifted to snake around his own. She was dissolving in his embrace, and this made him, in turn, pour himself into her throbbing hole.

Susan had gone down to lunch ahead of them. As Jacob and Normandie walked down alone, he told her about Susan's instant infatuation with Brandon.

'I wonder if that means she's not going to be our girlfriend any more,' said Normandie, only half-joking.

'And just when I was getting used to fucking with an audience,' said Jacob.

Normandie squeezed his hand, and he knew that they understood each other. The two of them were the unit; but their erotic association with Susan was not without meaning.

Susan did all the heavy lifting as far as the lunchtime flirting was concerned, but Brandon made it clear, in his vacant way, that her attention was very welcome. Jacob noticed, for example, that the specific manner in which Brandon stole Susan's french fries showed much more charm and tenderness than the guy had used to pilfer Jacob's own supply in San Francisco.

Back in Jacob and Normandie's room that night, a couple made romantic love in one of the beds … and the other bed rested empty.

## Chapter Thirty-two

'A GAME SHOW?' SAID Jacob. 'I suppose that might be fun. But I sort of wanted to tour the city. I've never been here before, after all, and this is our last free day.' What with one thing and another – and one thing *in* another – they had barely left the hotel at all the day before.

'Think of it this way,' said Normandie. 'You can tour *any* city … but game shows are only in Los Angeles.'

'I can't tour *Los Angeles* in another city.'

'True. Well, look, touring the city would be fine with me, really. But I think it only fair to tell you that *had* we gone to the game show taping, I had planned on attending without panties … and involving you in a little game of my own.'

Jacob sometimes liked to entertain Normandie by reading fine print aloud to her, and the registration form they were required to fill out before gaining admission to the *Think!* taping provided good material.

'*Eligibility is off-limits to employees of the network, their immediate families, their household pets, and their stuffed animals,*' he read. '*Any marionettes, ventriloquist dummies, porcelain figurines, or animatrons belonging to network employees are similarly barred from participating,*' he concluded. 'What do you think of that?'

'I think we'll have a splendid time regardless, Bergen,' said Normandie in her best Charlie McCarthy voice.

Though the free-tickets policy ensured that every taping session of *Think!* played to a full house, it was very easy for Normandie and Jacob to secure seats at the back. Most attendees, eager to get their money's worth out of their free tickets, were dying to sit near the front.

'Remember,' said Normandie. 'No panties.'

'Reminder appreciated but unnecessary.'

The lights went up on the stage, music began playing, and an announcer's voice came over the PA system. While everyone around them came to life with the electricity of a television show about to occur before their eyes, Jacob felt a different type of electricity coursing through him, with Normandie the source. She brought his hand onto her thigh and gave him an impish look.

Her light summer skirt was just billowy enough that a hand could slip under it without unduly stressing the fabric. Whether a hand was or wasn't making itself at home beneath this sort of skirt could be a woman's own secret – and, of course, that of the hand's owner.

With her bareness inviting him, it would have been easy for Jacob to tune out the hubbub of *Think!* – the drama, the music, the cheers. But that wasn't how Normandie's game was to be played.

'We have to keep watching, OK?' she said. 'We have to pay attention to the game, and make it look like we're just typical audience …' she stroked his crotch '… members.'

'Right.' He winked at her, and, in perfect synchronization, they turned their heads to watch what was happening under the lights.

On the stage, three contestants raced each other for the privilege of answering various difficult questions. They used buzzers – as recently described, and feared, by Brandon.

In the audience, a man's right hand found a path beneath some billows to encounter a friendly thigh.

On the stage, an emcee solemnly tested somebody's knowledge of geography.

In the audience, Jacob navigated without a map.

The show went to a commercial.

Jacob's hand went around back and fondled Normandie's bottom, right where it met the vinyl seat.

The show returned to play another round, and Jacob's hand returned from behind, easing its way around a naked hip.

Under the lights, the contestants made progress toward various prizes.

In the dark, Jacob made progress toward one specific prize.

They were getting close.

So was he.

On the stage, a contestant raised her fist triumphantly to celebrate a correct answer. '*Yesss!*' she shouted.

In the audience, a woman spread her legs generously to welcome a wandering hand. '*Yesss,*' she whispered.

The first-place contestant came forward to play a solo round. Slowly but surely, she made her way up a ladder of increasingly valuable questions.

Meanwhile, Jacob's fingers played a solo on Normandie, leading her up a ladder of her own. She was dripping for him, and her lips and clit responded tremulously to every touch.

He needed to unzip, and she was squirming right on the edge.

'*Oh, Jacob.*' When she breathed his name in her moment of ecstasy, he thought he heard it echo all around him.

He did. 'Jacob. Jacob Hastings,' said the emcee. 'You have been randomly selected from our audience today to help Marcy here.'

Inside his trousers, his erection twitched. 'What the hell am I supposed to do *now?*' his penis seemed to be asking him. As the studio filled with applause for Jacob, precum seeped into his briefs and perspiration rose to his brow. With difficulty, he stood. Fortunately, he was wearing a long sweater – a concession to the air conditioning – and he was reasonably confident that only Normandie knew how impossibly horny he was.

Marcy was a cute redhead, and when she smiled at Jacob he almost spilled the spunk he'd built up for Normandie. He tried to focus, instead, on the emcee, a bland-faced middle-aged man who Jacob imagined had made a lateral move into game shows from an earlier career as a bottle of salad dressing.

'Welcome to *Think!*, Jacob,' said the emcee, whose delivery was so dry the show title seemed to lose its exclamation point. The audience applauded again, as did Marcy. 'Where are you from?' asked the emcee, as if he couldn't possibly care less.

'Mountain Coll – er, *San Francisco*.'

'Are you ready to play?'

If only they knew how ready Jacob was to play. He nodded.

'We're going to show Marcy a *Think!* word, and she has to get you to guess the word, *without speaking*. Are you ready, Marcy?'

Jacob knew it was too much to hope that Marcy would say 'No.' She didn't.

'Your hint, Jacob,' continued the emcee, is ... '*reproduction*.'

The audience went wild.

'And here comes the *Think!* word, Marcy.' He pointed, evidently, to a monitor that could be seen by him, by Marcy, and by the audience ... but not by Jacob.

'Remember, Marcy, this is a family programme.'

Marcy made an obvious show of stifling bawdy laughter, and the audience went even wilder. Even the emcee was smirking now.

Marcy went to work, plunging into her pantomime assignment with the over-enthusiastic 'show face' of a high-school drama coach.

Jacob had always been good at charades, and he inferred that Marcy's antics were meant to evoke a person operating a photocopier – despite the fact that it really looked, for all the world, as if she were miming several concurrent acts of sexual intimacy ... followed by a few more consecutive acts, just for good measure. 'Photocopying,' he said weakly.

Marcy shrieked and rushed over to hug him. He thought he saw her eyes glow a little brighter when her thigh accidentally grazed his undiminished hard-on.

He returned to his seat, amid thunderous applause, and

collapsed. Normandie embraced him. 'Relax,' she whispered.

With his eyes on the next round of *Think!* – the final episode in Marcy's adventure – he felt the world opening up under his sweater. Normandie was busy with a zipper ... busy with the fly of underpants ... busy with a handful of Jacob.

'I won!' screamed Marcy from the stage.

Normandie's plan had been to start coaching Brandon over dinner, with the tutorial continuing into the evening. But though she and Jacob were able to persuade Brandon – and Susan – to join them for pasta at an agreeable-looking establishment down the block from the hotel, the rapport that had developed between their friends over the past twenty-four hours seemed to translate into a full-time job. During dinner, it monopolised even the attention of Jacob and Normandie, who greeted the other couple's under-the-table shenanigans with voyeuristic interest.

'Drop your napkin,' Normandie whispered to Jacob. When he'd done so, she said 'Oops,' and ducked down to retrieve it. She was slow to resurface, leaving Jacob to imagine – probably with a fair degree of accuracy – what she was seeing down there. When, at last, she returned to sea level, she indicated that she'd seen some hot stuff by means of a subtle wink in Jacob's direction. He noticed that Brandon and Susan each had only one hand visible above the table.

'OK,' said Normandie as dinner concluded. 'Fun is fun ...'

'And then some,' said Jacob.

'... but those of us who are going on TV tomorrow had better hit the books.'

'Me?' asked Brandon. 'No problem.'

Normandie looked at her watch. 'How about the rec room at 8?'

'Sure,' said Brandon, as though it didn't much matter, but what the heck.

'The rec room is perfect,' said Jacob quietly to Normandie as they walked back to the hotel. 'Because a wreck is exactly what I'm going to be if we don't see young Brandon applying himself.'

Jacob and Normandie had already played a game of ping-pong – and chased each other around the table for some reciprocal goosing – when they realised that it was 8:15 and they still had the room to themselves.

'Look!' said Normandie.

Jacob followed her gaze, through a window at one end of the room. He hadn't noticed it before, but it gave them a nice view of the hotel's indoor swimming pool. And of Susan and Brandon, stark naked, cavorting in it.

'They look great together,' said Normandie.

'You said a mouthful,' said Jacob.

Brandon had now lifted Susan by the ass and was holding her with her pussy at his face, while her legs dangled over his shoulders. The fluorescent lights tickled over their wet bodies, giving the onlookers in the rec room an extra-dazzling show.

'How about another game of ping-pong?' Normandie suggested.

# Chapter Thirty-three

'WHY ARE YOU SO nervous? *You're* not going in front of three television cameras at 5 this afternoon.'

Jacob stopped pacing the hotel room just long enough to look at Normandie and shrug.

'It's a good thing Susan's been sleeping elsewhere. You're filling up her entire side of the room with your lengthy, neurotic strides.'

'I know.'

'You're also kicking up dust.' She punctuated the observation with a diminutive sneeze.

'Junior gesundheit. And I'm sorry. But when I get this way, exercise is the only thing that relaxes me.'

'So, is it relaxing you?'

'No.'

'Hmm ...' said Normandie. 'Come here.'

Jacob paced his way back to her.

'Let's try a different kind of exercise.'

Soon she had both parties in a convenient state of nudity. 'You lie on your back on the bed, and I'll show you how this works.'

'Sounds good already. Can I keep pacing while I lie on the bed?'

By way of an answer, she pushed him onto the mattress.

She waited until he had properly situated himself, then she squatted over his face so that her pussy was a few inches above his mouth. 'We're going to do lick-ups.'

'Lick-ups?'

'They're sort of like sit-ups. You use your muscles to raise yourself up till your tongue can reach ... me. You keep your head in its raised position for – God, as long as you possibly

205

can, please – then you let it drop back onto the bed. Rest and repeat.'

'I see!' said Jacob.

'Trust me, it will be *great* … uh, exercise.'

That it was. Jacob's abs got a workout each time he strained to reach her. And the tender, exquisite reaction to every touch of his tongue was a more than adequate reward for his efforts. And he was beautifully motivated to repeat the effort time and again. It seemed as if Normandie might even come before he reached his lick-up limit.

The sound of the door opening startled them. Jacob was sure he had taken care to leave the FOR GOD'S SAKE DO NOT FUCKING DISTURB THIS PERPETUALLY HORNY COUPLE sign on the knob.

'Oh, sorry guys,' said Kate. 'Say, are you doing lick-ups?'

Jacob sat up for real as Normandie reluctantly shimmied off his face. 'Why does everyone know about lick-ups but me?' he asked. 'I was just getting the hang of it, too.'

'I can see that,' said Kate. 'And, if I may say so, well hung. As for why you didn't know about lick-ups – I can't answer that one. But I can, for what it's worth and in fifty words or fewer, explain why I barged into your room. I thought you were both still down at breakfast, and I wanted that David Sedaris book, which Normandie said I could borrow. I thought that was why she left the door unlocked – so I could help myself.'

'You left the door unlocked?' said Normandie.

'But I put the sign out,' he whined. 'Besides, I thought hotel room doors locked automatically these days.'

'This door didn't,' said Kate.

'The book is on the dresser,' said Normandie.

'Thanks, kid. I'll try to be quicker with this one than with that mystery you loaned me. That one's still lying around my living room, half-read.'

'That's all right,' said Normandie. 'You can leave a mystery lying around for months, and it won't spoil. Unless someone tells you the ending, that is. And now, Kate … well,

206

Jacob was just about to give me an orgasm when you walked in.'

'Perfect,' said Kate. 'That should be even more entertaining than Sedaris.' She settled herself into an armchair.

The door opened again.

Susan looked around – from the nude couple on the bed to the self-possessed woman in the armchair who was clutching a paperback.

'I've lost something,' she announced.

When Susan had told them that she hadn't seen Brandon since 2 a.m. and could not find him anywhere, Normandie's face had frozen. Now, while Jacob and Kate rattled off questions, comments, and a rather impressive assortment of expletives, Normandie continued to impersonate a particularly intelligent-looking mannequin.

Finally, she joined the chorus. 'You know, Susan, the last thing it looked like you were going to do was take your eyes off him,' she remarked.

Susan looked embarrassed. 'Uh, that's exactly it. Hide and seek.'

'*Hide and seek?*' said three well-harmonized voices.

'His idea. After we'd spent time together in the swimming pool ... and his room ... and the tennis court ... and the weight room ... we really couldn't fuck any more.'

'That makes sense so far,' said Jacob, with reserve.

'But we were still keyed-up. You know how it is when you're on vacation. So Brandon said, "Whoa!" – he actually said, y'know, "*whoa*" – "Whoa! We have the whole city to ourselves."'

'Give or take 10 million people,' said Kate.

'Counting was never Brandon's strong suit,' said Normandie.

'No,' said Jacob, 'that would be cunnilingus.'

'Jacob, you peeked,' said Susan. 'But I didn't. He suggested I give him a head start, and then try to find him.'

'*Find him?* In the *entire city of LA?*' asked Kate, incredulously.

'He said we should limit it to Hollywood and Burbank, for simplicity's sake.'

'For simplicity's sake,' Kate repeated. 'And you told him this game sounded like a good idea?'

'No, of course not. Just because Brandon is a very, very handsome idiot, it doesn't mean I'm an idiot, too. I told him it sounded, no offence, like a crazy and stupid idea. I think he may have taken that as a compliment.'

'So he ran out, while you … counted to 1,000?' asked Normandie.

'I, um, fell asleep at around 480.'

'But you just said you were keyed-up!'

'I made the mistake of counting the numbers as sheep,' said Susan. 'Baa,' she added, unhelpfully.

'So now it's just a matter of checking the 800 after-hours dance clubs in the area and finding out which one he passed out in,' said Jacob.

'Cinch,' said Kate. 'That's only 200 clubs apiece.'

'Except that they'd all be closed at ten o'clock in the morning,' said Normandie.

'Look,' said Kate. 'This is silly. Not as silly as Brandon, granted – but silly nonetheless. The guy's got to figure out that Susan hasn't found him – and possibly hasn't even gone looking for him – and he'll get his handsome behind back here in plenty of time to go on TV.'

'And to get to the studio in heavy LA traffic,' added Jacob.

'And to learn everything I need to teach him about astronomy,' said Normandie.

'So,' said Kate, with a little less assurance, 'all we have to do is sit tight, relax, and wait for him to come back, like any responsible adult would.'

The hotel room was silent for a few seconds. Then Normandie spoke.

'Come on,' she said. 'Let's go find the idiot.'

# Chapter Thirty-four

'WELL,' SAID NORMANDIE TO Jacob, 'you wanted a tour of LA.'

'Just Hollywood and Burbank,' Susan reiterated. 'Where is that, anyway?'

'Don't worry,' said Normandie. 'Jacob will drive, and you can keep counting to 1,000.'

'Baa,' said Susan.

If driving with Normandie and Susan as passengers had made Jacob feel like a dad, driving Normandie, Susan, and Kate made him feel like a school bus driver. A school bus driver who didn't know his destination ... or his route.

'According to my guidebook,' said Normandie, 'there's a high concentration of dance clubs in West Hollywood.'

'That doesn't sound promising,' said Jacob. 'Brandon doesn't seem very good at concentrating.'

'Nevertheless, I think we should head that way. The clubs, as discussed, will be closed ... but maybe he will have moved on to a video game arcade or a baseball card emporium or something.'

From the back seat, Susan snapped her gum.

Jacob slowed down to cruising speed when they arrived in the right part of town. 'So what are we looking for, exactly?'

'Anything that would attract a nimrod like Brandon,' said Normandie.

'A *lovable* nimrod,' Susan corrected.

'Stop!' said Kate.

'But he *is* lovable.'

'No – I meant stop the vehicle.'

Jacob stopped the vehicle.

'That little shop with the twin turntables set up in the

window. It looks like some sort of DJ place. And it's open.'

'Those aren't turntables, Kate, they're burners. That's a crêperie,' said Normandie.

'Oh,' said Kate.

Jacob began moving again.

'Stop!' said Kate.

'What now?' asked Normandie.

'Since you mentioned it, I could really go for some crêpes,' said Kate.

After breakfast, they resumed the search. This time, it was Susan who requested a stop.

'Look at them,' she said reverently.

She was alluding to a couple – she in a grey skirt, a black denim jacket, and fishnets; he in a thrift-shop seersucker jacket and retro-chic porkpie hat – standing against a brick wall, around the corner from a grocery store, photogenically making out.

'I'm glad I brought my camera,' said Susan. 'I'll be right back.'

Jacob and the others watched from an illegal parking space across the street while Susan negotiated for permission to take some shots of the passionate couple. Jacob could see how nicely the light was playing off their wall, and, despite everything, he couldn't blame Susan for interrupting the chase. When things were, evidently, settled, he watched Susan's efficient immortalization of their magical brick-wall snogging and groping. The woman's favourite pose seemed to be one in which her fishnet thigh teased the edge of her boyfriend's cords, while he kissed her throat.

One soft-core erotic photo session later, their car began moving again.

West Hollywood was, of course, full of storefronts that were open ... but none of them seemed particularly promising, Brandon-wise; and they certainly didn't have time to pop in and out of all of them indiscriminately.

'This was probably a stupid idea, to come running after him,' Normandie admitted at noon.

'I bet we'll have a better experience in Burbank,' said Susan.

'Why?' asked Jacob.

'Because it's a funny word.'

But they did not have a better experience in Burbank. In the absence of any further crêpe breakfasts or appealingly amorous couples, it could even be said that they had an inferior experience.

It was nearly quarter to two when Jacob suddenly pulled over.

'What is it?' asked Normandie.

'Just a hunch.'

He had stopped in front of a modest establishment, decorated with small, coloured lightbulbs and labelled as follows:

LI'L PEGGY'S DISCO TAQUERIA

'Ah,' said Normandie. 'I see what you mean.'

They never did learn if the 6'1" blonde Brandon was dancing with when they found him was Li'l Peggy. Nor did they learn whether Brandon had, technically, ordered the basket of spicy, deep fried filberts they were sharing on the dance floor – or whether those were compliments of the house.

'Hey!' said Brandon, with a grin of the shit-eating variety, to none of them in particular and without breaking out of his groove. 'Awesome place, huh?' Then he came toward them and addressed Susan. 'OK, so, now you get to hide.' He kissed her.

'Brandon!' said Normandie. 'We have to prepare for the taping. Professor Sinclair Jacobs, remember? Astronomy, remember? *Today,* remember?'

'Yeah, no problem,' said Brandon, as though he thought Normandie might feel bad about having brought the subject up. 'I was starting to wonder if it was about time to get ready for that.'

'Whoa – I don't know if I can learn stuff in a taxi,' Brandon advised Normandie.

'Well, we're going to find out,' she retorted. 'Because we're in a taxi, and I'm sure as hell going to be trying to teach you stuff. Fortunately, with traffic, we've got at least half an hour to work with.'

'Traffic's clear today, lady,' said the cabbie, a kid with a vaguely skate punk look who, Jacob decided, only called people 'lady' when he was on duty. Perhaps the dispatcher required it, Jacob speculated.

'Thanks a lot,' Normandie said to the driver.

'Don't thank me, lady. I didn't clear the traffic.'

She took a deep breath. 'OK, Brandon. I'm Priscilla, and I'm interviewing you. Remember, your name is Sinclair Jacobs, and you're an expert on astronomy. Got it?

'No,' said the cabbie. 'If his name is Sinclair Jaybert, why do you keep calling him "Brandon"?'

'*Jacobs,* not Jaybert,' said Jacob.

'Whatever.'

Normandie ignored the driver and continued to address Brandon. 'Professor Jacobs, what's your specialty?'

'I mix a pretty good martini,' said Brandon.

'No you don't,' said Normandie.

'*Yeah,* I do,' said Brandon, contentiously.

'I mean, you don't *say* that. You say – and repeat after me – "My research is chiefly in the area of galactic spectrum variations."'

Brandon swallowed. 'My research is chiefly in the area of galantic speculum variations.'

'Oh, good grief,' said Kate, who was sitting in the front-most passenger seat of the minivan and had hitherto been uncharacteristically silent.

'At least he got *variations* right,' said Jacob.

'*Galactic!*' shrieked Normandie. 'For crying out loud, haven't you ever watched *Star Trek?*'

'Oh yeah,' said Brandon. 'Right.'

'I love *Star Trek,*' said the driver amiably. 'Do you guys know the one where …'

'No,' said both Normandie and Jacob, with a certain finality in their tone.

Normandie took another deep breath. 'OK, I'm Priscilla again. Here's the next question …'

'Hey,' said Susan. 'If you're Priscilla, can I be Rhone Preston?'

'He's not on this programme,' said Jacob.

'I know. But we're just pretending.'

'No,' said Normandie officially. 'Nobody is Rhone Preston.'

'Sure, somebody is Rhone Preston,' said the driver. 'My brother up in SF watches him all the time. Doesn't look anything like *her*, either.' He jerked his thumb in Susan's direction. 'No offence, lady.'

'Please, Susan,' said Jacob gently. 'I'm afraid you're not helping. Doesn't it concern you that Brandon is going to make a complete fool of himself?'

Susan shrugged.

'All right,' said Normandie. 'Pay attention, *Professor Jacobs*.'

'Sorry,' said Jacob.

'Not you,' said Normandie.

'Sorry,' said Jacob.

'Could you tell us about the most important technique you've been using to identify the compositional elements of distant galaxies?'

'Hornstein optical blots that utilize hybridized, lichen-digested chlorophyll dye.'

Normandie's eyes widened. 'That's excellent, Brandon! How in the world did you know about that?'

'It's, like, a song lyric. Wanna hear the rest of it? It's kind of dirty.' Brandon chuckled.

'Yes, please,' said Susan.

'No, not now,' said Normandie, superseding her. 'In fact, we're almost there. So I suppose we'll just have to hope that Priscilla only asks you that one question, over and over.' She seemed ready to cast her fate to the winds.

'I thought *you* were Priscilla,' said the driver.

'Brandon looks so clever in his little necktie,' Susan informed Jacob.

'Maybe the necktie can answer the questions,' said Kate.

'So anyway,' said the cabbie, 'Kirk and Spock are standing on the bridge, and there's this …'

# Chapter Thirty-five

'I'M MARTY,' SAID A cherubic young man to Normandie, after they'd swept into the studio offices. 'I'm the fella who called you after we watched you on the transcript of Rhone's show. You were fab. Great television.'

The man was certainly an improvement over the haughty staffer who'd handled their *Insomnia* appearance.

'It's great to finally meet you, Dr Stephens.' He shook her hand enthusiastically. 'And you, Dr Jacobs.'

He extended a hand toward Jacob, who automatically moved to take it. But, in one swift motion, Normandie elbowed Jacob in the ribs and pushed Brandon forward.

'*This* is Professor Jacobs,' she said.

'But I thought –'

'Professor *Sinclair* Jacobs. He'll be sharing the spotlight with me today. You're probably a little confused because the *other* Dr Jacobs here – his brother, *Ernie* Jacobs – appeared with me on Rhone Preston.'

'Oh,' said Marty, uneasily.

'They do research as a team, and they divide up their public appearances to prevent any jealousy. You know how sibling rivalry is.' She laughed out an artificial trill. 'It's *Sinclair's* turn to be on TV today, isn't it, Sinclair?' She stood on tiptoes and patted Brandon's head.

'Oh,' said Marty again. He didn't seem quite satisfied. 'OK. I … uh … I don't want to be a problem, or cause any family arguments … but we were sort of expecting the same guy we saw before.'

'Trust me,' said Normandie smoothly. 'They're interchangeable.'

'They don't *look* interchangeable,' said Marty.

'That's only because they're brothers. Besides, Ernie *can't* go on TV today. He ...' Jacob saw the manic glint come into her eyes. 'He has laryngitis.'

'That's right,' said Jacob, without thinking, in his usual healthy baritone.

'You don't sound like you have laryngitis,' said Marty politely.

'No, but ... I will.' He assumed an air of authority and confidence. 'I'm subject to a very predictable form of laryngitis, and I'm scheduled to have a bout of it right around the time your taping begins.' He looked at his watch, as if that settled the matter.

'You see?' said Normandie, with a smile.

'Well ... OK,' said Marty. He made a note on his pad. Then he became cherubic again. 'We have a bit of time, folks, so just make yourselves at home here till they come to fetch you for make-up.'

'Psst.' As soon as Marty had disappeared, Normandie took Jacob aside. 'I'm excited now,' she said quietly.

'That's good to hear. Maybe you can actually relax and have some fun with this. You *do* like being on TV, after all.'

'Yes, yes,' said Normandie quickly. 'But that's not what I meant. I mean, I'm *excited* now. H-o-r-n-y.'

'Ah,' said Jacob. 'Then perhaps we can have some fun with *that,* too.' He looked around. 'They can't be using every storage room and closet in this great big building today, can they?'

Normandie twinkled. 'Let's go.' Then she spoke more loudly, to their friends. 'We'll be back soon.'

'Going to find the restrooms?' asked Kate.

'Going to find something,' said Jacob.

Once they were out the door, Normandie squeezed his hand tightly and practically ran him down the hallway. Jacob was glad to let her lead the way – he had learned that she had an instinct for cosy little closets and nice, empty stockrooms.

The otherwise immaculate studio corridor was strewn with segments of the Sunday funnies. As he dashed with

Normandie around this and that corner, Jacob tried to think of a plausible explanation for this ... but he failed. Some Hollywood mysteries were destined to remain mysteries, he told himself.

'In here.'

The room held a slightly ratty but comfortable-looking couch, along with a couple of wheeled costume racks. It was suitably devoid of occupants.

Jacob locked the door behind them, then turned to tackle Normandie's formidable libido.

'Wait a sec.'

He was surprised to hear her say this, at this particular juncture.

'Check out these costumes.'

Almost before he knew what was happening, she was cheerfully unbuttoning the cheerful buttons on her 'I'm going on television' dress. Then, underwear-delicious, she reached for a mini-dress that looked as if it had been soaking for four decades in an ocean of paisley. On the hanger with it was a garland of fake flowers, suitable for wearing in one's hair.

Jacob deduced that some sort of 1960s revue was in production at this studio.

'Fuck me in this ... man,' Normandie said.

'Groovy,' said Jacob, as he helped her into the hippie dress. 'I've always wanted to go to a love-in.'

He crowned her with the flowers. 'Crazy,' he said approvingly.

She pulled him onto the couch. Then she curled up on her side, in an erotic variant on the foetal position, letting her apricot-panty ass peek monochromatically out from the parti-coloured paisley.

He stroked her there. Then he reached up to tickle her under her arm. She laughed with sexual glee, then clenched her upper arm tightly against her torso, holding his finger still – the universal signal that the tickling was enough, for the moment. Jacob let her hold his finger there while he manoeuvred himself behind her. Still zipped, he pressed the

217

cloaked urgency of his erection against her bottom.

After a few seconds, she released her grip on his forefinger – the universal signal that he should tickle her again. Jacob could tell that this was one of those times when precise tickling would play a merry role in Normandie's orgasm. And he could tell, right through her panties and his pants, that she was already wonderfully wet.

He disengaged his finger from her underarm and stood up just long enough to strip from the waist down. Then he returned to his position behind her.

'Hey, man,' said the horny hippie chick, 'these panties just aren't making the scene any more.'

He took the hint, peeled and pulled them and, just for good measure, sniffed them – letting her see that he was doing so. 'Better than incense, baby,' he said before tossing them aside.

Then he gave her rear a slap and went after her in earnest, tickling a little behind her knees and a little inside her thighs, kissing her wetness and then, suddenly, the back of her neck. He could feel her arousal emanating from every inch of her skin as he flitted here and there to stroke and squeeze and tickle.

He was about to plunge into her when she sprang up from the foetal position and clambered on top of him, her eyes delirious with lust. Clearly, she wanted to get off by riding him; and Jacob was all for it. He leaned back and helped her lower her wet, soft groove onto his protrusion; then, as she gave herself a workout astride him, he seasoned her sensations with well-placed titillations, letting the crests of her laughter guide him.

When her hips no longer seemed to be moving by her command and seemed instead to be bouncing crazily of their own accord, Jacob let her delight find its own peak, removing his hands from this and that ticklish zone and resting them simply across the bosom of her dress.

It was a good thing, thought Jacob, as Normandie nearly shattered the walls with an ecstatic scream, that everything was soundproofed in a place like this. The thought repeated itself half a minute later, when a thick shout ripped out of his own mouth into the air, as a dose of bliss-wild fluid sailed forcefully into Normandie. He swallowed. Maybe that lie about the laryngitis would prove to be the truth.

Marty dropped Jacob, Susan, and Kate in the green room en route to taking Normandie and Brandon onto the set. Jacob wanted to send his lover off to television-land with a kiss, but the make-up prevented this. So he patted her shoulder and, ridiculously, shook her hand. Susan patted Normandie on the ass, making Jacob mutter a 'Why didn't I think of that?' Then Susan moved on to Brandon, insinuating her hand into his front trouser pocket while she straightened his clever necktie.

'Do you have that jpeg?' Normandie asked Marty.

'Yep, we're all set,' he replied agreeably, with a nod to Susan. 'Your assistant here gave us a flash drive.'

Once the stars had gone, the hangers-on settled onto the green room couch to watch the show.

'We need popcorn,' said Susan.

'Make mine scotch,' said Kate.

'It's starting,' said Jacob.

Priscilla Ray had matured since Jacob last saw her on a magazine cover. But she was more beautiful than ever. Part of it was simply the way her face appeared to be lit up with sheer delight at the very idea of hosting *Gimme Some Science!* Though the programme had been running for at least a year, Priscilla looked, upon introducing today's instalment, as if she'd just been given the good news that the show had been accepted by the network.

'It's hard choosing which one of them to look at,' said Kate, when the cameras showed Priscilla and Normandie together.

'That's why each of us has two eyes, I guess,' said Jacob. In truth, though, both of his were on Normandie – not only because he loved her and he was proud to see her in the spotlight, but also because he couldn't help thinking about how irresistible she'd looked, just a little while earlier, with

219

her panties off in the auxiliary costume lounge. He saw her smirk as her eyes momentarily greeted the camera – as if she'd read his mind.

Normandie's discussion with Priscilla went much like her discussion with Rhone, with the notable difference that on this occasion her spinning of the Rocking Horse Galaxy yarn was completely premeditated. Jacob could tell that she was excited – probably, once again, sexually excited, among other things – but completely in control.

Until, that is, the discussion grew to embrace Brandon.

'We'll be looking at an image of the fascinating Rocking Horse Galaxy discovery a little later,' said Priscilla. 'Personally, I can't wait,' she added, sounding like she really, really meant it and was possibly even a little bit sexually excited over the prospect herself. 'But I'd like to take a minute now to chat with Professor Sinclair Jacobs, who has come all the way from Mountain College to be with us today. Mountain College … where exactly is that, Professor?'

The camera picked up Brandon just in time for Jacob to see his eyes shifting uncomfortably. 'Oh, it's, y'know, around.'

Normandie looked concerned; but the studio audience laughed, and Priscilla rode their reaction like a pro. 'I suppose, to an astronomer, nothing on the *Earth* can really be considered very far,' she quipped.

Now Normandie laughed – over-enthusiastically, Jacob thought – apparently relieved that the entire interview had not yet fallen apart into a thousand intergalactic pieces.

Priscilla turned serious again. 'What would you say has been your most memorable moment as an astronomer, Professor Jacobs?'

Brandon swallowed. 'OK.' He hesitated. 'OK. There was this one galaxy, and one time a bunch of us scientists were looking at it, and we thought maybe it was *really, really* far away – like, even farther than they're supposed to be. Know what I mean?'

'I think so,' said Priscilla graciously. 'And what's your

current research specialty?'

Brandon spoke slowly and methodically. 'Galactic ... spectrum ... variations.'

The green room couch breathed a collective sigh of relief.

Priscilla smiled, with just a hint of condescension. 'I'm sure our audience appreciates your speaking slowly with the technical terminology, Professor.' The audience laughed self-consciously. 'But,' she said, addressing the theatre, 'he can speed it up a little, can't he?' A chorus of yeses and additional laughter rang out.

She turned back to Brandon. 'Don't overdo it, though,' she teased. 'If you hit 100 beats per minute, I understand the disco ball will automatically come down, and that will be the end of the show.' More laughter.

When the camera returned to Brandon, Jacob could see that the young man had tensed up. 'What do you mean, 100 beats per minute?'

'It was just a joke about dance music. Something the rest of us indulge in while you're up on the roof with your telescope.' The audience continued to titter.

Brandon snorted. 'Dance music? At 100 BPM? Yeah, *right*,' he sneered. 'Guess I'm not going dancing with *you*.'

Priscilla looked as close to nonplussed as television hosts get. 'Um ... that's fine. I don't remember inviting you, actually.'

'120 BPM *minimum*, dude,' Brandon explained. This was obviously very important to him.

Now Priscilla looked irritated. 'It doesn't matter.'

'Like, who the fuck dances at 100 BPM?'

Jacob guessed this was why many programmes – including this one – elected to tape in advance.

The camera pulled back, and Jacob saw a very different Normandie – a livid-with-smile-plastered-on, let's-control-the-damage-before-it's-too-late Normandie. 'I'm so excited about showing you our picture,' she volunteered.

'Yes!' said Priscilla, looking as grateful as if Normandie had just retrieved her cat from the nearest tree. She turned to

221

the camera. 'Can we see that thrilling image of the Rocking Horse Galaxy now? Folks, this has never been shown on TV before. In fact, even I haven't seen it.'

'I hope it comes out OK,' said Susan.

'They'll love it,' said Kate. 'Who wouldn't love a Rocking Horse Galaxy?'

Their attention was riveted on the monitor, as a wide shot of the three individuals on stage was replaced by a vivid image of...

Normandie and Jacob rocking carnally in Susan's studio, wearing nothing but socks.

'Um ... that's my ass,' said Jacob, to nobody in particular.

'Don't overlook Normandie's,' said Kate. 'Her ass is showing up pretty well, too.'

'Oops,' said Susan. 'I must have named both images *rocking.jpg*.'

The monitor returned to an out-of-control studio audience and a host who was now several steps beyond nonplussed.

'Susan!' Normandie was shouting.

'Who the fuck is Susan?' Priscilla Ray demanded, looking helplessly for guidance into the eye of the camera.

# Chapter Thirty-six

JACOB RAISED HIS GLASS. 'Congratulations, darling,' he said. 'Here's to you … and here's to the Hauser University Department of Media Studies.'

Normandie clinked with him. 'It *is* awfully nice of them,' she pronounced, referring to their decision to offer her a tenured position – from which she could continue to teach a smattering of astronomy for Kate, along with the special group of classes that Media had created with her in mind.

'What do they call it again?' asked Jacob.

'The Science in the Popular Mind programme. Otherwise known as "How to invent your own galaxies for fun and profit."'

'And pose *in flagrante* on talk shows.'

'Yes. That's for extra credit.'

Jacob glanced at the menu. 'We'd better order, if we're going to be done in time to make the opening.'

The 'opening' was the kick-off party at the Rocking Horse Palace, a hot new dance spot that Brandon and Susan had created in what had formerly been the Living Museum of the American Rocking Horse. When the museum – which had never really been open – had decided to really close, all concerned had been delighted to discover that by leaving a few of the sturdier 'horsies' with the property, the LMARH foundation snagged a tax write-off while Susan and Brandon snagged an instant theme for their décor.

It had indeed been a momentous month since the aborted, but widely talked about, *Gimme Some Science!* taping – and the awkward sessions that had succeeded it in Kate's and Tommy's offices, resulting in an unceremonious end to the Rocking Horse Galaxy. So Jacob was enjoying the relative placidity of tonight's celebratory restaurant meal. His eyes roamed the soothing environment with approval.

'Oh, no,' he suddenly said.

'What?' said Normandie.

He pointed behind her. 'Sylvia Hodgeport. That grandmotherly rocking horse nut with whom I rubbed elbows – or whatever the clean version of that expression is – at the drugstore. She's coming this way. I swear, if she mentions the name Osbert, I'll scream.'

Sylvia was soon at Jacob's aforementioned elbow. 'Where in the world have you been?' she demanded, by way of initiating conversation.

'I'm sorry,' said Jacob curtly. 'I didn't realise we had a standing appointment at the drugstore.' Then he decided to try to relax, to steer things in a direction of greater civility. 'This is Normandie.'

Sylvia smiled at her. 'I have a rocking horse named Normandie.' Then she focussed once again on Jacob. 'That's what I need to speak to you about.'

'About the fact that you allegedly have a rocking horse named Normandie?' For some reason – probably, he realised, pure stubbornness – he didn't quite believe that Sylvia did.

'About rocking horses in general.'

'Look, Ms Hodgeport, I think you've misunderstood my relationship to …'

'No business of mine!' she assured him brusquely. 'What you and *your* Normandie do, or don't do, behind closed doors…'

'Or on national television …' Normandie muttered.

'… is no business of mine.'

'What I was going to say, Ms Hodgeport, is that I think you've misunderstood my relationship – my level of *commitment,* if you will – to rocking horses.'

'But you and I could have such fun!' Sylvia protested.

'Yes, well …' He felt awkward. 'That's the other thing. I'm sorry, but I'm just not interested, you see, in …'

'But I don't understand,' said Sylvia petulantly. 'Helen at

the *Inveigler* told me that you were looking for work. And you've obviously got a track record on the subject. I would think it would be the perfect job for you.'

'Job? I'm sorry … I don't …'

'Jacob Hastings, are you a total shithead? I'm offering you the editorship of my new specialty magazine about rocking horses, based right here in San Francisco. What in the world did you think I wanted from you?'

'You don't want to know.'

'Well?'

Jacob raised his glass respectfully to Sylvia Hodgeport. 'May I drop by your office in the morning?'

'No.'

'Excuse me?'

'I don't have an office yet. It will have to be at my house. We'll have tea among my horsies and get everything settled. I believe it's Jennifer Cranberry's turn to be the chief tea-horsy.' She fished in her purse for a business card. Jacob knew it would have much too much purple ink on it, and it did. 'Ten o'clock,' she said, as she handed it to him. 'Goodnight, Normandie, dear.' And she left them.

Jacob thought for a minute, twirling the stem of his wineglass. 'So now I'm editor-in-chief. Editor-in-chief of a rocking horse rag. I don't know whether to feel proud or ashamed, broadened or denatured. Or indifferent.'

Then Normandie's sympathetic laughter rolled across the table toward him in kind, reassuring waves, and her toes brushed little pulses of *joie de vivre* across his ankle.

Jacob sipped his wine, gazed straight ahead, and savoured the feeling of being exactly where he wanted to be.

THE END

225

## About the Author

The erotic fiction of Jeremy Edwards has been published in numerous anthologies, including *A is for Amour; Afternoon Delight; Coming Together: At Last,* vol. 1; *Coming Together: For the Cure; Coming Together: Into the Light; Coming Together: Under Fire; The Cougar Book; Erotic Tales 2; F is for Fetish; Five Minute Fantasies 1; Five Minute Fantasies 2; Frenzy; Girl Fun 1; Got a Minute?; J is for Jealousy; K is for Kinky; Love Notes; The Mammoth Book of Best New Erotica,* vols. 7, 8, and 9; *The Mile High Club; Never Have the Same Sex Twice; Open for Business; Oysters and Chocolate; Playing with Fire; Rubber Sex; Satisfy Me; Seriously Sexy 1; Seriously Sexy 3; Sex and Satisfaction; Sex and Satisfaction 2; Sex and Seduction; Sex and Shoes; Sex, Love and Valentines; Swing!; Tasting Her; Tease Me;*

*Ultimate Burlesque;* and *Ultimate Decadence.* His stories have appeared frequently in *Forum* and *Scarlet* magazines, and at online venues such as Clean Sheets, Good Vibrations, Oysters and Chocolate, Ruthie's Club, Sex-Kitten, and The Erotic Woman.

A popular guest on the Web circuit, Jeremy has been seen or heard such places as Erotica Readers and Writers Association, Lust Bites, LoveHoney, Dr. Dick's Sex Advice, and Cult of Gracie Radio. In the nonvirtual world, he has read at the In the Flesh series in New York, the Erotic Literary Salon in Philadelphia, and (via telephone) In the Flesh: L.A. His work has also been featured in the literary showcase of the Seattle Erotic Art Festival.

Jeremy's greatest goal in life is to be sexy and witty at the same moment—ideally in lighting that flatters his profile. Readers can drop in on him unannounced (and thereby catch him in his underwear) at his website, www.jeremyedwardserotica.com.